Ethan of Athos

Ethan of Athos

Lois McMaster Bujold

NESFA Press
Post Office Box 809
Framingham, MA 01701

Ethan of Athos copyright 1986, 2003

by Lois McMaster Bujold

Foreword copyright 2003 by Marna Nightingale

Cover art copyright 2003 by Nicholas Jainschigg

Dust jacket photograph of Lois McMaster Bujold
by Beth Gwinn, copyright 1995

ISBN: 1-886778-39-6

Printed in the United States of America

For those who listened in the beginning: Dee, Dave, Laurie, Barbara, R.J., Wes, and the patient ladies of the M.A.W.A.

Contents

Foreword   xi

Ethan of Athos   1

Editor's Note   201

Foreword

We who are loud, joyous, unabashed lovers and partisans of science fiction have learned to greet the remark that a book, or a writer, "transcends the genre" with narrowed eyes and brusque demands to be told exactly what the speaker means by *that*. Our response is remarkably similar to the one which used to baffle and sometimes hurt the well-meaning souls who once roamed the earth telling especially bright or competent women that they thought "just like men". We've learned to see the dismissal beneath some 'compliments'—what's wrong with being a science fiction writer? What's wrong with being a woman? The analogy I am drawing—between gender and genre—is not accidental, and it's not casual. The words are almost the same for a reason—*genre* is the French word for kind, or type, and our word *gender* comes from the same root. A certain kind of book, or writer. A particular type of person. Not, clearly, the finest kind, if telling someone they are good means negating their genre, or their gender.

Genre is important, though not all-important—it's the bones under the flesh, the underlying structure. *Ethan of Athos* could not be what it is, could not ask the questions it asks in the way it asks them, and be anything but a science-fiction novel, and it is a supremely good one: herein is fascinating new technology, space adventure, and mystery. Here are richly textured cultures at once utterly alien and instantly recognizable, endlessly surprising and at the same time inevitably and always products of their particular intersection of basic axioms and advanced technology. *Ethan of Athos* has suspense and trouble, people shooting at each other, and people falling in love with each other. It's got spaceships and space stations. It's got genetically engineered superhumans, heroes and villains, nice normal folks trying to get through the day. It's got a wonderfully twisty plot, as Lois' books always do. It's even got a Mad Scientist (and a few who are just really really annoyed).

(This is as good a time as any for a few public service announcements. First of all, if you're wondering whether you came in halfway through, you should know that *Ethan of Athos* is, as are all of the books of the Vorkosigan Saga, intentionally freestanding—in theory, you *can* read just one (though as far as I know, nobody ever has). Secondly, this foreword therefore contains no synopsis. If you want to, you can skip the rest of it and dive straight into the book, maybe drop by here again after if you care to. I may have promised to get up here and juggle, but you're under no obligation to hang around and watch. Lastly, you may wish to know that there is a mailing list for fans of Lois' work, which you can find out about by going to www.dendarii.com. (This may come in handy once you've finished reading every Bujold published to date and need some understanding people to keep you good company until the next book comes out.)

If genre is the bones of a story, the fundamental understanding of gender which a story reveals might be described as a look at the skin which covers the flesh of our common humanity. I would be grievously underrating the capacities of men to say that *Ethan of Athos* could only have been written by a woman, but it *is* fair to say that it could only have been written by someone who has a deep knowledge of and respect for that half of the human experience—the skills and the collective knowledge—which we have until recently regarded as the almost-exclusive province of women.

The question of gender in science-fiction has had a long but curiously tame history, remarkably similar to the treatment of gender in that other would-be-time-traveler's delight, historical fiction: everything else about a novel's setting may be "rich and strange", and suited to the time in which the novel is set, but the gender roles portrayed generally fall safely within at least the broad limits of what is acceptable to the time in which the author is living, at least by the end of the book. Exceptions exist, but are rare enough to be memorable: *Herland. The Left Hand Of Darkness. The Gate to Women's Country*. The Darkover books.

With the exception of *The Left Hand of Darkness*, which concerns itself primarily with beings who are both men and women, and the partial exception of *The Gate to Women's Country*, however, when we talk about "gender roles in science fiction" we're talking about women's roles. There it is again, that assumption that women are the troublesome—and troubled—gender, the gender that needs to 'transcend their type' if we're ever going to get anywhere. These days science fiction—in lock-step with Western society—takes it for granted that women *can* transcend 'their type'; women's options should and will be expanded, but in very specific directions, towards greater access to 'men's stuff'. The 'problematic' female characters, now, are not the ones who try to be more like men, but the ones who do not. And the men? Well, there they are, doing pretty much what fictitious men have usually done (and wanted to do), and actual men have generally done and at least pretended to enjoy, conquering new worlds, getting into fights, working at the office, running the country, or the planet, seducing women, all that. Sometimes we might get a world where war has been abolished, or farmed out somehow, but those are dystopic tales, and if the question is even raised, the effect on the male role is not to change it, but to transfer it—the warriors, whoever they are, become the new *real* men, the ones to be reckoned with, while the 'original' men become something else, something less, at least until they see the error of their ways.

In these new takes on gender roles, it's not just the potential for male change which is largely ignored; all that messy 'womanstuff' is generally left behind, too—some way is found to get the meals cooked and the children raised, the clothes made, washed and ironed, the relationships maintained, and so forth—some machine will be built or some inferior race or underclass will be there, economically created or conquered, or maybe cloned. Possibly the underclass will be made up of those problematic women who just can't, or won't, learn to play a man's game by the men's rules. It's a simple enough bit of handwaving, and after all, it's really not very important, right?

But of course it's not quite that simple, and it *is* that important. While there is no shortage of women, freed by technological and cultural change from confinement to 'women's work', doing the things that we traditionally think of as adventurous and powerful in Lois' fiction, she is equally fascinated by the other side of the coin. When women are no longer biologically bound to childbearing, and to the home-based role that this bio-logic seems invariably to create, men are no longer biologically bound to 'not childbearing', nor to the 'men's work' that we consider appropriate for those appointed to the supporting role in human evolution. When reproduction and parenting and love are no longer inexorably linked either to gender or to sex, gender relations: sexuality, love, and partnership, are freer to change than ever before. In *Ethan of Athos*, Lois sets out to explore these two neglected aspects of the gender role question—what happens to men's roles, and to women's work, when technology sets them free of biological sex? (Remembering the title of a certain high-school class in which, as a suburban substitute for a more solemn Initiation Into Womanhood, we were taught the "mysteries of womanhood:" menstruation and mending, IUDs and ironing, and I learned to make, though never to like, tuna casserole, I want to say that this book belongs to an entirely new genre: Domestic Science Fiction—but I can't bring myself to be quite that much of a brat. I do want to say, however, that I have reconsidered my disdain both for the title of the course, which at the time I considered pretentious, and for the curriculum, which I considered deeply inferior to Shop.)

The central, and the most fascinating, piece of technology in Lois' writing is the uterine replicator. This seemingly innocuous piece of equipment, which had its beginnings as a bit of convenient handwaving in *Shards of Honor*, has gone on to become one of the greatest agents of social change in the Nexus, (the series of star systems which provide the context for *Ethan of Athos*, as well as for the

Vorkosigan adventures), on each planet according to its cultural assumptions. In *Ethan of Athos* we see Lois' early consideration of the impact that the uterine replicator will have on gender roles, still sketchy in spots, but full of hints as to the directions she will later take—in particular, we get a sense of the genre (and the gender) conventions she proposes to play the very best sort of merry hell with. The most obvious form that this consideration takes is the social structure of Athos, a planet with no women and a great many children. There is the evolving understanding and partnership between Elli Quinn and Ethan Urquhart—the woman who wants to be a mercenary fleet commander, and the man who just wants to go home, settle down, and raise a bunch of kids. There is the very proper Athosian Ethan's progress from terror at the mere thought of a woman to understanding and acceptance of the human women—the mothers, in a sense— whose ovarian cultures helped build his world. There is Elli's sideways look at the path she has rejected, and her own coming to terms with it.

So we have the bones, and we have the skin, but what of the flesh, our common humanity? We are thinking creatures and tool-using mammals, we are usually either men or women, but beyond the first and underneath the second, we are members of the human race. (Another word for *race*, from the same root as *genre* and *gender*, is *genus*; to speak of ourselves as "members of the human race" is to make yet another series of statements—about the kind or type of being we think we are, and about who we do and do not think counts as a member.) Because this is science fiction, Bujold considers the question of humanity through the mechanism of technological change; because this is a book about gender and sex, the particular focus is reproductive technology. And because this is a book about how we create, become, remain, and treat members of the human race, as well as about how we decide who qualifies, Lois' use of the advantages and perils of bio-tech's capacity to give us almost total control over the creation of human life never degenerates into the easy and cheap answers so common in science fiction and in our own society. She never makes technology the villain, destroying our hu-

manity, nor does she cast it as the hero—which is why, at this re-
printing, *Ethan of Athos* is one of that rarest of science fiction stories:
a story which, as time has passed and the breakthroughs it discusses
have come nearer to fruition in the real world, instead of becoming
dated, it has become *more* relevant, *more* timely, because it relies for
its power on increasingly urgent human questions, instead of on rapidly aging technological answers. The question is another common
theme of science fiction, given a quarter turn. Lois has said that her
early works all turned out, often unbeknownst to her until long after
their publication, to be about 'the price of parenthood,' and when in
Ethan of Athos she asks how far we can go before we cease to be truly
human, the question applies not only to the products of replicator
gestation and precision genetic design, but even more so to the progenitors, the choosers, the parents. As we follow the adventures of
Terrance Cee we see not only what his creators and their technology
have made of him, but also what their work has made of them. As
we watch Ethan chase frantically around the galaxy to retrieve his—
and all of Athos'—future offspring, or as Elli Quinn considers her
options, we see how their choices about parenting change them forever. And just to make sure we haven't mislaid the point under all the
futuristic machinery, Ecotech Helda and her absent son, are there to
remind us that our worst nightmares about biotech may be no worse
than the things we've been doing to our children for centuries. Whatever tools we may have at our disposal, the issue most central to our
success or failure when we set out to create and raise children surely
remains the same—are we using our things to make people, or are
we trying to make people into things? (What is important about the
notion of a "superhuman" versus the notion of a "subhuman" is not
the difference, it seems, but the similarity—to label a person as either
makes it terrifyingly easy for us to think of them as a thing.)

The question of "people versus things" is not limited to the
parents, or progenitors, in Lois' fiction, but rather one which we all
have to answer, whenever we have power over another person, or
even when we are called to make decisions about who we are going
to be and what we are going to do. What is most intriguing, and

most important, about Terrence Cee is not what his progenitors intended him to be—a genetically advanced, fanatically loyal super-spy—but the person he himself decides to become. Being human is simple, though not easy, it turns out—you become a human being when you choose to be one and then keep choosing it, over and over. And so, Terrence Cee both fulfills and overturns another science-fiction trope: he becomes something beyond his creators' wildest dreams

As we all do, sooner or later. Because animating the bones (genre), the skin (gender) and the flesh (genus)—whether of a novel or a human being—is one more thing: the unique spark of life that properly belongs to any creation—and, of course, there is a word from the same root for that as well—*sui generis*, one of a kind, the only of its type. The aspect of a story that no analysis can capture; the part that turns A Great Book into A Life-Changing Story. The piece of us that neither nature nor nurture can account for. The inexplicable, unlooked-for capacity within us that makes atrocities and miracles happen; that can inspire a provincial, out of his depth, frightened Ethan to respond to something as completely outside of his experience as Terrence Cee by seeing him, and naming him, as exactly what he is: "You are my brother, of course."

Of course.

- Marna Nightingale
May, 2003

Ethan of Athos

CHAPTER ONE

The birth was progressing normally. Ethan's long fingers carefully teased the tiny cannula from its clamp.

"Give me hormone solution C now," he ordered the medtech hovering beside him.

"Here, Dr. Urquhart."

Ethan pressed the hypospray against the circular end-membrane of the cannula, administering the measured dose. He checked his instrumentation: placenta tightening nicely, shrinking from the nutritive bed that had supported it for the last nine months. Now.

Quickly he broke the seals, unclamped the lid from the top of the canister, and passed his vibra-scalpel through the matted felt of microscopic exchange tubing. He parted the spongy mass and the medtech clamped it aside and closed the stopcock that fed it with the oxy-nutrient solution. Only a few clear yellow droplets beaded and brushed off on Ethan's gloved hands. Sterility obviously uncompromised, Ethan noted with satisfaction, and his touch with the scalpel had been so delicate that the silvery amniotic sac beneath the tubing was unscored. A pink shape wriggled eagerly within. "Not much longer," he promised it cheerfully.

A second cut and he lifted the wet and vernix-covered infant from its first home. "Suction!"

The medtech slapped the bulb into his hand and he cleared the baby's nose and mouth of fluid before its first surprised inhalation.

1

The child gasped, squawked, blinked, and cooed in Ethan's secure and gentle grip. The medtech wheeled the bassinet in close and Ethan laid the infant under the warming light and clamped and cut the umbilical cord. "You're on your own now, boy," he told it.

The waiting engineering technician pounced on the uterine replicator that had incubated the fetus so faithfully for three-quarters of a year. The machine's multitude of little indicator lights were now all darkened. The tech began disconnecting it from its bank of fellows, to take downstairs for cleaning and re-programming.

Ethan turned to the infant's waiting father. "Good weight, good color, good reflexes. I'd give your son an A-plus rating, sir."

The man grinned and sniffed and laughed and brushed a surreptitious tear from the corner of one eye. "It's a miracle, Dr. Urquhart."

"It's a miracle that happens about ten times a day here at Sevarin." Ethan smiled.

"Do you ever get bored with it?"

Ethan gazed down with pleasure at the tiny boy, who was waving his fists and flexing in his bassinet. "No. Never."

Ethan was worried about the CJB-9. He quickened his pace down the quiet, clean corridors of the Sevarin District Reproduction Center. He was ahead of the shift change, having come in early especially to attend the birth. The last half hour of the night shift was the busiest, a crescendo of completing logs and signing off responsibilities to the yawning incomers. Ethan did not yawn, but did pause to punch two cups of black coffee from the dispenser in the rear of the medtech's station before joining the night shift team leader in his monitoring cubicle.

Georos waved greeting, his arm continuing in a smooth pounce on the proffered cup. "Thanks, sir. How was vacation?"

"Nice. My little brother had a week's leave from his army unit to coincide with it, so we were both home together for a change. South

Province. Pleased the old man no end. My brother got a promotion—he's first piccolo now in his regimental band."

"Is he going to stay in, then, past the two years' mandatory?"

"I think so. At least another two years. He's developing his musicianship, which is what he really wants anyway, and that extra slew of social duty credits in his bag won't hurt a bit."

"Mm," Georos agreed. "South Province, eh? I wondered why you weren't haunting us in your off-hours."

"It's the only way I can really vacate—get out of town," Ethan admitted wryly. He stared up at the rows of readouts lining the cubicle. The night team leader fell silent, sipping his coffee, watching Ethan over the rim, disturbingly silent after exhausting the small talk.

Uterine Replicator Bank 1 was on-line now. Ethan keyed directly to Bank 16, where the CJB-9 embryo dwelt.

"Ah, hell." The breath went out of him in a long sigh. "I was afraid of that."

"Yeah," agreed Georos, pursing his lips in sympathy. "Totally non-viable, no question. I took a sonic scan night before last—it's just a wad of cells."

"Couldn't they tell last week? Why hasn't the replicator been recycled? There are others waiting, God the Father knows."

"Waiting on paternal permission to flush the embryo." Georos cleared his throat. "Roachie scheduled the father to come in for a conference with you this morning."

"Aw…" Ethan ran his hand through his short dark hair, disarranging its trim professional neatness. "Remind me to thank our dear chief. Have you saved any more wonderful dirty work for me?"

"Just some genetic repairs on 5-B—possible enzyme deficiency. But we figured you'd want to do that yourself."

"True."

The night team leader began the routine report.

Ethan was almost late for the conference with the father of the CJB. During morning inspection he walked into one replicator chamber to find the tech in charge bopping happily through his duties to the loud and raucous strains of "Let's Stay Up All Night," a screechy dance tune currently popular among the undesignated set, blaring out of the stimu-speakers. The driving beat set Ethan's teeth on edge; this could scarcely be the ideal pre-natal sonic stimulation for the growing fetuses. Ethan left with the soothing strains of the classic hymn "God of Our Fathers, Light the Way" rendered by the United Brethren String Chamber Orchestra swelling gently through the room and the grumpy tech yawning pointedly.

In the next chamber he found one bank of uterine replicators running 75% saturated in the waste toxins carried off by the exchange solution; the tech in charge explained he'd been waiting for it to hit the regulation 80% before doing the mandatory filter changes. Ethan explained, clearly and forcefully, the difference between minimum and optimum, and oversaw the filter changes and the subsequent drop back to a more reasonable 45% saturation.

The receptionist beeped him twice before penetrating his lecture to the tech on the exact shade of lemon-colored crystal brightness to be expected in an oxygen and nutrient exchange solution operating at peak performance. He dashed up to the office level and stood panting a moment outside his door, balancing the dignity of a spokesman for the Rep Center versus the discourtesy of making a patron wait. He took a deep breath that had nothing to do with his gallop upstairs, fixed a pleasant smile on his face, and pushed open the door with the DR. ETHAN URQUHART, CHIEF OF REPRODUCTIVE BIOLOGY raised in gold letters on its ivory plastic surface.

"Brother Haas? I'm Dr. Urquhart. No, no—sit down, make yourself comfortable," Ethan added as the man popped nervously to his feet, ducking his head in greeting. Ethan sidled around him to his own desk, feeling absurdly grateful to be so shielded.

The man was huge as a bear, red from long days in sun and wind; the hands that turned his cap around and around were thick with muscle and callus. He stared at Ethan. "I was expecting an older man," he rumbled.

Ethan touched his shaved chin, then became self-conscious of the gesture and put his hand down hastily. If only he had a beard, or even a mustache, people would not be constantly mistaking him for a twenty-year-old despite his six-foot frame. Brother Haas was sporting a beard, about a two-week growth, scrubby by comparison to the luxuriant mustache that proclaimed him a long-standing designated alternate parent. Solid citizen. Ethan sighed. "Sit, sit." He gestured again.

The man sat on the edge of his chair, clutching his headgear in earnest supplication. His formal clothes were out of fashion and fit, but painfully clean and tidy; Ethan wondered how long the fellow'd had to scrub this morning to get *every speck* of dirt from under those horny nails.

Brother Haas slapped his cap absently against his thigh. "My boy, doctor—is—is there something the matter with my son?"

"Uh—didn't they tell you anything on the comlink?"

"No, sir. They just told me to come. So I signed out the ground car from my commune motor pool and here I am."

Ethan glanced at the dossier on his desk. "You drove all the way up here from Crystal Springs this morning?"

The bear smiled. "I'm a farmer. I'm used to getting up early. Anyway, nothing's too much trouble for my boy. My first, y'know"— he ran a hand over his chin and laughed—"well, I expect that's obvious."

"How did you end up here at Sevarin, instead of your district Rep Center at Las Sands?" asked Ethan curiously.

"It was for the CJB. Las Sands said they didn't have a CJB."

"I see." Ethan cleared his throat. "Any particular reason you decided on CJB stock?"

The farmer nodded firmly. "It was the accident last harvest decided me. One of our fellows tangled wrong-end-to with a thresher— lost an arm. Typical farm accident, but they said, if only he'd got to a doctor sooner, they mighta saved it. The commune's growing. We're right on the edge of the terraforming. We need a doctor of our own. Everybody knows CJBs make the best doctors. Who knows when

I'll get enough social duty credits for a second son, or a third? I meant to get the best."

"Not all doctors are CJBs," said Ethan. "And most certainly not all CJBs are doctors."

Haas smiled polite disagreement. "What are you, Dr. Urquhart?"

Ethan cleared his throat again. "Well—in fact, I'm a CJB-8."

The farmer nodded confirmation to himself. "They said you were the best." He stared hungrily at the Rep doctor, as if he might trace the lineaments of his dream son in Ethan's face.

Ethan tented his hands together upon his desk, trying to look kindly and authoritative. "Well. I'm sorry they didn't tell you more over the comlink—there was no reason to keep you in the dark. As you no doubt suspected, there is a problem with your, uh, conceptus."

Haas looked up. "My son."

"Uh—no. I'm afraid not. Not this round." Ethan inclined his head in sympathy.

Haas's face fell, then he looked up again, lips compressed with hope. "Is it anything you can fix? I know you do genetic repairs—if it's the cost, well, my commune brethren will back me—I can clear the debt, in time—"

Ethan shook his head. "There are only a couple dozen common disorders we can do something about—some types of diabetes, for example, that can be repaired by one gene splice in a small group of cells, if you catch them at just the right stage of development. Some can even be pulled from the sperm sample when we filter out the defective double-X-chromosome-bearing portion. There are many more that can be detected in the early check, before the blastula is implanted in the replicator bed and starts forming its placenta. We routinely pull one cell then and put it through an automated check. But the automated check only finds problems it's programmed to find—the hundred or so most common birth defects. It's not impossible for it to miss something subtle or rare—it happens half-a-dozen times a year. So you're not alone. We usually pull it and just fertilize another egg—it's the most cost-effective solution, with only six days invested at that point."

Haas sighed. "So we start over." He rubbed his chin. "Dag said it was bad luck to start growing your father-beard before birthday. Guess he was right."

"Only a setback," Ethan reassured his stricken look. "Since the source of the difficulty was in the ovum and not the sperm, the Center isn't even going to charge you for the month on the replicator." He made a hasty note to that effect in the dossier.

"Do you want me to go down to the paternity ward now, for a new sample?" asked Haas humbly.

"Ah—before you go, certainly. Save you another long drive. But there's one other little problem that needs to be ironed out first." Ethan coughed. "I'm afraid we can't offer CJB stock any more."

"But I came all the way here just for CJB!" protested Haas. "Damn it—I have a right to choose!" His hands clenched alarmingly. "Why not?"

"Well…" Ethan paused, careful of his phrasing. "Yours is not the first difficulty we've had with the CJB lately. The culture seems to be—ah—deteriorating. In fact, we tried very hard—all the ova it produced for a week were devoted to your order." No need to tell Haas how frighteningly scant that production was. "My best techs tried, I tried—part of the reason we took a chance on the current conceptus was that it was the only fertilization we achieved that was viable past the fourth cell division. Since then our CJB has stopped producing altogether, I'm afraid."

"Oh." Haas paused, deflated, then swelled with new resolve. "Whose does, then? I don't care if I have to cross the continent. CJB is what I mean to have."

Ethan wondered glumly why resolution was classed as a virtue. More of a damned nuisance. He took a breath and said what he'd hoped to avoid saying: "No one, I'm afraid, Brother Haas. Ours was the last working CJB culture on Athos."

Haas looked appalled. "No more CJBs? But where will we get our doctors, our medtechs—"

"The CJB *genes* are not lost," Ethan pointed out swiftly. "There are men all over the planet who carry them and who will pass them on to their sons."

"But what happened to the, the cultures? Why don't they work any more?" asked Haas in bewilderment. "They haven't— been poisoned or anything, have they? Some damned Outlander vandalism—"

"No, no!" Ethan said. Ye gods, what a riot *that* fabulous rumor could start. "It's perfectly natural. The first CJB culture was brought by the Founding Fathers when Athos was first settled—it's almost two hundred years old. Two hundred years of excellent service. It's just— senescent. Old. Worn out. Used up. Reached the end of its life-cycle, already dozens of times longer than it would have lived in a, ah"—it wasn't an obscenity, he was a doctor and it was correct medical termi- nology—"woman." He hurried on, before Haas could make the next logical connection. "Now, I'm going to offer a suggestion, Brother Haas. My best medtech—does superb work, most conscientious—is a JJY- 7. Now, we happen to have a very fine JJY-8 culture here at Sevarin that we can offer you. I wouldn't mind having a JJY myself, if only…" Ethan cut himself off, lest he tip into a personal bog and wallow in front of this patron. "I think you'd be very satisfied."

Haas reluctantly allowed himself to be talked into this substi- tute and was sent off to the sampling room he had first visited with such high hopes a month before. Ethan sighed, sitting at his desk after the patron had departed, and rubbed the worry around his temples. The action seemed to spread the tension rather than dissipate it. The next logical connection…

Every ovarian culture on Athos was a descendant of those brought by the Founding Fathers. It had been an open secret in the Rep Centers for two years and more—how much longer could it be until the general public picked up on it? The CJB was not the first culture to die out re- cently. Some sort of bell curve, Ethan supposed; they were on the up- slope and rising dizzily. Sixty percent of the infants growing cozily, pla- centas tucked in their soft nests of microscopic exchange tubing in the replicators downstairs, came from just eight cultures. Next year, if his secret calculations were borne out, it would be even worse. How long before there was not enough ovarian material to meet growth demand—or even population replacement? Ethan groaned, picturing his future unemployment prospects—if he wasn't ripped apart by angry mobs of ursine non-fathers before then....

He shook himself from his depression. Something would be done before things came to that pass, surely. Something *had* to break.

The worry made an ominous bass note under Ethan's pleasant routine for three months after his return from vacation. Another ovarian culture, LMS-10, curled up and died altogether and EEH-9's egg cell production declined by half. It would be the next to go, Ethan calculated. The first break in the downward slide arrived unexpectedly.

"Ethan?" Chief of Staff Desroches' voice had an odd edge, even over the intercom. His face bore a peculiar look of suppressed excitement; his lips, framed by glossy black beard and mustache, kept twitching at the corners. Not at all the morose pout that had been threatening over the past year to become permanent. Ethan, curious, laid his micropipette down carefully on the lab bench and went to the screen.

"Yes, sir?"

"I'd like you to come up to my office right away."

"I just started a fertilization—"

"As soon as you're done, then," Desroches conceded with a wave of his hand.

"What's up?"

"The annual census ship docked yesterday." Desroches pointed upward, although in fact Athos's only space station rode in a synchronous orbit above another quadrant of the planet. "Mail's here. Your magazines were approved by the Board of Censors—you've got a year's back issues sitting on my desk. And one other thing."

"Another thing? But I just ordered the journal—"

"Not your personal property. Something for the Rep Center." Desroches' white teeth flashed. "Finish up and come see." The screen blanked.

To be sure. A year's back issues of *The Betan Journal of Reproductive Medicine* imported at hideous expense, although of the highest degree of interest, would scarcely make Desroches' black eyes dance with joy. Ethan scurried, albeit meticulously, through the fertilization, placed the pod in the incubation chamber from which, in six or seven days time if things went well, the blastula would be transferred to a uterine replicator in one of the banks in the next room, and zipped upstairs.

A dozen brightly labeled data disks were indeed neatly stacked on the corner of the Chief's comconsole desk. The other corner was occupied by a holocube of two dark-haired young boys riding a spotted pony. Ethan scarcely glanced at either, his attention instantly overwhelmed by the large white refrigeration container squarely in the center. Its control panel lights burned a steady, reassuring green.

L. Bharaputra & Sons Biological Supply House, Jackson's Whole, the shipping label read. *Contents: Frozen Tissue, Human, Ovarian, 50 units. Stack with heat exchange unit clear of obstruction. This End Up.*

"We *got* them!" Ethan cried in delight and instant recognition, clapping his hands.

"At last." Desroches grinned. "The Population Council's going to have one hell of a party tonight, I'll bet—what a relief! When I think of the hunt for suppliers—the scramble for foreign exchange—for a while I thought we were going to have to send some poor son out there personally to get them."

Ethan shuddered and laughed. "Whew! Thank the Father nobody had to go through *that*." He ran a hand over the big plastic box, eagerly, reverently. "Going to be some new faces around here."

Desroches smiled, reflective and content. "Indeed. Well—they're all yours, Dr. Urquhart. Turn your routine lab work over to your techs and get them settled in their new homes. Priority."

"I should say so!"

Ethan set the carton tenderly on a bench in the Culture Lab and adjusted the controls to bring the internal temperature up somewhat. There would be a wait. He would only thaw twelve today, to fill the culture support units waiting, cold and empty, for new life. Soberly, he touched the darkened panel behind which the CJB-9 had dwelt so long and fruitfully. It made him feel sad and strangely adrift.

The rest of the tissue must wait for thawing until Engineering installed the bank of new units along the other wall. He grinned, thinking of the frantic activity that must now be disrupting that department's placid routine of cleaning and repairs. Some exercise would be good for them.

While he waited, he carried his new journals to the comconsole for a scan. He hesitated. Since his promotion to department head last year, his censorship status had been raised to Clearance Level A. This was the first occasion he'd had to take advantage of it; the first chance to test the maturity and judgment supposed necessary to handle totally uncut, uncensored galactic publications. He moistened his lips, nerving himself to prove that trust not misplaced.

He chose a disk at random, stuck it into the read-slot, and called up the table of contents. Most of the two dozen or so articles dwelt, predictably but disappointingly, on problems of reproduction in vivo in the human female, hardly apropos. Virtuously, he fought down an impulse to peek at them. But there was one article on early diagnosis of an obscure cancer of the vas deferens and better still one encouragingly titled, "On an Improvement in Permeability of Exchange Membranes in the Uterine Replicator." The uterine replicator had originally been perfected on Beta Colony—long famous for its leading-edge technologies—for use in medical emergencies. Most of its refinements still seemed to come from there, even at this late date, a fact not widely appreciated on Athos.

Ethan called up the entry and read it eagerly. It mostly seemed to involve some fiendishly clever molecular meshing of lipoproteins and polymers that delighted Ethan's geometric reason, at least on the second reading when he finally grasped it. He lost himself for a while in calculations about what it would take to duplicate the work here at Sevarin. He would have to talk to the head of Engineering....

Idly, as he mentally inventoried resources, he called up the author's page. "On an Improvement..." came from a university hospital at some city named Silica—Ethan knew little of off-planet geography, but it sounded appropriately Betan. What ordered minds and clever hands must have come up with that idea....

"Kara Burton, M.D., Ph.D., and Elizabeth Naismith, M.S. Bioengineering..." He found himself suddenly looking, on screen, at two of the strangest faces he had ever seen.

Beardless, like men without sons, or boys, but devoid of a boy's bloom of youth. Pale, soft faces, thin-boned, yet lined and time-scored; the engineer's hair was nearly white. The other was thick-bodied, lumpy in a pale blue lab smock.

Ethan trembled, waiting for the insanity to strike him from their level, medusan gazes. Nothing happened. After a moment, he unclutched the desk edge. Perhaps then the madness that possessed galactic men, slaves to these creatures, was something only transmitted in the flesh. Some incalculable telepathic aura? Bravely, he raised his eyes again to the figures in the screen.

So. That was a woman—two women, in fact. He sought his own reaction; to his immense relief, he seemed to be profoundly unaffected. Indifference, even mild revulsion. The Sink of Sin did not appear to be draining his soul to perdition on sight, always presuming he had a soul. He switched off the screen with no more emotion than frustrated curiosity. As a test of his resolution, he would not indulge it further today. He put the data disk carefully away with the others.

The freezer box was nearly up to temperature. He readied the fresh buffer solution baths and set them super-cooling to match the current temperature of the box's contents. He donned insulated gloves, broke the seals, lifted the lid.

Shrink wrap? *Shrink wrap?*

He peered down into the box in astonishment. Each tissue sample should have been individually containerized in its own nitrogen bath, surely. These strange gray lumps were wrapped like so many packets of lunch meat. His heart sank in terror and bewilderment.

Wait, wait, don't panic—maybe it was some new galactic technology he hadn't heard of yet. Gingerly, he searched the box for instructions, even rooting down among the packets themselves. Nothing. Look and guess time.

He stared at the little lumps, realizing at last that these were not cultured tissue at all, but the raw material itself. He was going to have to do the growth culturing personally. He swallowed. Not impossible, he reassured himself.

He found a pair of scissors, cut open the top packet, and dropped its contents, plop, into a waiting buffer bath. He contemplated it in some dismay. Perhaps it ought to be segmented, for maximum penetration of the nutrient solution—no, not yet, that would shatter the cellular structure in its frozen state. Thaw first.

He poked through the others, driven by growing unease. Strange, strange. Here was one six times the size of the other little ovoids, glassy and round. Here was one that looked revoltingly like a lump of cottage cheese. Suddenly suspicious, he counted packets. Thirty-eight. And those great big ones on the bottom—once, during his youthful army service, he had volunteered for K.P. in the butcher's department, fascinated by comparative anatomy even then. Recognition dawned like a raging sun.

"That," he hissed through clenched teeth, "is a *cow's* ovary!"

The examination was intense and thorough and took all afternoon. When he was done, his laboratory looked as though a first-year zoology class had been doing dissections all over it, but he was quite, quite sure.

He practically kicked open the door to Desroches' office and stood hands clenched, trying to control his ragged breathing.

Desroches was just donning his coat, the light of home in his eye; he never turned off the holocube until he was done for the day. He stared at Ethan's wild, disheveled face. "My God, Ethan, what is it?"

"Trash from hysterectomies. Leavings from autopsies, for all I know. A quarter of them are clearly cancerous, half are atrophied, five aren't even *human,* for God's sake! *And every single one of them is dead.*"

"What?" Desroches gasped, his face draining. "You didn't botch the thawing, did you? Not you—!"

"You come look. Just come look," Ethan sputtered. He spun on his heel and shot over his shoulder, "I don't know what the Population Council paid for this crud, but we've been *screwed.*"

CHAPTER TWO

"Maybe," the senior Population Council delegate from Las Sands said hopefully, "it was an honest error. Maybe they thought the material was intended for medical students or something."

Ethan wondered why Roachie had dragged him along to this emergency session. Expert witness? Another time, he might have been awed by his august surroundings: the deep carpeting, the fine view of the capital, the long polished ripple-wood table and the grave, bearded faces of the elders reflected in it. Now he was so angry he barely noticed them. "That doesn't explain why there were thirty-eight in a box marked fifty," he snapped. "Or those damned cow ovaries—do they imagine we breed minotaurs here?"

The junior representative from Deleara remarked wistfully, "Our box was totally empty."

"Faugh!" said Ethan. "Nothing so completely screwed up could be either honest or an error—" Desroches, looking exasperated, motioned him down and Ethan subsided. "Gotta be deliberate sabotage," Ethan continued to him in a whisper.

"Later," Desroches promised. "We'll get to that later."

The chairman finished recording the official inventory reports from all nine Rep Centers, filed them in his comconsole, and sighed. "How the hell did we pick this supplier, anyway?" he asked, semirhetorically.

The head of the procurement subcommittee dropped two tablets of medication into a glass of water and laid his head on his

15

arms to watch them fizz. "They were the lowest bidder," he said
morosely.

"You put the future of Athos into the hands of the lowest bidder?" snarled another member.

"You all approved it, remember?" replied the procurement head,
stung into animation. "You insisted on it, in fact, when you found
the next bidder would only send thirty for the same price. Fifty different cultures promised for each Rep Center—you practically peed
yourselves with glee, as I recall—"

"Let us keep these proceedings official, please," the chairman
warned. "We have no time to waste either apportioning or evading
blame. The galactic census ship breaks orbit in four days and is the
only vector for our decisions until next year."

"We should have our own jump ships," remarked a member.
"Then we wouldn't be treed like this, at the mercy of their schedule."

"Military's been begging for some for years," said another.

"So which Rep Centers do you want to trade in to pay for them?"
asked a third sarcastically. "We and they are the two biggest items in
the budget, next to the terraforming that grows the food for our
children to eat while they're growing up—do you want to stand up
and tell the people that their child-allotment is to be halved to give
those clowns a pile of toys that produce nothing for the economy in
return?"

"Nothing until now," muttered the second speaker cogently.

"Not to mention the technology we'd have to import—and
what, pray tell, are we going to export to pay for it? It took all our
surplus just to—"

"So make the jump ships pay for themselves. If we had them, we
could export *something* and obtain enough galactic currency to—"

"It would directly contravene the purposes of the Founding Fathers to seek contact with that contaminated culture," interjected a
fourth man. "They put us at the end of this long pipeline in the first
place precisely to protect us from—"

The chairman tapped the table sharply. "Debates on larger issues belong in the General Council, gentlemen. We are met today to

address a specific problem, and quickly." His flat, irritated tone did not invite contradiction. There was a general stirring and shuffling of notes and straightening of spines.

The junior member from Barca, poked by his senior, cleared his throat. "There is one possible solution, without going off-planet. We could grow our own."

"It's exactly because our cultures *won't* grow any more that we—" began another man.

"No, no, I understand that—none better," the Barca man, a Chief of Staff like Desroches, said hastily. "I meant, ah…" He cleared his throat again. "Grow some female fetuses of our own. They need not even be brought to term, quite. Then raid them for ovarian material and, er, begin again."

There was a revolted silence around the table. The chairman looked like a man sucking on a lemon. The member from Barca shrank in his seat.

The chairman said at last, "We're not that desperate yet. Although it may be well to have spoken what others will surely think of eventually."

"It needn't be public knowledge," the Barca man offered.

"I should hope not," agreed the chairman dryly. "The possibility is noted. Members will mark this section of the record classified. But I point out, for all, that this proposal does not address the other, perennial problem faced by this Council and Athos: maintaining genetic variety. It had not pressed on our generation—until now—but we all knew it had to be faced in the future." His tones grew more mellow. "We would be shirking our responsibilities to ignore it now and let it be dumped on our grandsons in the form of a crisis."

There was a murmur of relief around the table, as logic safely propped emotional conviction. Even the junior member from Barca looked happier. "Quite." "Exactly." "Just so—" "Better to kill two chickens with one stone, if we can—"

"Immigration would help," put in another member, who doubled, one week a year, as Athos's Department of Immigration and

Naturalization. "If we could get some."

"How many immigrants came on this year's ship?" asked the man across from him.

"Three."

"Hell. Is that an all-time low?"

"No, year before last there were only two. And two years before that there weren't any." The Immigration man sighed. "By rights we ought to be flooded with refugees. Maybe the Founding Fathers were just too thorough about picking a planet away from it all. I sometimes wonder if anyone out there has heard of us."

"Maybe the knowledge is suppressed, by, you know—*them*."

"Maybe the men trying to get here are turned away at Kline Station," opined Desroches. "Maybe only a few are allowed to trickle in."

"It's true," agreed the Immigration man, "the ones we do get tend to be a little—well—strange."

"No wonder, considering they're all products of that, uh, traumatic genesis. Not their fault."

The chairman tapped the table again. "We shall continue this later. We are agreed, then, to pursue our first choice of an off-planet supply of cultured tissue—"

Ethan, still fuming, steamed into speech. "Sirs! You're not thinking of going back to those scalpers—" Desroches pulled him firmly back into his seat.

"From some more reputable source," the chairman finished smoothly, with an odd look at Ethan. Not disapproval; a sort of smiling, silky smugness. "Gentlemen delegates?"

A murmur of approval rose around the table.

"The ayes have it; it is so moved. I think we also agree not to make the same mistake twice: no more sight-unseen purchases. It follows that we must now choose an agent. Dr. Desroches?"

Desroches stood. "Thank you, Mr. Chairman. I have given some thought to this problem. Of course, the ideal purchasing agent must first of all have the technical know-how to evaluate, choose, package, and transport the cultures. That narrows the possible choices considerably, right there. He must also be a man of proven integrity, not merely because he will be responsible for nearly all the foreign exchange Athos can muster this year—"

"All of it," the chairman corrected quietly. "The General Council approved it this morning."

Desroches nodded. "And not only because the whole future of Athos will depend on his good judgment, but also that he have the moral fiber to resist, er, whatever it is out there that, ah, he may encounter."

Women, of course, and whatever it was they did to men. Was Roachie volunteering, Ethan wondered? He certainly knew the technical end. Ethan admired his courage, even if his self-description was bordering on the swelled-headed. Probably needed it, to psych himself up. Ethan did not begrudge it. For Desroches to leave his two sons, on whom he doted, behind for a whole year…

"He should also be a man free of family responsibilities, that his absence not put too great a burden on his designated alternate," Desroches went on.

Every bearded face around the table nodded judiciously.

"—and finally, he should be a man with the energy and conviction to carry on regardless of the obstacles fate or, uh, whatever, may throw in his path." Desroches' hand fell firmly to Ethan's shoulder; the expression of smug approval on the chairman's face broadened to a smile.

Ethan's half-formed words of congratulation and commiseration froze in his throat. Running through his formerly-teeming brain was only one helpless, recycling phrase: *I'll get you for this, Roachie.…*

"Gentlemen, I give you Dr. Urquhart." Desroches sat and grinned cheerily at Ethan. "*Now* stand up and talk," he urged.

The silence in Desroches' ground car on the drive back to Sevarin was long and sullen. Desroches broke it a little nervously. "Are you willing to admit you can handle it yet?"

"You set me up for that," growled Ethan at last. "You and the chairman had it all cooked up in advance."

"Had to. I figured you'd be too modest to volunteer."

"Modest, hell. You just figured I'd be easier to nail if I wasn't a moving target."

"I thought you were the best man for the job. Left to its own devices, God the Father knows what the committee would have picked. Maybe that idiot Frankin from Barca. Would you want to put the future of Athos in his hands?"

"No," Ethan began to agree reluctantly, then hardened. "Yes! Let *him* get lost out there."

Desroches grinned, teeth glinting in the faint tinted light from the control panel. "But the social duty credits you'll be getting—think of it! Three sons, a decade's accumulation in the normal course of events, earned in just one year. Generous, I think."

Ethan had a sudden poignant vision of a holocube for his own desk, filled with life and laughter. Ponies, indeed, and long holidays sailing in the sunshine, passing on the subtleties of wind and water as his father had taught him, and the tumble, noise, and chaos of a home teeming with the future.... But he said glumly, "*If* I succeed and *if* I get back. And anyway, I have enough social duty credits for a son and a half. It would have meant a hell of a lot more if they'd coughed up enough credits to qualify my designated alternate."

"If you'll forgive my frankness, people like your foster brother are just the reason social duty credits may not be transferred," said Desroches. "He's a charming young man, Ethan, but even you must admit he's totally irresponsible."

"He's young," argued Ethan uneasily. "He just needs a bit more time to settle."

"Three years younger than you, I believe? Bull. He'll never settle as long as he can sponge off you. I think you'd do a lot better for yourself to find a qualified D.A. and make him your partner than try to make a D.A. out of Janos."

"Let's leave my personal life out of this, huh?" snapped Ethan, secretly stung; then added somewhat inconsistently, "which this mission is going to totally disrupt, by the way. Thanks heaps." He hunched down in the passenger side as the car knifed the night.

"It could be worse," said Desroches. "We really could have activated your Army Reserve status, made it a military order, and sent
you out on a corpsman's pay. Fortunately, you saw the light."

"I didn't think you were bluffing."

"We weren't." Desroches sighed and grew less jocular. "We didn't
pick you casually, Ethan. You're not going to be an easy man to replace at Sevarin."

Desroches dropped Ethan off at the garden apartment he shared
with his foster brother and continued on out of town with a reminder
of an early start at the Rep Center tomorrow. Ethan sighed acknowl-
edgment. Four days. Two only allowed to orient his chief assistant to
his sudden new duties and wind up his own personal affairs—should
he make a will?—one day of briefing in the capital by the Population
Council, and then report to the shuttleport. Ethan's brain balked at
the impossibility of it all.

So much would simply have to be left hanging at the Rep Center. He thought suddenly of Brother Haas's JJY son, successfully
started three months ago. Ethan had planned to personally officiate
at his birthday, as he had personally seen to his fertilization: alpha and
omega, to savor however briefly and vicariously the joyous fruits of
his labors. He would be long gone before that date.

Approaching his door, he tripped over Janos's electric bike,
dumped carelessly between the flower tubs. Much as Ethan admired
Janos's fine idealistic indifference to material wealth, he wished he'd
take better care of his things—but it had always been so.

Janos was the son of Ethan's own father's D.A.. The two had
raised all their sons together, as they had run their business together,
an experimental and ultimately successful fish farm on the South
Province coast, as they had melded their lives together, seamlessly.
Between son and foster-son no line was ever drawn. Ethan the eldest,
bookish and inquisitive, destined from birth to higher education and
higher service; Steve and Stanislaus, born each within a week of the
other, each flatteringly bred from their father's partner's ovarian cul-

ture stock; Janos, boundlessly energetic, witty as quicksilver; Bret, the baby, the musical one. Ethan's family. He had missed them, achingly, in the army, in school, in his too-good-to-be-passed-up new job at Sevarin.

When Janos had followed Ethan to Sevarin, eager to trade country life for town life, Ethan had been comforted. No matter that it had interrupted Ethan's tentative social experimentation. Ethan, shy in spite of his achievements, loathed the singles scene and was glad of an excuse to escape it. They had fallen comfortably back into the pattern of their early teenage sexual intimacy. Ethan sought comfort tonight, more inwardly frightened than even his sarcastic banter with Desroches had revealed.

The apartment was dark, too quiet. Ethan made a rapid pass through all the rooms, then, reluctantly, checked the garage.

His lightflyer was gone. Custom-built, first fruits of a year's savings from his recently augmented salary as department head; Ethan had owned it all of two weeks. He swore, then choked back the oath. He really had intended to let Janos try it, once the newness had worn off. Too little grace time left to start an argument over trifles.

He returned to the apartment, dutifully considered bed. No—too little time. He checked the comconsole. No message, naturally. Janos had doubtless intended to be home before Ethan. He tried the comlink to the lightflyer's number. No answer. He smiled suddenly, punched up a city grid on the comconsole, and entered a code. The beacon was one of the little refinements of the luxury model—and there it was, parked not two kilometers away at Founders' Park. Janos partying nearby? Very well, Ethan would get out of his domestic rut and join him tonight and doubtless startle him considerably by not being angry about the unauthorized borrowing.

The night wind ruffled his dark hair and chilled him awake as he neared Founders' Park on the purring electric bike. But it was the sight of the emergency vehicles' flashing yellow lights that froze his bones. God the Father—no, no: no need to assume that just because Janos and the rescue squad were in the same vicinity, there was some causal connection.

No ambulance, no city police, just a couple of garage tows. Ethan relaxed slightly. But if there was no blood on the pavement, why the fascinated crowd? He brought the bike to a halt near the grove of rustling oak trees and followed the spectators' upturned faces and the white fingers of the searchlights into the high leafy foliage.

His lightflyer. Parked in the top of a twenty-five-meter-tall oak tree.

No—*crashed* in the top of the twenty-five-meter oak tree. Vanes bent all to hell and gone, half-retracted wings crumpled, doors sprung open, gaping to the ground; his heart nearly failed him at the sight of the dangling empty pilot restraint harness hanging out. The wind sighed, the branches creaked ominously, and the crowd did a hasty prudent backstep. Ethan surged through them. No blood on the pavement...

"Hey, mister, you better not stand under there."

"That's my flyer," Ethan said. "It's in a damned tree..." He cleared his throat to bring his voice back down an octave to its normal range. There *was* a certain hypnotizing fascination to it. He tore himself away, whirled to grab the garage man by his jacket.

"The guy who was flying that—where...?"

"Oh, they took him off hours ago."

"General Hospital?"

"Hell, no. *He* was feeling no pain at all. His friend got a cut on the head, but I think they just sent him home in the ambulance. City police station, I imagine, for the driver. He was singing."

"Aw, sh—"

"You say you own this vehicle?" a man in a city parks department uniform accosted Ethan.

"I'm Dr. Ethan Urquhart, yes?"

The parks man pulled out a com panel and punched up a half-completed form. "Do you realize that tree is nearly two hundred years old? Planted by the Founders themselves—irreplaceable historic value. And it's split halfway down—"

"Got it, Fred," came a shout from on high.

"Lower away!"

"—responsibility for damages—"

A creak of strained wood, a rustle from above, an "Ah" from the crowd—a high-pitched rising whine as an antigrav unit suddenly failed to phase properly.

"Oh, shit!" came a yowl from the treetops. The crowd scattered with cries of warning.

Five meters per second, thought Ethan with hysterical irrelevancy. Times twenty-five meters times *how* many kilograms?

The nose-down impact on the granite cobblestones starred the gleaming red outer shell of the flyer with fracture lines from front to rear. In the sudden silence after the great crunch Ethan could quite clearly hear an elfin tinkle of expensive electronic instrumentation within, coming to rest a little out of phase with the main mass.

Janos's blond head turned, startled, at Ethan's tread upon the tiles of the Sevarin City Police Station.

"Oh, Ethan," he said plaintively. "I've had a *hell* of a day." He paused. "Uh—did you find your flyer?"

"Yeah."

"It'll be all right, just leave it to me. I called the garage."

The bearded police sergeant with whom Janos was dealing across the counter snickered audibly. "Maybe it'll hatch out some tricycles up there."

"It's down," said Ethan shortly. "And I've paid the bill for the tree."

"The tree?"

"Damages thereto."

"Oh."

"How?" asked Ethan. "The tree, I mean."

"It was the birds, Ethan," Janos explained.

"The birds. Force you down, did they?"

Janos laughed uneasily. Sevarin's avian population, all descendants of mutated chickens escaped from the early settlers and gone feral, were a diverse lean lot already hinting at speciation, but still not exactly great flyers. They were considered something of a municipal nuisance; Ethan glanced covertly at the police sergeant's face and was relieved by a marked lack of concern at the birds' fate. He didn't think he could face a bill for chickens.

"Yeah, uh," said Janos, "you see, we found out we could tumble 'em—make a close pass, they'd go whipping around like a whirligig. Just like flying a fighter and dive-bombing the enemy…" Janos's hands began to make evocative passes through the air, heroic starfighters.

Athos had had no military enemies in two hundred years. Ethan gritted his teeth, maintained reason. "And ended up dive-bombing the tree in the dark instead. I suppose I can see how that could happen."

"Oh, it was before dark."

Ethan made a quick calculation. "Why weren't you at work?"

"It was your fault, really. If you hadn't left before dawn on that joy junket to the capital, I wouldn't have overslept."

"I reset the alarm."

"You know that's never enough."

True. Getting Janos upright and correctly aimed out the door in the morning was exhausting as setting-up exercises.

"Anyway," Janos continued, "the boss got shitty about it. The upshot was, uh—I got fired this morning." He seemed to be finding his boots suddenly very interesting.

"Just for being late? That's unreasonable. Look, I'll talk to the guy in the morning—somehow—if you want, and—"

"Uh, don't—don't bother."

Ethan looked at Janos's sunny, even features more closely. No contusions, no bandages on those long lithe limbs, but he was definitely favoring his right elbow. It might just be from the flyer accident—but Ethan had seen that particular pattern of barked knuckles before.

"What happened to your arm?"

"The boss and his pet goon got a little rough, showing me out the door."

"Damn it! They can't—"

"It was after I took a swing at him," Janos admitted reluctantly, shifting.

Ethan counted to ten and resumed breathing. No time. No time. "So you spent the afternoon getting drunk with—who?"

"Nick," said Janos and hunched, waiting for the explosion.

"Mm. I suppose that accounts for the onslaught on the birds, then." Nick was Janos's buddy for all the competitive games that left Ethan cold; in his darker and more paranoid moments, Ethan occasionally suspected Janos of having something on the side with him. No time now. Janos unhunched, looking surprised, when no explosion came.

Ethan dug out his wallet and turned politely to the police sergeant. "What will it take to spring the Scourge of the Sparrows out of here, Officer?"

"Well, sir—unless you wish to make some further charge with respect to your vehicle…"

Ethan shook his head.

"It's all been taken care of in the night court. He's free to go."

Ethan was relieved, but astonished. "No charges? Not even for—"

"Oh, there were charges, sir. Operating a vehicle while intoxicated, to the public danger, damaging city property—and the fees for the rescue teams…" The sergeant detailed these at some length.

"Did they give you severance pay, then?" Ethan asked Janos, running a confused mental calculation from his foster brother's last known financial balance.

"Uh, not exactly. C'mon, let's go home. I've got a hell of a headache."

The sergeant counted back the last of Janos's personal property; Janos scribbled his name on the receipt without even glancing at it.

Janos made the noise of the electric bike an excuse not to continue the conversation during the ride home. This was a strategic error, as it allowed Ethan time to review his mental arithmetic.

"How'd you buy your way out of that?" Ethan asked, closing the front door behind him. He glanced across the front room at the digital; in three hours he was supposed to be getting up for work.

"Don't worry," said Janos, kicking his boots under the couch and making for the kitchen. "It's not coming out of your pocket this time."

"Whose, then? You didn't borrow money from Nick, did you?" Ethan demanded, following.

"Hell, no. He's broker than I am." Janos pulled a bulb of beer from the cupboard, bit the refrigeration tube, and drew. "Hair of the dog. Want one?" he offered slyly.

Ethan refused to be baited into a diversionary lecture on Janos's drinking habits, clearly the intent. "Yeah."

Janos raised a surprised eyebrow and tossed him a bulb. Ethan took it and flopped into a chair, legs stretched out. A mistake, sitting; the day's emotional exhaustion washed over him. "The fines, Janos."

Janos sidled off. "They took them out of my social duty credits, of course."

"Oh, God!" Ethan cried wearily. "I swear you've been going backwards ever since you got out of the damned army! *Anyone* could have enough credits to be a D.A. by now, without volunteering for *anything*." A red urge shook him to take Janos and bash his head into the wall, restrained only by the terrible effort required to stand up again. "I can't leave a baby with you all day if you're going to go on like this!"

"Hell, Ethan, who's asking you to? I got no time for the little shit-factories. They cramp your style. Well—not *your* style, I suppose. You're the one who's all hot for paternity, not me. Working at that Center overtime has turned your brain. You used to be fun." Janos, apparently recognizing he had crossed the line of Ethan's amazing tolerance at last, was retreating toward the bathroom.

"The Rep Centers are the heart of Athos," said Ethan bitterly. "All our future. But you don't care about Athos, do you? You don't care about anything but what's inside your own skin."

"Mm." Janos, judging from his brief grin about to try to turn Ethan's anger with an obscene joke, took in his dark face and thought better of it.

The struggle was suddenly too much for Ethan. He let his empty beer bulb drop to the floor from slack fingers. His mouth twisted in sardonic resignation. "You can have the lightflyer, when I leave."

Janos paused, shocked white. "Leave? Ethan, I never meant—"

"Oh. Not that kind of leave. This has nothing to do with you. I forgot I hadn't told you yet—the Population Council's sending me on some urgent business for them. Classified. Top secret. To Jackson's Whole. I'll be gone at least a year."

"Now who doesn't care?" said Janos angrily. "Off for a year without so much as a by-your-leave. What about me? What am I supposed to do while you're…" Janos's voice plowed into silence. "Ethan—isn't Jackson's Whole a *planet*? Out there? With—with—*them* on it?"

Ethan nodded. "I leave in four—no, three days, on the galactic census ship. You can have all my things. I don't know…what's going to happen out there."

Janos's chiseled face was drained sober. In a small voice he said, "I'll go clean up."

Comfort at last, but Ethan was asleep in his chair before Janos came out of the bathroom.

CHAPTER THREE

Kline Station was an accretion of three hundred years. Even so, Ethan was unprepared for the size of it and the complexity. It straddled a region of space where no less than six fruitful jump routes emerged within a reasonable sublight boost of each other. The dark star nearby hosted no planets at all and so Kline Station rode a slow orbit far out of its gravity well, cresting the stygian cold.

Kline Station had been full of history even when Athos was first settled; it had been the jumping-off point for the Founding Fathers' noble experiment. A poor fortress, but a great place to do business, it had changed hands a number of times as one or another of its neighbors sought it as a guardian of its gates, not to mention a source of cash flow. Presently it maintained a precarious political independence based on bribery, determination, suppleness in business practice, and a stiffness in internal loyalty bordering on patriotism. A hundred thousand citizens lived in its mazy branches, augmented at peak periods of traffic by perhaps a fifth as many transients.

So much Ethan had learned from the crew of the census courier. The crew of eight was all male not, Ethan found, out of regular rule or respect for the laws of Athos, but from the disinclination of female employees of the Bureau to spend four months on the round-trip voyage without a downside leave. It gave Ethan a little breather, before being plunged into galactic culture. The crew was courteous to him, but not so encouraging as to break through Ethan's own timid

29

reserve, and so he had spent much of the two months en route in his own cabin, studying and worrying.

As preparation, he'd decided to read all the articles by and about women in his *Betan Journals of Reproductive Medicine.* There was the ship's library, of course, but its contents certainly had not been approved by the Athosian Board of Censors and Ethan was not really sure what degree of dispensation he was supposed to have on this mission. Better to stock up on virtue, he reasoned glumly; he was probably going to need it.

Women. Uterine replicators with legs, as it were. He was not sure if they were supposed to be inciters to sin, or sin was inherent in them, like juice in an orange, or sin was caught from them like a virus. He should have paid more attention during his boyhood religious instruction, not that the subject had ever been anything but mysteriously talked around. And yet, when he'd read one *Journal* edited of names as a scientific test, he'd found the articles indistinguishable as to the sex of the author.

This made no sense. Maybe it was only their souls, not their brains, that were so different? The one article he'd been sure was a man's work turned out to be by a Betan hermaphrodite, a sex which hadn't even existed when the Founding Fathers had fled to Athos, and where did they fit in? He lost himself, for a while, imagining the flap in Athosian Customs should such a creature present itself for entry, as the bureaucrats tried to decide whether to admit its maleness or exclude its femaleness—it would probably be referred to a committee for about a century, by which time the hermaphrodite would have conveniently solved the problem by dying of old age.

Kline Station Customs were made nearly equally tedious by the most thorough microbiological inspection and control procedure Ethan had ever seen. Kline Station, it appeared, cared not if you were smuggling guns, drugs, or political refugees, as long as your shoes harbored no mutant fungi. Ethan's terror and—he admitted to himself—ravenous curiosity had mounted to a fever when he was at last permitted to walk through the flex tube from the courier into the rest of the universe.

The rest of the universe was disappointing at first glance, a dingy chilly freighter docking bay. The mechanical working side of Kline Station, to be sure, like the backside of a tapestry that probably made a fine show from some more intended perspective. Ethan puzzled over which of a dozen exits led to human habitation. The ship's crew was obviously busy, or out of sight; the microbial inspection team had dashed off as soon as its task was done, like as not to another job. A lone figure was leaning casually against a wall at the mouth of an exit ramp in the universal languid pose of idleness watching work. Ethan approached it for directions.

The crisp gray-and-white uniform was unfamiliar to Ethan, but obviously military even without the clue of the sidearm on the hip. Only a legal stunner, but it looked well cared for and not at all new. The slim young soldier looked up at Ethan's step, inventoried him, he felt, with one glance, and smiled politely.

"Pardon me, sir," Ethan began and halted in uncertainty. Hips too wide for the wiry figure, eyes too large and far apart above a small chiseled nose, jaw thin-boned and small, beardless skin fine as an infant's—it *might* have been a particularly elegant boy, but...

Her laughter pealed like a bell, entirely too loud for the reddening Ethan. "You *must* be the Athosian," she chuckled.

Ethan began to back away. Well, she didn't look like the middle-aged scientists portrayed in the *Betan Journal*. It was a perfectly natural mistake, surely. He had resolved earlier to avoid speaking to women as much as humanly possible and here he was already—"How do I get out of here?" he mumbled, darting cornered glances around the docking bay.

She raised her eyebrows. "Didn't they give you a map?"

Ethan shook his head nervously.

"Why, that's practically criminal, turning a stranger loose in Kline Station without a map. You could go out looking for the commode and starve to death before you found your way back. Ah ha, the very man I'm looking for. Hi! Dom!" she hailed a courier crewman just now crossing the docking bay with a duffel slung over his shoulder. "Over here!"

The crewman changed course, his annoyance melting into the look of a man eager to please, if slightly puzzled. He stood straighter than Ethan had ever seen him, sucking in his gut. "Do I know you, ma'am—I hope?"

"Well, you ought to—you sat next to me in disaster drill class for two years. I admit it's been a while." She ran a hand through her dark cropped curls. "Picture longer hair. C'mon, the re-gen didn't change my face *that* much! I'm Elli."

His mouth made an "o" of astonishment. "By the gods! Elli Quinn? What have you done to yourself?"

She touched one molded cheekbone. "Complete facial regeneration. Do you like it?"

"It's fantastic!"

"Betan work, you know—the best."

"Yeah, but—" Dom's face puckered. "Why? It's not like you were so hard to look at before you ran off to join the mercenaries." He gave her a grin that was like a sly poke in the ribs, although his hands were clasped behind his back like a boy's at a bakery window. "Or did you strike it rich?"

She touched her face again, less cheerfully. "No, I haven't taken up hijacking. It was sort of a necessity—caught a plasma beam to the head in a boarding battle out Tau Verde way, a few years back. I looked a little funny with no face at all, so Admiral Naismith, who does not do things by halves, bought me a new one."

"Oh," said Dom, quelled.

Ethan, who found his enthusiasm over the woman's facial aesthetics a trifle baffling, had no trouble sympathizing with this; any plasma burn was horrendous—this one must have come close to killing her. He eyed the face with a new medical interest.

"Didn't you start out with Admiral Oser's group?" asked Dom. "That's still his uniform, isn't it?"

"Ah. Allow me to introduce myself. Commander Elli Quinn, Dendarii Free Mercenary Fleet, at your service." She bowed with a flourish. "The Dendarii sort of annexed Oser and his uniforms and me—and it's been a step up in the world, let me tell you. But I, sir, have home leave for the first time in ten years and intend to enjoy it. Popping up beside old classmates and giving them heart failure—flashing my credit rating in front of all the people who predicted I'd come to a bad end—speaking of coming to a bad end, you seem to have turned your passenger here loose without a map."

Dom eyed the mercenary officer suspiciously. "That wasn't intended as a pun, was it? I've been on this run for four years and I am so damned tired of coming back to a lot of half-witted bend-over jokes—"

The mercenary woman's laughter burst against the overhead girders, her head thrown back. "The secret of your abandonment revealed, Athosian," she said to Ethan. "Should I take him in hand, then, being by virtue of my sex innocent of the suspicion of, er, unnatural lusts?"

"For all of me, you can," allowed Dom, shrugging. "*I* have a wife to get home to." He walked pointedly around Ethan.

"Good-oh. I'll look you up later, all right?" said the woman.

The crewman nodded to her, rather regretfully, and trod off up the exit ramp. Ethan, left alone with the woman, suppressed an urge to run after him begging protection. Recalling vaguely that economic servitude was one of the marks of the damned, he had a sudden horrible suspicion that she might be after his money—and he was carrying Athos's entire purse for the year. He became intensely conscious of her sidearm.

Amusement livened her strange face. "Don't look so worried. I'm not going to eat you." She snickered suddenly. "Conversion therapy not being my line."

"Glck," blurted Ethan and cleared his throat. "I am a faithful man," he quavered. "To, to Janos. Would you like to see a picture of Janos?"

"I'll take your word for it," she replied easily. The amusement softened to something like sympathy. "I really have you spooked, don't I? What, am I by chance the first woman you've met?"

Ethan nodded. Twelve exits, and he had to pick this one....

She sighed. "I believe you." She paused thoughtfully. "You could use a faithful native guide, though. Kline Station has a reputation for travelers' aid to uphold—it's good for business. And I'm a friendly cannibal."

Ethan shook his head with a paralyzed smile.

She shrugged. "Well, maybe when you get over your culture shock I'll run across you again. Are you going to have a long layover?" She pulled an object from her pocket, a tiny holovid projector. "You get one of these automatically when you get off a proper passenger ship—I don't need mine." A colorful schematic sprang into the air. "We're here. You want to be here, in the branch called Transients' Lounge—nice facilities, you can get a room—actually, you can get most anything, but I fancy you'd prefer the staid end of things. This section. Up this ramp and take the second cross-corridor. Know how to operate this thing? Good luck—" She pressed the map module into his hand, flashed a last smile, and vanished into another exit.

He gathered his meager belongings and found his way to the transients' area eventually, after only a few wrong turns. He passed many more women en route, infesting the corridors, the bubble-car tubes, the slidewalks and lift-tubes and arcades, but thankfully none accosted him. They seemed to be everywhere. One had a helpless infant in her arms. He stifled a heroic impulse to snatch the child out of danger. He could hardly complete his mission with a baby in tow and besides, he couldn't possibly rescue them all. It also occurred to him, belatedly, as he dodged a squad of giggling children racing across his path to swoop like sparrows up a lift-tube, that there was a fifty percent chance the infant was female anyway. It assuaged his conscience a little.

Ethan chose a room on the basis of price, after an alarming tele-conference between the transient hostel's concierge, the Kline Station public computer system, a Transients' Ombudsman, and no less than four live human officials on ascending rungs of the station's governing hierarchy about the exchange rate to be assigned to Ethan's Athosian pounds. They were actually quite kind in computing the most favorable translation of his funds, via two currencies of which Ethan had never heard, into the maximum possible number of Betan dollars. Betan dollars were one of the harder and more universally acceptable currencies available. Still, he ended with what seemed far fewer dollars than he had had pounds before and he passed hastily over the proffered Imperial Suite in favor of an Economy Cabin.

Economy proved more cabinet than cabin. When he was asleep, Ethan assured himself, he wouldn't mind. Now, however, he was wide-awake. He touched the pressure pad to inflate the bed and lay on it anyway, mentally reviewing his instructions and trying to ignore an odd myopic illusion that the walls were pressing inward.

When the Population Council had finally sat down to calculate it, returning the shipment to Jackson's Whole with Ethan to demand their money back cost more than the dubious refund, so Jackson's Whole was scrubbed. Ethan was at last, after much debate, given broad discretionary powers to choose another supplier on the basis of the freshest information available at Kline Station.

There were subsidiary instructions. Keep it under budget. Get the best. Go as far afield as needed. Don't waste money on unnecessary travel. Avoid personal contact with galactics; tell them nothing of Athos. Cultivate galactics to recruit immigrants; tell them all about the wonders of Athos. Don't make waves. Don't let them push you around. Keep an eye peeled for additional business opportunities. Personal use of Council funds will be considered peculation and prosecuted as such.

Fortunately, the Chairman had spoken to Ethan privately after the committee briefing.

"Those your notes?" He nodded to the clutch of papers and discs Ethan was juggling. "Give them to me."

And he dropped them into his oubliette.

"Get the stuff and get back," he told Ethan. "All else is gas."

Ethan's heart lifted at the memory. He smiled slowly, sat up, tossed his map module in the air and caught it in a smooth swipe, pocketed it, and went for a walk.

In Transients' Lounge Ethan found the bright face of the tapestry at last by the simple expedient of taking a bubble car through the tubes to the most luxurious passenger dock, turning around, and walking back the other way. Framed in crystal and chrome were sweeping panoramas of the galactic night, of other branches of the Station shot with candy-colored lights, of the glittering wheels of the earliest sections turning forever for the sake of their obsolete centrifugal gravities. Not abandoned—nothing was ever wholly abandoned in this society—but some put to less urgent uses, others half-dismantled for salvage that Kline Station might grow, like a snake eating its tail.

Within the soaring transparent walls of Transients' Lounge rioted a green fecundity of vines, trees in tubs, air ferns, orchids, muted tinkling chimes, bizarre fountains running backward, upside down, spiraling around the dizzy catwalks, lively intricate trickery with the artificial gravity. Ethan paused to stare in fascination for fifteen minutes at one fountain, sheeting water suspended in air, running endlessly in the form of a moebius strip. A breath away, across the transparent barrier, a cold that could turn all to stone in an instant lurked in deathly silence. The artistic contrast was overwhelming and Ethan was not the only downsider transient who stood transfixed in open wonder.

Bordering the parks section were cafes and restaurants where, Ethan calculated, if he only ate once a week he might dine and hostelries where patrons who could afford the restaurants four times a day dwelt. And theaters and feelie-dream booths and an arcade which, according to its directory, offered travelers the solace of some eighty-six officially established religions. Athos's, of course, was not among them. Ethan passed what was obviously the funeral procession of some philosophic person who spurned cryogenic storage in favor of microwave cremation—Ethan, eyes still full of the endless dark beyond the trees, thought he could understand a preference for fire over ice—and some mysterious ceremony whose principals, a woman wrapped in red silk and a man in spangled blue, were pelted with rice by giggling friends who then tied dozens of strings around the pair's wrists.

Coming to the core of the section, Ethan got down to business. Here were the consuls, embassies, and offices of commercial agents from a score of planets who shipped through the nexus of Kline Station's local space. Here, presumably, he would get a lead on a biological supplier who could fulfill Athos's needs. Then buy a ticket for the chosen planet, then—but Kline Station itself was sensory overload enough for one day.

Dutifully, Ethan at least peeked into the Betan Embassy. Unfortunately, its commercial directory computer interface was manned by what was obviously a female expediter. Ethan withdrew hastily without speaking to her. Perhaps he'd try later, during another shift. He pointedly ignored the collection of consuls representing the great syndicated houses of Jackson's Whole. Ethan did resolve to send House Bharaputra a stiff note of complaint, though, later.

Passing back through from this direction, Ethan's chosen hostel did indeed look staid. He estimated he'd walked a couple of kilometers through various levels from the luxury docks, but a curiosity that grew rather than faded with each new sight and discovery drew him out of Transients' Lounge entirely, into the Stationers' own sections. Here the decor diminished from staid to utilitarian.

The odors from a small cafeteria, tucked between a customized plastics fabricator and a pressure suit repair facility, reminded Ethan suddenly that he hadn't eaten since leaving shipboard. But there were a great many women within. He reversed the impulse and withdrew, feeling very hungry. A random walk led him down two more little tubes into a narrow, rather grubby commercial arcade. He was not far from the docking area by which he'd entered Kline Station. His wanderings were arrested by the smell of overused frying grease drifting from one doorway. He peered into the dimly lit interior.

A number of men in a kaleidoscope of Stationer work uniforms were lounging at tables and along a counter in attitudes of repose. It was evidently some sort of break room. There were no women present at all. Ethan's oppressed spirits lifted. Perhaps he could relax here, even get something to eat. He might even strike up a conversation. Indeed, remembering his instructions from the Athosian Department of Immigration, he had a duty to do so. Why not start now?

Ignoring a queasy subliminal feeling of unease—this was no time to let his shyness rule him—he entered, blinking. More than a break room. Judging from the alcoholic smell of the beverages, these men must be off-duty altogether. It was some sort of recreational facility, then, though it resembled an Athosian club not at all. Ethan wondered wistfully if one could get artichoke beer here. Being Stationer, it would more likely be based on algae or something. He suppressed a homesick twinge, moistened his lips, and walked boldly up to a group of half-a-dozen men in color-coded coveralls clustered around the counter. Stationers must be used to seeing Transients far more bizarrely dressed than his plain casual Athosian shirt, jacket, trousers, and shoes, but for a moment he wished for the doctor's whites he wore at the Rep Center, all clean and crisp from the laundry, that always lent him their reassuring sense of official identity.

"How do you do," Ethan began politely. "I represent the Bureau of Immigration and Naturalization of the Planet Athos. If I may, I'd like to tell you about the pioneering opportunities for settlement still available there—"

The sudden dead silence of his audience was interrupted by a large worker in green coveralls. "Athos? The Planet of the Fags? You on the level?"

"Can't be," said another, in blue. "Those guys never stick their noses off their home dirtball."

A third man, all in yellow, said something extremely coarse.

Ethan took a breath and began again, valiantly. "I assure you, I am indeed on the level. My name is Ethan Urquhart; I am myself a doctor of reproductive medicine. A crisis has arisen recently in our birth rate—"

Green-coveralls gave a bark of laughter. "I'll bet! Let me tell you what you're doing wrong, buddy—"

The coarse one, from whom alcoholic esters were wafting in high concentration, said something depressingly one-track. Green-coveralls chortled and patted Ethan familiarly on the stomach. "You're in the wrong store, Athosian. Beta Colony's the place to go for a change-of-sex operation. After that, you can get knocked up in no time."

One-track repeated himself. Ethan turned to him, his outrage and confusion taking refuge in stiff formality. "Sir, you seem to have some sadly narrow preconceptions about my planet. Personal relationships are a matter of individual preference and entirely private. In fact there are many communes, strict interpreters of the Founding Fathers, who take vows of chastity. They are highly respected—"

"Yeech!" cried Green-coveralls raucously. "That's even *worse*!" A roar of laughter went up from his co-workers.

Ethan felt his face flush. "Excuse me. I am a stranger here. This is the only place I've seen on Kline Station that is free of women and I thought some reasonable discourse might be possible. It's a very serious—"

One-track made a loud remark in the same vein.

Ethan wheeled around and slugged him.

Then froze, horror-stricken at his own dreadful breach of control. This wasn't the behavior of an ambassador—he must apologize at once—

"Free of women?" One-track snarled, scrambling back to his feet, his eyes red and drunken and feral. "Is that why you came in here—bloody procuring? I'll show you—"

Ethan found himself secured abruptly from behind by two of One-track's burlier friends. He trembled, suppressing a terrified impulse to struggle and break free. If he stayed cool maybe he could still—

"Hey, fellows, take it easy," Green-coveralls began anxiously. "He's obviously just a transient—"

The first blow doubled Ethan over, his breath whistling between clenching teeth. The two pinioning him straightened him up again. "—what we do to your type," *wham!* "around here!"

Ethan found he had no breath left with which to apologize. He hoped desperately One-track wasn't going to make a very long speech. But One-track continued, punctuating Ethan regularly.

"—bloody—damned—nosing around our—"

A light, sardonic, alto voice interrupted. "Aren't you a little worried by the odds? What if he gets loose and gangs up on the six of you?"

Ethan twisted his head around; it was the mercenary woman, Commander Quinn. She bounced lightly on her feet, head cocked alertly.

Green-coveralls swore reverently under his breath; One-track just swore. "Come on, Zed," said Green-coveralls, laying a hand on his comrade's arm, although never taking his eyes from the woman's face, "That's enough, I'm thinking."

One-track shook himself free. "And what's this dirt-sucker to you, Sweetie?" he snapped.

One corner of the woman's carved mouth twisted up; Blue-coveralls' lips parted in entrancement. "Suppose I say I'm his military advisor?" she said.

"Fag-loving women," One-track swore, "are worse than the fags themselves—" and continued in crudeness.

"Zed," muttered Blue-coveralls, "can it. She's not a tech, she's a troop. Combat vet—look at her insignia." There was a stir in the back of the room, as several neutral observers made prudent exits.

"All drunks are a pain," drawled the woman to the air, "but aggressive drunks are just plain disgusting."

One-track shoved toward her, mouthing confused obscenities. She waited in stillness until he crossed some invisible boundary. There was a sudden buzz and a flash of blue light. Ethan realized as the weapon spun in her hand and melted soundlessly back into its holster that the pause had been for stunner nimbus; all others in the group were out of range and untouched.

"Take a nap," she sighed. She glanced up at the two men still holding Ethan. "That your friend?" She nodded to the prone One-track, unconscious on the floor. "You should be more choosy. Friends like that can get you killed."

Ethan was hastily dropped. His knees buckled as he folded over his aching belly. The mercenary woman pulled him back to his feet. "C'mon, pilgrim. Let me take you back where you belong."

"I should have said, 'Why, are you missing yours?'" Ethan decided. "That's what I should have said to him. Or maybe—"

Commander Quinn's lips curved. Ethan wondered irritably why everyone around here seemed to find Athosians so amusing, except for the ones who acted as though he were offering them a dose of leprosy. A sudden new fear put him so off-balance he very nearly clutched the mercenary's arm. "Oh, God the Father. Are those constables?"

A pair of men was nearing them in the corridor. Their uniforms were pine green slashed with sky blue and an intimidating array of equipment hung from their utility belts. Ethan felt a sudden stab of guilt. "Maybe I should turn myself in—get it over with. I did assault that man—"

Commander Quinn's mouth quivered with amusement. "Not unless you're incubating some rare new plant virus under your fingernails. Those guys are Biocontrol—the ecology cops. Underfoot all over Kline Station." She paused to exchange polite nods with the men, who passed on, and added under her breath, "Bunch of compulsive hand-washers." She continued after a meditative moment, "Don't cross them, though. They have unlimited powers of search and seizure—you could find yourself being forcibly deloused, with no appeal."

Ethan thought about that. "I suppose station ecology is much less resilient than planetary."

"Balanced on a wire, between fire and ice," she agreed. "Some places have religion. Here we have safety drills. By the way, if you ever see a patch of frost forming anywhere but a docking bay, report it at once."

They re-entered Transients' Lounge. Her eyes were too penetrating, edgy with seriousness, for her quirking mouth and they made Ethan hideously uneasy. "Hope that little incident doesn't put you off Stationers," she said. "What say I take you to dinner, to make up for my fellow citizens' bad manners?"

Was this some sort of proposition, a ploy to get him alone and
helpless? He edged farther from her, as she paced softly beside him
like a predatory cat.

"I—I'm not ungrateful," he stammered, his voice rising in pitch,
"but, uh, I have a stomach ache," quite true, "thank you anyway," there
was a lift-tube to the next level, the one his hostel was on, "good-bye!"

He bolted for the tube, leaped in. Reaching upward did nothing to speed his ascent. His last shreds of dignity kept him from flapping his arms. He offered her a strained smile through the crystal sides
of the tube as her level fell away in dreamy slowness, distorted, fore-
shortened, blinked out.

He nipped out of the tube at his exit, darting behind a sort of
free-form sculpture with plants nearby in the mallway. He peered
through the leaves. She did not chase him. He unwound eventually,
slumping on a bench for a long, numb time. Safe at last.

He heaved a sigh and pushed to his feet and dragged off up the
mall. His little cubicle seemed newly attractive. Something very bland
to eat from the room service console, a shower, and bed. No more
exploratory adventures. Tomorrow he would get right to business.
Gather his data, choose the supplier, and ship out on the first available transport...

A man dressed in some planetary fashion of dull neutrality, plain
gray tunic and trousers, approached Ethan on the esplanade, smiling.
"Dr. Urquhart?" He grasped Ethan's arm.

Ethan smiled back in uncertain courtesy. Then stiffened, his
mouth opening to cry indignant protest as the hypospray prickled
his arm. A heartbeat and his mouth slackened, the cry unspent. The
man guided him gently toward a bubble car in the tubeway.

Ethan's feet felt vague, like balloons. He hoped the man
wouldn't let go, lest he bob helplessly up to the ceiling and hang upside
down with things falling out of his pockets on the passersby. The
mirrored canopy of the bubble car closed over his unfocused gaze like
a nictating membrane.

CHAPTER FOUR

Ethan came to awareness in a hostel room much larger and more luxurious than his own. His reason flowed with slow clarity, like honey. The rest of him floated in a sweet, languid euphoria. Distantly, under his heart, or down in his throat, something whined and cried and scratched frantically like an animal locked in a cellar, but there was no chance of its getting out. His viscous logic noted indifferently that he was bound tightly to a hard plastic chair and certain muscles in his back and arms and legs burned painfully. So what.

Far more intriguing was the man emerging from the bathroom, rubbing his damp reddened face vigorously with a towel. Gray eyes like granite chips, hard-bodied, average height, much like the fellow who'd picked Ethan off the mall and who even now sat on a nearby float chair, watching his prisoner closely.

Ethan's kidnapper was of so ordinary an appearance Ethan could hardly keep him before his mind even when he was looking directly at him. But Ethan had the oddest insight, like x-ray vision, that his bones contained not marrow but ice stone-hard as that outside the Station. Ethan wondered how he manufactured red blood cells with this peculiar medical condition. Maybe his veins ran liquid nitrogen. They were both utterly charming and Ethan wanted to kiss them.

"Is he under, Captain?" asked the man with the towel.

"Yes, Colonel Millisor," replied the other. "A full dose."

The man with the towel grunted and flung it on the bed next to the contents of Ethan's pockets and all his clothes, arrayed there.

43

Ethan noticed his own nakedness for the first time. There were a few Kline Station tokens, a comb, an empty raisin wrapper, his map module, his credit chit for his Betan funds for purchasing the new cultures—the creature under his heart howled, unheard, at that sight. His captor poked among the spoils. "This stuff scan clean?"

"Ha. Almost," said the cold captain. "Take a look at this." He picked up Ethan's map module, cracked open its back, and fixed an electron viewer over its microscopic circuit board. "We shook him down in the loading zone. See that little black dot? It was caused by a bead of acid in a polarized lipid membrane. When my scanner beam crossed it, it depolarized and dissolved and burned out—whatever had been there. Tracer for sure, probably an audio recorder as well. Very neat, tucked right in the standard map circuitry, which incidentally masked the bug's electronic noise with its own. He's an agent, all right."

"Were you able to trace the link back to its home base?"

The captain shook his head. "No, unfortunately. To find it was to destroy it. But we blinded them. They don't know where he is now."

"And who is 'they'? Terrence Cee?"

"We can hope."

The leader, the one Ethan's kidnapper had named Colonel Millisor, grunted again and approached Ethan to stare into his eyes. "What's your name?"

"Ethan," said Ethan sunnily. "What's yours?"

Millisor ignored this open invitation to sociability. "Your full name. And your rank."

This struck an old chord and Ethan barked smartly, "Master Sergeant Ethan CJB-8 Urquhart, Blue Regiment Medical Corps, U-221-767, *sir!*" He blinked at his interrogator, who had drawn back, startled. "Retired," he added after a moment.

"Aren't you a doctor?"

"Oh, yes," said Ethan proudly. "Where does it hurt?"

"I hate fast-penta," growled Millisor to his colleague.

The captain smiled coldly. "Yes, but at least you can be sure they're not holding anything back."

Millisor sighed, lips compressed, and turned to Ethan again. "Are you here to meet Terrence Cee?"

Ethan stared back, confused. See Terrence? The only Terrence he knew was one of the Rep Center techs. "They didn't send him," he explained.

"Who didn't send him?" Millisor asked sharply, all attention.

"The Council."

"Hell," the captain worried. "Could he have found himself some new backing, so soon after Jackson's Whole? He can't have had time, or the resources! I took care of every—"

Millisor held up a hand for silence, probed Ethan again. "Tell me everything you know about Terrence Cee."

Dutifully, Ethan began to do so. After a few moments Millisor, his face reflecting increasing frustration, cut him off with a sharp chop of his hand. "Stop."

"Must have been some other fellow," opined the cold captain. His leader shot him a look of exasperation. "Try another subject. Ask him about the cultures," the captain suggested in placation.

Millisor nodded. "The human ovarian cultures shipped to Athos from Bharaputra Biologicals. What did you do with them?"

Ethan began to describe, in detail, all the tests he'd put the material through that memorable afternoon. To his growing dismay, his captors didn't look at all pleased. Horrified, then mystified, then angry, but not happy. And he so wanted to make them happy....

"More garbage," the cold captain interrupted. "What is all this nonsense?"

"Can he be resisting the drug?" asked Millisor. "Increase the dose."

"Dangerous, if you still mean to put him back on the street with a gap in his memory. We're running short of time for that scenario to pass."

"That scenario may have to be changed. If that shipment has arrived on Athos and been distributed already, we may have no choice but to call in a military strike. And deliver it in less than seven months, or instead of a limited commando raid to torch their Reproduction Centers, we'll be forced to sterilize the whole damned planet to be sure of getting it all."

"Small loss." The cold captain shrugged.

"Big expense. And increasingly hard to keep covert."

"No survivors, no witnesses."

"There are always survivors at a massacre. Among the victors, if nowhere else." The granite chips sparked and the captain looked uncomfortable. "Dose him."

A prickle in Ethan's arm. Methodical and relentless, they asked him detailed questions about the shipment, his assignment, his superiors, his organization, his background. Ethan babbled. The room expanded and shrank. Ethan felt as if he were being turned inside out, with his stomach lining exposed to the world and his eyes twisted around and staring at each other. "Oh, I love you all," he crooned and retched violently.

He came to with his head under the shower. They gave him a different drug, replacing his euphoria with disjointed terror, and badgered him endlessly about Terrence Cee, the shipment, his mission, together and by turns.

Their frustration and hostility mounting, they gave him a drug that vastly increased the firing rate of his sensory nerves and applied instruments to his skin in areas of high nerve density that left no mark but induced incredible agony. He told them everything, anything, whatever they asked—he would gladly have told them what they wanted to hear, if only he could have guessed what it was—but they were merciless and unmoved, surgical in their concentration. Ethan became plastic, frantic, until at last all sensation was obliterated in a series of uncontrollable convulsions that nearly stopped his heart. At this they desisted.

He hung in his chair, breath shallow and shocky, staring at them through dilated eyes.

The leader glared back, disgusted. "Damnation, Rau! This man is a total waste of time. The shipment that he unpacked on Athos is definitely not what was sent from Bharaputra's laboratory. Terrence

Cee has pulled a switch somehow. It could be anywhere in the galaxy by now."

The captain groaned. "We were so close to wrapping up the entire case on Jackson's Whole! No, damn it! It has to be Athos. We all agreed, it *had* to be Athos."

"It may still be Athos. A plan within a plan—within a plan...." Millisor rubbed his neck wearily, looking suddenly much older than Ethan's first estimate. "The late Dr. Jahar did too good a job. Terrence Cee is everything Jahar promised—except loyal. Well, we'll get no more out of this one. You sure that wasn't just a speck of dirt in that circuit board?"

The captain started to look indignant, then frowned at Ethan as though he were something he had found sticking to the bottom of his boot. "It wasn't dirt. But that's sure as hell not any agent of Terrence Cee's. Think he has any use as a stalking-goat?"

"If only he were an agent," said Millisor regretfully, "it would be worth a try. Since he evidently isn't, he has no value at all." He glanced at his chronometer. "My God, have we been at this seven hours? It's too late now to blank him and turn him loose. Have Okita take him out and arrange an accident."

The docking bay was cold. A few safety lights splashed color on walls and silvered the silhouettes of silent equipment isolated in the thick stretches of dimness. The metal catwalks arched through a high, echoing hollowness, emerging from shadows, converging in darkness, a spider's skyway. Mysterious mechanical bundles dangled from the girders like a spider's preserved victims.

"This should be high enough," muttered the man called Okita. He was almost as average looking as Captain Rau, but for the compact density of his muscles. He manhandled Ethan to his knees. "Here. Drink up."

He forced a tube into Ethan's mouth and squeezed the bulb, for the nth time. Ethan choked and perforce swallowed the burning, aromatic liquid. The dense man let Ethan drop. "Absorb that a minute," Okita told him, as though he had some choice in the matter.

Ethan clung to the mesh flooring of the catwalk, dizzy and belching, and stared through it at the metal floor far below. It seemed to gleam and pulsate in slow, seasick waves. He thought of his smashed lightflyer.

Captain Rau's chosen henchman leaned against the safety railing and sniffed reflectively, also looking down. "Falls are funny things," he mused. "Freaky. Two meters are enough to kill you. But I heard of a case where a fellow fell three hundred meters and survived. Depends on just how you hit, I guess." The bland eyes flickered over the bay, checking entrances, checking for Ethan knew not what. "They run their gravity a little light here. Better break your neck first," Okita decided judiciously. "Just to be sure."

Ethan could not press his fingers through the narrow mesh to cling, though he tried. For an insane moment he thought of trying to bribe his assassin-to-be with his Betan credit chit, that his captors had carefully returned to his pockets along with all their other contents before sending them off like a pair of lovers looking for a dark place to tryst. Like a drunk and his loyal friend trying to guide him back to his hostel before he wandered drunkenly into the maze of the station and got lost. Ethan reeked of alcoholic esters and his mumbled whimperings for help had been unintelligible to the amused passers-by in the populated corridors. His tongue seemed less thick now, but this place was unpopulated in the extreme.

A surge of loyalty and nausea shook him. No. He would die with his purse intact. Besides, Okita looked remarkably unbribable. Ethan didn't think he'd even be interested in delaying his execution for a little rape. At least the money could be taken from his crumpled body and returned to Athos....

Athos. He did not want to die, dared not die. The terrifying scraps of conversation he'd overheard between his interrogators worried him like savage dogs. Bomb the Rep Centers? Banks of helpless babies crashing down, flames shooting up to boil away their gentle waterbeds—he shuddered and shivered and moaned, but could not drive his half-paralyzed muscles to his straining will. Vile, inhuman plans—so reasonably discussed, so casually dispatched... all insane here...

The dense man sniffed and stretched and scratched and sighed and checked his chronometer for the third time. "All right," he said at last. "Your biochemistry should be muddled enough by now. Time for your flying lesson, boy-o."

He grasped Ethan by the scruff of his neck and the seat of his pants, boosting him up to the railing.

"Why are you doing this to me?" squeaked Ethan in a last desperate attempt to communicate.

"Orders," grunted the dense man with finality. Ethan stared into the bored, flat eyes and gave himself up for murdered for the crime of being innocent.

Okita yanked his head back over the railing by the hair and folded his hand around the squeeze bottle. The murky ceiling of the docking bay, crossed by girders above, blurred in Ethan's eyes. The cold metal rail bit his neck.

Okita studied the positioning, cocking his head and narrowing his eyes. "Right." Bracing Ethan's arching body against the railing with his knees, he raised doubled fists for a powerful blow.

The catwalk shook, a rattling jar. The panting figure raising the stunner in both hands did not pause to cry warning, but simply fired. She seemed to have dropped out of the sky. The shock of the stunner nimbus scarcely made any difference in Ethan's inventory of discomfort. But Okita was caught square on and followed the momentum of his aimed blow over the railing. His legs, picking up speed, tilted up and slid past Ethan's nose, like a ship sinking bow-first.

"Aw, *shit*," yelled Commander Quinn and bounded forward. The stunner clattered across the catwalk and spun over the side to whistle through the air and burst to sizzling shards far below. Her clutching swipe was just too late to connect with Okita's trouser leg. Blood winked from her torn fingernail. Okita followed the stunner, headfirst.

Ethan slithered bonelessly down to crouch on the mesh. Her boots, at his eye level, arched to tiptoe as she peered down over the side. "Gee, I feel really bad about that," she remarked, licking her bleeding finger. "I've never killed a man by accident before. Unprofessional."

"You again," Ethan croaked.

She gave him a cat's grin. "What a coincidence."

The body splayed on the deck below stopped twitching. Ethan stared down whitely. "I'm a doctor. Shouldn't we go down there and, um…"

"Too late, I think," said Commander Quinn. "But I wouldn't get too misty-eyed over that creep. Quite aside from what he almost did to you just now, he helped kill eleven people on Jackson's Whole, five months ago, just to cover up the secret I'm trying to find out."

His syrup-slow logic spoke. "If it's a secret people are killed just for knowing, wouldn't it make a lot more sense to try to *avoid* finding it out?" He clutched his shredded acuity. "Who are you really, anyway? Why are you following me?"

"Technically, I'm not following you at all. I'm following Ghem-colonel Luyst Millisor and the so-charming Captain Rau and their two goons—ah, one goon. Millisor is interested in you, therefore I am too. Q.E.D.—Quinn Excites Dismay."

"Why?" he whimpered wearily.

She sighed. "If I had arrived at Jackson's Whole two days ahead of them instead of two days behind them, I could tell you. As for the rest—I really am a commander in the Dendarii Mercenaries and everything I've told you is true, except that I'm not on home leave. I'm on assignment. Think of me as a rent-a-spy. Admiral Naismith is diversifying our services."

She squatted beside him, checked his pulse, eyes and eyelids, battered reflexes. "You look like death warmed over, Doctor."

"Thanks to you. They found your tracer. Decided *I* was a spy. Questioned me…" He found he was shivering uncontrollably.

Her lips made a brief grim line. "I know. Sorry. I did save your life just now, I hope you noticed. Temporarily."

"Temporarily?"

She nodded toward the deck below. "Colonel Millisor is going to be quite excited about you, after this."

"I'll go to the authorities—"

"Ah—hm. I hope you'll think better of that. In the first place, I don't think the authorities would be able to protect you quite well enough. Secondly, it would blow my cover. Until now I don't think Millisor suspected I existed. Since I have an awful lot of friends and relatives around here, I'd just as soon keep it that way, Millisor and Rau being—what they are. You see my point?"

He felt he ought to argue with her. But he was sick and weak—and, it also occurred to him, still very high in the air. Green vertigo plucked at him. If she decided to send him after Okita... "Yeah," he mumbled. "Uh, what—what are you going to do with me?"

She planted her hands on her hips and frowned thoughtfully down upon him. "Not sure yet. Don't know if you're an ace or a joker. I think I'll keep you up my sleeve for a while, until I can figure out how best to play you. With your permission," she added in palpable afterthought.

"Stalking-goat," he muttered darkly.

She quirked an eyebrow at him. "Perhaps. If you can think of a better idea, trot it out."

He shook his head, which made shooting pains ricochet around inside his skull and yellow pinwheels counter-rotate before his eyes. At least she didn't seem to be on the same side as his recent captors. The enemy of my enemy—my ally...?

She hoisted him to his feet and pulled his arm across her shoulders to thread their way down stairs and ladders to the docking bay floor. He noticed for the first time that she was several centimeters shorter than himself. But he had no inclination to spot her points in a free-for-all.

When she released him he sank to the deck in a dizzy stupor. She poked around Okita's body, checking pulse points and damages. Her lips thinned ironically. "Huh. Broken neck." She sighed and stood regarding the corpse and Ethan with much the same narrow calculation.

"We could just leave him here," she said. "But I rather fancy giving Colonel Millisor a mystery of his own to solve. I'm tired of being on the damn defensive, lying low, always one move behind. Have you ever given thought to the difficulty of getting rid of a body on a space station? I'll bet Millisor has. Bodies don't bother you, do they? What with your being a doctor and all, I mean."

Okita's fixed stare was exactly like that of a dead fish, glassily reproachful. Ethan swallowed. "I actually never cared much for that end of the life-cycle," he explained. "Pathology and anatomy and so forth. That's why I went for Rep work, I guess. It was more, um... hopeful." He paused a while. His intellect began to crunch on in spite of himself. "*Is* it hard to get rid of a body on a space station? Can't you just shove it out the nearest airlock, or down an unused lift-tube, or something?"

Her eyes were bright with stimulation. "The airlocks are all monitored. Taking anything out, even an anonymous bundle, leaves a record in the computers. And it would last *forever* out there. Same objection applies to chopping it up and putting it down an organics disposer. Eighty or so kilos of high-grade protein leave too big a blip in the records. Besides, it's been tried. Very famous murder case, a few years back. The lady's still in therapy, I believe. It would definitely be noticed."

She flopped down beside him to sit with her chin on her knees, arms wrapped around her boots and flexing, not rest but nervous energy contained. "As for stashing it whole anywhere inside the Station—well, the safety patrols are nothing compared to the ecology cops. There isn't a cubic centimeter of the Station that doesn't get checked on a regular schedule. You *could* keep moving it around, but..."

"I think I have a better idea. Yes. Why not? As long as I'm going to commit a crime, let it be a perfect one. Anything worth doing is worth doing well, as Admiral Naismith would say."

She rose to make a wandering circuit of the docking bay, selecting bits of equipment with the faintly distracted air of a housekeeper choosing vegetables at the market.

Ethan lay on the floor in misery, envying Okita, whose troubles were over. He had been on Kline Station, he estimated, just about a day and had yet to have his first meal. Beaten up, kidnapped, drugged, nearly murdered, and now rapidly becoming accessory-after-the-fact to a crime which if not exactly a murder was surely the next best thing. Galactic life was every bit as bad as anything he had imagined. And he had fallen into the hands of a madwoman, to boot. The Founding Fathers had been right…. "I want to go home," he moaned.

"Now, now," Commander Quinn chided, plunking down a float pallet next to Okita's body and rolling a squat cylindrical shipping canister off it. "That's no way to be, just when my case is showing signs of cracking open at last. You just need a good meal"—she glanced at him—"and about a week in a hospital bed. Afraid I shan't be able to supply that, but as soon as I finish cleaning up here I'll take you to a place where you can rest a bit while I get the next phase started. All right?"

She unlatched the shipping canister and, with some difficulty, folded Okita's body into it. "There. That doesn't look too coffin-like, does it?" She made a rapid but thorough pass over the impact area with a sonic scrubber, emptied its receptacle bag in with Okita, hopped the canister back onto the pallet with a hand-tractor, and replaced everything else where she had found it. Lastly, and somewhat mournfully, she collected all the pieces of her stunner.

"So. That gives the project its first deadline. Pallet and drum must be returned here within eight hours, before the next scheduled docking, or they'll be missed."

"Who were those men?" he asked her, as she had him crawl onto the pallet and settle himself for the ride. "They were insane. I mean, everyone I've met here is crazy, but they—they were talking about bombing Athos's reproduction clinics! Killing all the babies—maybe killing everyone!"

"Oh?" she said. "That's a new wrinkle. First I've heard of that scenario. I am extremely sorry I didn't get to listen in on that interrogation and I hope you will, ah, fill me in on what I missed. I've been trying to plant a bug in Millisor's quarters for three weeks, but his counter-intelligence equipment is, unfortunately, superb."

"You mainly missed a lot of screaming," said Ethan morosely.

She looked rather embarrassed. "Ah—yes. I'm afraid I didn't think they'd need to use anything but fast-penta."

"Stalking-goat," Ethan grumbled.

She cleared her throat, sitting cross-legged beside him with the control lead in her hand. The pallet rose into the air like a magic carpet.

"Not—not too high," Ethan choked, scrambling for a non-existent handhold. She brought it back down to a demure ten centimeters altitude and they started off at a walking pace.

She spoke slowly, seeming to choose her words with great care. "Ghem-colonel Luyst Millisor is a Cetagandan counter-intelligence officer. Captain Rau and Okita and another brawn by the name of Setti, are his team."

"Cetagandan! Isn't that planet pretty far from here to be interested in, um"—he glanced at the Stationer woman—"us? This nexus node, I mean."

"Not far enough, evidently."

"But why, in God the Father's name, should they want to destroy Athos? Is Cetaganda—controlled by women or something?"

A laugh escaped her. "Hardly. I'd call it a typical male-dominated totalitarian state, only slightly mitigated by their rather artistic cultural peculiarities. No. Millisor is not, per se, interested in either Athos or the Kline Station nexus. He's chasing—something else. The big secret. The one I was hired to find out."

She paused to maneuver the float pallet around a tricky ascending corner. "Apparently there was, on Cetaganda, a long-range, military-sponsored genetics project. Until about three years ago, Millisor was the security chief for that project. And the security was tight. In twenty-five *years*, no one had been able to find out what they were up to, beyond the fact that it seemed to be the one-man show of a certain Dr. Faz Jahar, a moderately bright Cetagandan geneticist who vanished from view about the time it started. Do you have any idea how incredibly long that is to keep a secret in this business? The thing has really been Millisor's life work, as well as Jahar's.

"In any event, something went wrong. The project went up in smoke—literally. The laboratory blew up one night, taking Jahar with it. And Millisor and his merry men have been chasing *something* around the galaxy ever since, blowing people away with the careless abandon of either homicidal lunatics, or—men scared out of their wits. And, ah, while I'm not sure I'd vouch for Captain Rau, Ghem-colonel Millisor does not strike me as a madman."

"You couldn't prove it by me," said Ethan glumly. There was still something not quite right with his vision and tremula came and went in his muscles.

They came to a large hatch in the corridor wall. RENOVA-TION, said a bright sign. DO NOT ENTER. AUTHORIZED PERSONNEL ONLY.

Commander Quinn did something Ethan could not quite see to the control box and the hatch slid open. She floated the pallet through. There came a voice and a laugh from the corridor they had just vacated. She closed the hatch quickly, leaving them in total darkness.

"There," she muttered, switching on a hand light. "Nobody saw us. Undeserved luck. Bloody time for it to start averaging out."

Ethan blinked at his surroundings. An empty rectangular basin was the centerpiece for a large airy chamber full of columns, pierced lattices, mosaics, and elaborate arches.

"It's supposed to be an exact replica of some famous palace on Earth," Commander Quinn explained. "The Elhamburger or something. A very wealthy shipper was having it done—all finished, in fact—when his assets were suddenly tied up in litigation. The suits have been going on for four months now and the place is still pad-locked. You can baby-sit our friend here till I get back." She rapped on the lid of the canister.

Ethan decided that all that was needed to make his day complete would be for it to rap back. But she had grounded the pallet and was piling up some cushions. "No blankets," she muttered. "I gotta keep my jacket. But if you sort of burrow in here, you should be warm enough."

It was like falling into a bank of clouds. "Burrow," Ethan whispered. "Warm…"

She dug into her jacket pocket. "And here's a candy bar to tide you over."

He snatched it; he couldn't help himself.

"Ah, one other thing. You can't use the plumbing. It would register on the computer monitors. I know this sounds terrible, but—if you've gotta go, use the canister." She paused. "It's not, after all, like he didn't deserve it."

"I'd rather die," said Ethan distinctly around a mouthful of nuts and goo. "Uh—are you going to be gone long?"

"At least an hour. Hopefully not more than four. You can sleep, if you like."

Ethan jerked himself awake. "Thank you."

"And now," she rubbed her hands together briskly, "phase two of the search for the L-X-10-Terran-C."

"The what?"

"That was the code name of Millisor's research project. Terran-C for short. Maybe some part of whatever they were working on originated on Earth."

"But Terrence Cee is a man," said Ethan. "They kept asking me if I was here to meet *him*."

She was utterly still for a moment. "Oh…? How strange. How very strange. I never knew that." Her eyes were bright as mirrors. Then she was gone.

CHAPTER FIVE

Ethan awoke with a startled gasp as something landed on his stomach. He thrashed up, looking around wildly. Commander Quinn stood before him in the wavering illumination of her hand light. The fingers of her other hand tapped a nervous, staccato rhythm on her empty stunner holster. Ethan's hands encountered a bulky bundle of cloth in his lap, which proved to be a set of Stationer coveralls wrapped around a matching pair of boots.

"Put those on," she ordered, "and hurry. I think I've found a way to get rid of the body, but we have to get there before shift change if I'm going to catch the right people on duty."

He dressed. She helped him impatiently with the unfamiliar tabs and catches, and made him sit again on the float pallet. It all made him feel like a backward four-year-old. After a quick reconnoiter by the mercenary woman, they left the chamber as unseen as they had entered it, drifting off through the maze of the Station.

At least he no longer felt as though his brains were suspended in syrup in a jar, Ethan thought. The world parted around him now with no more than natural clarity and colors did not flash fire in his eyes, nor leave scorched trails across his retinas. This was fortunate, as the Stationer coveralls Quinn had brought him to wear over his Athosian clothes were bright red. But waves of nausea still pulsed slowly in his stomach like moon-raised tides. He slouched, trying to lower his center of gravity still further onto the moving float pallet, and ached for something more than the three hours of sleep the mercenary woman had allowed him.

"People are going to see us," he objected as she turned down a populated corridor.

"Not in that outfit." She nodded toward the coveralls. "Along with the float pallet it's the next best thing to a cloak of invisibility. Red is for Docks and Locks—they'll all think you're a porter in charge of the pallet. As long as you don't open your mouth or act like a downsider."

They passed into a large chamber where thousands of carrots were aligned in serried ranks, their white beards of roots dripping in the intermittent misting from the hydroponics sprayers, their fluffy green tops glowing in the grow-lights. The air of the room through which, Quinn assured him, they were taking a short cut, tasted cool and moist with a faint underlying tang of chemicals.

His stomach growled. Quinn, guiding the float pallet, glanced over at him. "I don't think I should have eaten that candy bar," Ethan muttered darkly.

"Well, for the gods' sakes don't throw up in *here*," she begged him. "Or use the—"

Ethan swallowed firmly. "No."

"Do you think a carrot would settle your stomach?" she asked solicitously. She reached over, tipping the pallet terrifyingly, and plucked one from the passing row. "Here."

He took the damp hairy thing dubiously and after a moment stuffed it into one of the coverall's many closured pockets. "Maybe later."

They rose past a dozen stacked banks of growing vegetables to take an exit high in the chamber wall. NO ADMITTANCE, it said in glowing green letters. Quinn ignored the admonition with a verve bordering, Ethan thought, on the anti-social. He glanced back at the door as it hissed closed behind them. NO ADMITTANCE, it repeated on this side. So, they had committees on Kline Station too....

She brought the pallet down in the next cross-corridor beside a door marked ATMOSPHERE CONTROL. NO ADMITTANCE. AUTHORIZED PERSONNEL ONLY, by which Ethan reasoned it must be their destination.

Commander Quinn unfolded herself from a half-lotus. "Now, whatever happens, try not to talk. Your accent would give you away at once. Unless you'd rather stay out here with Okita until I'm ready for you."

Ethan shook his head quickly, struck by a vision of himself trying to explain to some passing authority that he was *not*, despite appearances, a murderer searching for a place to bury the body.

"All right. I can use the extra pair of hands. But be prepared to move on my order when the chance comes." She led on through the airseal doors, float pallet following like a dog on a leash.

It was like stepping into a chamber beneath the sea. Viridescent lines of light and shadow waved and scintillated across the floor, the walls—Ethan gaped at the walls. Three-story-high transparent barriers held back clear water stuffed with green and pierced with brilliant light. Millions of tiny silver bubbles galloped merrily through the minute fronds of aquatic plants, now pausing, now streaming on. An amphibian fully half a meter long pushed through this underwater jungle to stare at Ethan through its beady eyes. Its skin was black and shiny as patent leather, striped in scarlet. It shot away in a spray of silver to vanish in the green lace.

"Oxy-CO_2 exchange for the Station," Commander Quinn explained in an undertone. "The algae is bioengineered for maximum oxygen generation and CO_2 absorption. But of course, it grows. So to save having the chambers down half the time while we, ah, bale hay, the newts—specially bred—crop it for us. But then, naturally, you end up with a lot of newts...."

She broke off as a blue-suited technician shut down a monitor at a control station and turned to frown at them. She waved at him cheerily. "Hi, Dale, remember me? Elli Quinn. Dom told me where to look you up."

His frown flipped to a grin. "Yes, he told me he'd seen you." He advanced as if he might hug her, but settled on a bashful handshake instead.

They exchanged small talk while Ethan, unintroduced, tried not to shift about nervously, or open his mouth or act like a downsider. The first two were easy enough, but what was it that marked a downsider in Stationer eyes? He stood by the float pallet and tried desperately to act like nobody at all.

Quinn ended what seemed to Ethan an unnecessarily lengthy digression about the Dendarii Mercenaries with the remark, "And do you know, those poor troops have never tasted fried newt legs!"

The tech's eyes glinted with a humor baffling to Ethan. "What! Can there be a soul in the universe so deprived? No cream of newt soup, either, I suppose?"

"No newt creole," confided Commander Quinn with mock horror. "No newts 'n' chips."

"No newt provençal?" chorused the tech. "No newt stew? No newt mousse in aspic? No slither goulash, no newt chowder?"

"Bucket o' newts is unknown to them," confirmed Quinn. "Newt caviar is a delicacy unheard of."

"No newt nuggets?"

"Newt nuggets?" echoed the commander, looking suddenly really nonplused.

"Latest thing," explained the tech. "They're really boned leg meat, chopped, reformed, and fried."

"Oh," said the mercenary woman. "I'm relieved. For a moment there I was picturing some form of, er, newt organettes."

They both burst into laughter. Ethan swallowed and looked around surreptitiously for some kind, any kind, of basin. A couple of the slick black creatures swam to the barrier and goggled at him.

"Anyway," Quinn went on to the tech, "I thought if you were about due for the culling this shift you might spare me a few, to freeze and take back with me. Assuming you're not short, of course."

"We are never," he groaned, "short of newts. Help yourself. Take a hundred kilos. Take two. Three."

"A hundred would be plenty. All I can afford to ship. Make it a treat for officers only, eh?"

He chuckled and led her up a ladder to an access port. Ethan skittishly followed her come-along gesture, bringing up the float pallet.

The tech picked his way delicately across a mesh catwalk. Beneath them the waters hissed and rushed in little eddies; a fresh draft from below cooled Ethan's skin and cleared his aching head. He kept one hand on the safety railing. Some of the whirlpools below suggested powerful suction pumpers at work somewhere in the silver-green. Another water chamber was visible beyond this one and beyond that another, retreating out of sight.

The catwalk widened to a platform. The hiss became a roar as the tech pulled back a cover above an underwater cage. The cage roiled with black and scarlet shapes, slipping and splashing over each other.

"Oh, lord, yes," yelled the tech. "Full house. Sure you don't want to feed your whole army?"

"Would if I could," called Quinn back. "Tell you what, though. I'll trot the excess down to Disposal for you, once I pick out my choice. Does Transients' Lounge need any?"

"No orders this shift. Help yourself."

He opened a housing over a control box, did something; the newt trap rose slowly, draining water, compressing the wriggling black and scarlet mass. Another motion at the controls, a buzz, a blue light. Ethan could feel the nimbus of a powerful stun beam even where he stood. The mass stopped writhing and lay still and shining.

The tech heaved a large green plastic carton from a stack of identical ones and positioned it on a digital scale under a trap door in the bottom of the cage. He aligned a chute and opened the trap. Dozens of limp newts slithered down into the carton. As the digital readout approached 100 kilograms he slowed the flow and tossed a last black body in by hand. He then removed the carton with a hand-tractor, replaced it with another, and repeated the process. A third carton did not quite make it to full capacity. The tech entered the exact biomass removed from the system into his computer log.

"Want me to help you pack your canister?" he offered.

Ethan blanched, but the mercenary woman said lightly, "Naw, go on back down to your monitors. I'm going to sort through these by hand a bit, I think—no point in shipping any but the best."

The tech grinned and started back across the catwalk. "Find 'em some nice juicy ones," he called. Quinn gave him a friendly wave as he vanished back through the access port.

"Now," she turned back to Ethan, her face gone intent, "let's make these numbers match. Help me get that dirt-sucker up on this scale."

It wasn't easy; Okita had stiffened, wedged in the canister. The mercenary woman stripped him of clothes and a variety of lethal weapons and made them into a compact bundle.

Ethan shook off the paralysis of his confusion to attempt a task he at last felt sure of and weighed the corpse. Whatever this madness was he had fallen into, it threatened Athos. His original impulse to escape the mercenary woman was becoming, in his gradually clearing head, an equally strenuous desire not to let her out of his sight until he could discover, somehow, everything she knew about it.

"Eight-one-point-four-five kilograms," he reported in his best clipped scientific tone, the one he used for visiting VIPs back at Sevarin. "Now what?"

"Now get him into one of these cartons and fill it to, ah, one hundred point six two kilos with newts," she instructed with a glance at the first carton's readout. When this was done—the last fraction of a kilo was accomplished by her pulling a vibra-knife from her jacket and adding slightly less than half a newt—she switched data discs and sealed the carton.

"Now eighty-one point forty-five kilos of newts into that shipping canister," she instructed. It came out even, leaving them with three cartons and a canister as before.

"Will you please tell me what we're doing?" Ethan begged.

"Turning a rather difficult problem into a much simpler one. Now instead of an extremely incriminating drum full of dead downsider, all we have to get rid of is eighty or so kilos of stunned newts."

"But we haven't got rid of the body," Ethan pointed out. He stared down into the bright waters. "Are you going to dump the newts back in?" he asked hopefully. "Can they swim all right, stunned?"

"No, no, no!" said Quinn, looking quite shocked. "That would unbalance the system! It's very finely tuned. The whole point of this exercise is to keep the computer records straight. As for the body—you'll see."

"All set?" called the tech as they floated out of the access port, canister, cartons and all stacked on the pallet.

"No, darn it," said Quinn. "I realized when I was about halfway through that I'd grabbed the wrong size shipping canister. I'll have to come back later. Look, give me the receipt and I'll still run this load down to Disposal for you. I want to look up Teki there anyway."

"Oh, sure, all right," said the tech, brightening. "Thanks." He punched up the records, put them on a data disk, and handed it over. Commander Quinn retreated with all seemly haste.

"Good." She slumped as the airseal doors slid shut behind them, the first hint of weariness Ethan had seen in her. "I'll get to oversee the final act myself." She added to Ethan's bewildered look, "We could have just left them to go down to Disposal on the regular schedule, but I kept having this horrible vision of a last-minute order arriving from Transients' Lounge and Dale opening a carton to fill it...."

"An order for newts?" Ethan floundered.

She snickered. "Yes, but up there they're sold to the downsiders as Premium Fresh Frog Legs, on the restaurant menus. We stiff 'em for a sweet price, too."

"Is—is that, er, ethical?"

She shrugged. "Gotta make a profit somewhere. Snob appeal keeps the demand up. You can hardly give the wee beasties away on the Stationer side, everybody's so sick of them. But Biocontrol refuses to diversify the weed-grazers on account of the system working at max efficiency for oxygen generation as is. And everyone has to agree, the oxygen comes first. The newts are just a by-product."

They re-mounted the float pallet and drifted off down the corridor. Ethan glanced sideways at the mercenary woman's abstracted profile. He must try…

"What kind of genetics project?" he asked suddenly. "Millisor's thing, I mean. Don't you know any more about it than that?"

She spared him a thoughtful glance. "Human genetics. And in truth, I know very little more than that. Some names, a few code words. God only knows what they were up to. Making monsters, maybe. Or raising supermen. The Cetagandans have always been a bunch of aggressive militarists. Maybe they meant to raise battalions of mutant super-soldiers in vats like you Athosians and take over the universe or something."

"Not likely," remarked Ethan. "Not battalions, anyway."

"Why not? Why not clone as many as you want, once you've made the mold?"

"Oh, certainly, you could produce quantities of infants—although it would take enormous resources to do so. Highly trained techs, as well as equipment and supplies. But don't you see, that's just the beginning. It's nothing, compared to what it takes to raise a child. Why, on Athos it absorbs most of the planet's economic resources. Food of course—housing—education, clothing, medical care—it takes nearly all our efforts just to maintain population replacement, let alone to increase. No government could possibly afford to raise such a specialized, non-productive army."

Elli Quinn quirked an eyebrow. "How odd. On other worlds, people seem to come in floods and they're not necessarily impoverished, either."

Ethan, diverted, said, "Really? I don't see how that can be. Why, the labor costs alone of bringing a child to maturity are astronomical. There must be something wrong with your accounting."

Her eyes screwed up in an expression of sudden ironic insight. "Ah, but on other worlds the labor costs aren't added in. They're counted as free."

Ethan stared. "What an absurd bit of double thinking! Athosians would never sit still for such a hidden labor tax! Don't the primary nurturers even get social duty credits?"

"I believe"—her voice was edged with a peculiar dryness—"they call it women's work. And the supply usually exceeds the demand—non-union scabs, as it were, undercutting the market."

Ethan was increasingly puzzled. "Are not most women combat soldiers, then, like you? Are there men Dendarii?"

She hooted, then lowered her voice as a passer-by stared. "Four-fifths of the Dendarii are men. And of the women, three out of four are techs, not troops. Most military services are skewed that way, except for ones like Barrayar that have no women at all."

"Oh," said Ethan. After a disappointed pause he added, "You are an atypical sample, then." So much for his nascent Rules of Female Behavior.

"Atypical." She was still a moment, then snorted. "Yeah, that's me all over."

They passed through an archway framing airseal doors labeled ECOBRANCH: RECYCLING. Ethan ate his carrot as they threaded the corridors, stripping off roots and top and, after a glance around his immaculate white surroundings, stuffing them back in his pocket. By the time he had crunched down the last mouthful they arrived at a door marked ASSIMILATION STATION B: AUTHORIZED PERSONNEL ONLY.

They entered a brightly-lit chamber lined with banks of intimidating-looking monitors. A lab bench and sink in the center seemed half familiar to Ethan, for it was jammed with equipment for organic analysis. A number of color-coded conduits with access ports—for sampling?—crowded one end of the room. The other end was entirely occupied by a strange machine connected to the larger system by pipes; Ethan could not begin to guess its function.

A pair of legs in pine-green trousers with sky-blue piping were sticking out between a couple of the conduits. A high-pitched voice muttered unintelligibly. After a few more savage sibilants there was a clang and the whine of a sealing mechanism and the legs' owner wriggled out and stood.

She wore plastic gloves to her armpits and was clutching an unidentifiable crumpled metal object perhaps a third of a meter long that dripped vile-smelling brown liquid. *F. Helda*, read the nametag over her left breast pocket, *Biocontrol Warden*. Her face was red and angry, and terrified Ethan. Her voice cleared, "—unbelievable stupid downsider jerks…" She broke off as she saw Ethan and his companion. Her eyes narrowed and her frown deepened. "Who are you? You don't belong in here. Can't you read?"

Dismay flashed in Quinn's eyes. She recovered and smiled winningly. "I just brought down the newt cull from Atmosphere. A little favor for Dale Zeeman."

"Zeeman should do his own work," the ecotech woman snapped, "not entrust it to some ignorant downsider. I'll write him up for this."

"Oh, I'm Stationer born and bred," Quinn assured her hastily. "Let me introduce myself—Elli Quinn's the name. Maybe you know my cousin Teki—he works in this department. As a matter of fact, I rather thought he d be here."

"Oh," said the woman, only slightly mollified. "He's in A Station. But don't you go over there now. They're cleaning the filters. He won't have time to chat until after the system is back up. Work shifts are not the place for personal visiting, you know—"

"What in the world is that?" Quinn diverted her lecture with a nod at the metal object.

Ecotech Helda's clutch tightened on the tortured metal as if she might strangle it. Her chill toward her unauthorized visitors struggled with her need to vent her rage and lost. "My latest present from Transients' Lounge. You wonder how illiterates can afford space travel— damn it, even illiterates have no excuse, the rules are demonstrated on the holovid! It *was* a perfectly good emergency oxygen canister, until some asshole stuffed it down an organics disposer. He must have had to smash it flat first to fit it in. Thank the gods it was discharged, or it might have blown out a pipe. Unbelievable stupidity!"

She stalked across the room to fling it into a bin with a number of other obviously non-organic bits of trash. "I hate downsiders," she growled. "Careless, dirty, inconsiderate animals…" She stripped off the gloves and disposed of them, mopped the drips with a sonic scrubber and antiseptic, and turned to the sink to scrub her hands with violent thoroughness.

Quinn nodded toward the big green cartons. "Can I help you get these out of the way?" she asked brightly.

"There was absolutely no point in bringing them down ahead of schedule," said the ecotech. "I have an interment scheduled in five minutes and the degrader is programmed to break down all the way to simple organics and vent to Hydroponics. It will just have to wait. You can take yourselves off and tell Dale Zeeman—" she broke off as the door slid open.

Half a dozen somber Stationers followed a covered float pallet through the door. Quinn motioned Ethan silently to an inconspicuous seat on their own float pallet as the procession entered the chamber. Ecotech Helda hastily straightened her uniform and composed her features to an expression of grave sympathy.

The Stationers gathered around while one of them intoned a few platitudes. Death was a great leveler, it seemed. The turns of phrase were different, but the sense would have passed at an Athosian funeral, Ethan thought. Maybe galactics weren't so wildly different after all.

"Do you wish a final view of the deceased?" Helda inquired of them.

They shook their heads, a middle-aged man among them remarking, "Ye gods, the funeral was enough." He was shushed by a middle-aged woman beside him.

"Do you wish to stay for the interment?" asked Helda, formally and unpressingly.

"Absolutely not," said the middle-aged man. At a look of embarrassed disapproval from his female companion, he added firmly, "I saw Grandpa through five replacement operations. I did my bit when he was alive. Watching him get ground up to feed the flowers won't add a thing to my karma, love."

The family filed out and the ecotech returned to her original aggressively businesslike demeanor. She stripped the corpse—it was an exceedingly ancient man—and took the clothes to the corridor, where presumably someone had lingered to collect them. Returning, she checked a data file, donned gloves and gown, wrinkled her lip, and attacked the deceased with a vibra-knife. Ethan watched with a professional fascination as a dozen mechanical replacement parts clanked into a tray—a heart, several tubes, bone pins, a hip joint, a kidney. The tray was taken to a washer and the body to the strange machine at the end of the room.

Helda unsealed a large hatch and swung it down and shifted the body on its catch basin onto it. She clamped the catch basin to the inner side, swung it up—there was a muffled thump from within—and resealed it. The ecotech pressed a few buttons, lights lit, and the machine whined and hissed and grunted with a demure even rhythm that suggested normal operation.

While Helda was occupied in the other end of the room, Ethan risked a whisper. "What's happening in there?"

"Breaking the body down to its components and returning the biomass to the Station ecosystem," Quinn whispered back. "Most clean animal mass—like the newts—is just broken down into higher organics and fed to the protein culture vats—that's where we grow steak meat and chicken and such for human consumption—but there's a sort of prejudice against disposing of human bodies that way. Smacks of cannibalism, I guess. And so that your next kilo cube of pork doesn't remind you too much of your late Uncle Neddie, the humans get broken down much finer and fed to the plants instead. A purely aesthetic choice—it all goes round and round in the end—logically, it doesn't make any difference."

His carrot had turned to lead in his stomach. "But you're going to let them put Okita—"

"Maybe I'll turn vegetarian for the next month," she whispered. "Sh."

Helda glanced irritably at them. "What are you hanging about for?" She focused on Ethan. "Have you no work to do?"

Quinn smiled blandly and rapped the green cartons. "I need my float pallet."

"Oh," said the ecotech. She sniffed, hitched up one sharp, bony shoulder, and turned away to tap a new code into the degrader's control panel. Stamping back with a hand tractor, she lifted the top carton and locked it into position on the hatch. It flipped up; there was a slithery rumble from within the machine. The hatch flopped down again and the first carton was replaced by the second. Then the third. Ethan held his breath.

The third carton emptied with a startling thump.

"What the hell…?" muttered the ecotech and reached for the seals. Commander Quinn turned white, her fingers twitching over her empty stunner holster.

"Look, is that a cockroach?" cried Ethan loudly in what he prayed might pass for a Stationer accent.

Helda whirled. "Where?"

Ethan pointed to a corner of the room away from the degrader. Both the ecotech and the commander went to inspect. Helda got down on her hands and knees and ran a finger worriedly along a seam between floor and wall. "Are you sure?" she said.

"Just a movement," he murmured, "in the corner of my eye…"

She frowned fiercely at him. "More like a damned hangover in the corner of your eye. Slovenly muscle-brain."

Ethan shrugged helplessly.

"Better call Infestation Control anyway," she muttered. She hit the start button on the degrader on her way to the comconsole and jerked her thumb back over her shoulder. "Out."

They complied immediately. Floating down the corridor Commander Quinn said, "My gods, Doctor, that was inspired. Or—you didn't really see a roach, did you?"

"No, it was just the first thing that popped into my head. She seemed like the sort of person who is bothered by bugs."

"Ah." Her eyes crinkled in amused approval.

He paused. "Do you have a roach problem here?"

"Not if we can help it. Among other things, they've been known to eat the insulation off electrical wiring. You think about fire on a space station a bit and you'll see why you got her attention."

She checked her chronometer. "Ye gods, we've got to get this float pallet and canister back to Docking Bay 32. Newts, newts, who will buy my newts…? Ah ha, the very thing."

She made a sharp right turn into a cross corridor, nearly dumping Ethan, and speeded up. After a moment she brought the pallet to a halt before a door marked "Cold Storage Access 297-C."

Inside they found a counter and a plump, bored-looking young woman on duty eating little fried morsels of something from a bag.

"I'd like to rent a vacuum storage locker," Quinn announced.

"This is for Stationers, ma'am," the counter girl began, after a hungry, wistful look at the mercenary woman's face. "If you go up to Transients' Lounge, you can get—"

Quinn slapped an ID down on the counter. "A cubic meter will do and I want it in removable plastic. Clean plastic, mind you."

The counter girl glanced at the ID. "Ah. Oh." She shuffled off, returning a few minutes later with a big plastic-lined case.

The mercenary woman signed and thumbprinted and turned to Ethan. "Let's lay them in nicely, eh? Impress the cook, when he thaws 'em out."

They packed the newts in neat rows. The counter girl, looking on, wrinkled her nose, then shrugged and returned to her comconsole where the holovid was displaying something that looked suspiciously more like play than work.

They were just in time, Ethan gauged; some of their amphibian victims were beginning to twitch. He almost felt worse about them than he did about Okita. The counter girl bore the box off.

"They won't suffer long, will they?" Ethan asked, looking back over his shoulder.

Commander Quinn snorted. "I should die so quick. They're going into the biggest freezer in the universe—outside. I think I really will ship them back to Admiral Naismith, later, when things calm down."

" 'Things,' " echoed Ethan. "Quite. I think you and I should have a talk about 'things'." His mouth set mulishly.

Hers turned up on one side. "Heart to heart," she agreed cordially.

CHAPTER SIX

After sneaking the float pallet back to its docking bay, Commander Quinn brought him by a roundabout route to a hostel room not much larger than Ethan's own. This hostel was, Ethan was dimly aware, in yet another section of Transients' Lounge, although he was not quite sure where they had recrossed that unmarked border. Quinn had dropped behind several times, or parked him abruptly in some cul-de-sac while she scouted ahead, or once wandered off quite casual-seeming, her arm draped across the shoulders of some uniformed Stationer acquaintance as she gesticulated gaily with her free hand. Ethan prayed she knew what she was doing.

She at any rate seemed to feel he had been successfully smuggled to some kind of home base, for she relaxed visibly when the hostel room doors sealed shut behind them, kicking off her boots and stretching and diving for the room service console.

"Here. Real beer." She handed him a foaming tumbler, after pausing to squirt something into it from her Dendarii issue medkit. "Imported."

The aroma made his mouth water, but he stood suspiciously, without raising it to his lips. "What did you put in it?"

"Vitamins. Look, see?" She snapped a squirt out of the air from the same vial and washed it down with a long swallow from her own tumbler. "You're safe here for now. Drink, eat, wash, what-you-will."

He glanced longingly toward the bathroom. "Won't double use show up on the computer monitors? What if someone asks questions?"

She smirked. "It will show that Commander Quinn is enter-
taining a handsome Stationer acquaintance in her room, at length.
Nobody'd dare ask anything. Relax."

The implications were anything but relaxing, but Ethan was by
that time ready to risk his life for a shave; his stubbled chin was per-
ilously close to pretending to paternal honors to which he had no right.

The bathroom, alas, had no second exit. He gave up and drank
his beer while he washed. If Millisor and Rau had not found useful
intelligence in him, he doubted Commander Quinn could either, no
matter what she'd doctored his drink with.

He was horrified by the haggard face that stared back at him
from the mirror. Sandpaper chin, red-rimmed eyes, skin blotched and
puffy—no patron in his right mind would trust his infant to that
ruffian. Fortunately, a few minutes work returned him to his normal
reassuring squeaky-clean neatness: merely tired, not degraded. There
was even a sonic scrubber that cleaned his clothes while he showered.

He emerged to find Commander Quinn occupying the room's
sole float chair, her jacket off, feet propped up and luxuriating in their
decompression. She opened her eyes and gestured him toward the bed.
He stretched himself out nervously, the pillow to his back; but there
was no other choice of seating. He found a fresh beer and a tray of
edibles, anonymous Stationer tidbits, ready to hand. He tried not to
think about the food's possible sources.

"So," she began. "There seems to be an awful lot of interest focused on this shipment of biologicals Athos ordered. Suppose you
start there."

Ethan swallowed a bite and gathered all his resolve. "No. We
trade information. Suppose *you* start there." His burst of assertiveness
ran down in the face of her bland raised eyebrows and he added weakly,
"If you don't mind."

She cocked her head and smiled. "Very well." She paused to wash
down a bite of her own. "Your order was filled, apparently, by
Bharaputra Laboratories' top genetics team. They spent a couple of
months at it, under need-to-know security. This probably saved several lives, later. The order was sent off on a non-stop freight run to

Kline Station, where it sat in a warehouse for two months waiting for the yearly census courier to take it to Athos. Nine big white freezer boxes—" she described them in precise detail, right down to the serial numbers. "Is that what you got?"

Ethan nodded grimly.

She went on. "Just about the time the shipment was leaving Kline Station for Athos, Millisor and his team arrived on Jackson's Whole. They went through Bharaputra's lab like—well, professionally speaking, it was a very successful commando raid." Her lips closed on some angrier private judgment. "Millisor and his team escaped right through House Bharaputra's private army, vaporizing the laboratory and all its contents behind them. The contents included most of the genetics team, quite a few innocent bystanders, and the technical records of the work done on your shipment. I gather they must have spent some time questioning the Bharaputra people before they crisped them, because they got it all. Pausing only to murder the wife and burn down the house of one of the geneticists, Millisor and company vanished from the planet, to turn up under new identities here just three weeks too late to catch your shipment.

"So then I arrived on Jackson's Whole, innocently asking questions about Athos. House Bharaputra Security about had a colonic spasm. Fortunately, I was finally able to persuade them I had no connection with Millisor. In fact, they think I'm working for them, now." She smiled slowly.

"The Bharaputrans?"

Her smile became a grimace. "Yes. They hired me to assassinate Millisor and his team. A lucky break for me, since now I'm not racing one of their own hit squads to the target. I seem to have made a start in spite of myself. They'll be so pleased." She sighed and drank again. "Your turn, Doctor. What was in those boxes to be worth all those lives?"

"Nothing!" He shook his head in bewilderment. "Valuable, yes, but not worth killing for. The Population Council had ordered four hundred and fifty live ovarian cultures, to produce egg cells, you know, for children—"

"I know how children are produced, yes," she murmured.

"They were to be certified free of genetic defects and taken only from sources in the top twenty intelligence percentiles. That's all. A week's routine work for a good genetics team such as you describe. But what we got was *trash!*" He detailed the shipment received with increasingly irate fervor, until she cut him off.

"All right, Doctor! I believe you. But what left Jackson's Whole was not trash, but something very special. Somebody therefore took your shipment somewhere in transit and replaced it with garbage—"

"Very odd garbage, when you think about it," Ethan began slowly, but she was going on.

"What somebody, then, and when? Not you, not me—although I suppose you've only my word for that—and not, obviously, Millisor, although he would have liked to."

"Millisor seemed to think it was this Terrence Cee—person, or whatever he is."

She sighed. "Whatever-he-is had plenty of time for it. It could have been switched on Jackson's Whole, or on shipboard en route to Kline Station, or anytime before the census courier left for Athos— ye gods, do you have any idea how many ships dock at Kline Station in the course of two months? And how many connections they in turn make? No wonder Millisor has been going around looking as if his stomach hurts. I'll get a copy of the Station docking log anyway, though…." She made a note.

Ethan used the pause to ask, "What is a *wife?*"

She choked on her beer. For all that she waved it about, Ethan noticed that its level was dropping very slowly. "I keep forgetting about you…. Ah, wife. A marriage partner—a man's female mate. The male partner is called a husband. Marriage takes many forms, but is most commonly a legal, economic, and genetic alliance to pro- duce and raise children. Do you copy?"

"I think so," he said slowly. "It sounds a little like a designated alternate parent." He tasted the words. "Husband. On Athos, 'to husband' is a verb meaning to conserve resources. Like stewardship." Did this imply the male maintained the female during gestation? So, this supposedly organic method had hidden costs that might make a real Rep Center seem cheap, Ethan thought with satisfaction.

"Same root."

"What does it mean 'to wife,' then?"

"There is no parallel verb. I think the root is just some old word meaning simply, 'woman'."

"Oh." He hesitated. "Did the geneticist whose house was burned and his—his *wife* have any children?"

"A little boy, who was in nursery school at the time. Strangely enough, Millisor didn't bother to torch it, too. Can't imagine how he overlooked that loose thread. The wife was pregnant." She bit rather savagely into a protein cube.

Ethan shook his head in frustration. "Why? Why, why, why?"

She smiled elliptically. "There are moments when I think you might be a man after my own heart—that was a joke," she added as Ethan lurched, recoiling. "Yes. Why. My very own assigned question. Millisor seemed convinced that what Bharaputra's labs produced was actually intended for Athos, in spite of the subsequent diversion. Now, if nothing else, I've learned in the past few months that what Millisor thinks had better be taken into account. Why Athos? What does Athos have that nobody else does?"

"Nothing," said Ethan simply. "We're a small, agriculturally based society with no natural resources worth shipping. We're not on a nexus route to anywhere. We don't go around bothering anyone."

" 'Nothing'," she noted. "Think of a scenario where a planet with 'nothing' would be at a premium... You have privacy, I suppose. Other than that, only your insistence upon reproducing yourselves the hard way sets you apart." She sipped her beer. "You say Millisor was talking about attacking your Reproduction Centers. Tell me about them."

Ethan needed little encouragement to wax enthusiastic about his beloved job. He described Sevarin and its operations and the dedicated cadre of men who made it work. He explained the beneficent system of social duty credits which qualified potential fathers. He ran down abruptly when he found himself describing the personal troubles that prevented him from achieving his own heart's desire for a son. This woman was getting entirely too easy to talk to—he wondered anew what was in his beer.

She leaned back in her chair and whistled tunelessly a moment. "Damn that diversion anyway. But for that, I'd say the cuckoo's-egg scenario had the most appeal. It accounted so nicely for Millisor's activities. Rats."

"The what scenario?"

"Cuckoo's-egg. Do you have cuckoos on Athos?"

"No... Is it a reptile?"

"An obnoxious bird. From Earth. Principally famous for laying its eggs in other birds' nests and skipping out on the tedious work of raising them. Now found galaxy-wide mainly as a literary allusion, since by some miracle nobody was dumb enough to export them off-planet. All the rest of the vermin managed to follow mankind into space readily enough. But do you see what I mean by a cuckoo's-egg scenario?"

Ethan, seeing, shivered. "Sabotage," he whispered. "Genetic sabotage. They thought to plant their monsters on us, all unawares..." He caught himself up. "Oh. But it wasn't the Cetagandans who sent the shipment, was it? Uh—rats. It wouldn't work anyway, we have ways of weeding out gene defects..." He subsided, more puzzled than ever.

"The shipment may have incorporated material stolen from the Cetagandan research project, though. Thus accounting for Millisor's passion for retrieving or destroying it."

"Obviously, but—why should Jackson's Whole want to do that to us? Or are they enemies of Cetaganda?"

"Ah—hm. How much do you know about Jackson's Whole?"

"Not much. They're a planet, they have biological laboratories, they submitted a bid to the Population Council in response to our advertisement year before last. So did half a dozen other places."

"Yes, well—next time, order from Beta Colony."

"Beta Colony was the high bid."

She ran a finger unconsciously across her lips; Ethan thought of plasma burns. "I'm sure, but you get what you pay for. Actually, that's misleading. You can get what you pay for on Jackson's Whole too, if your purse is deep enough. Want to have a young clone made of yourself, grown to physical maturity in vitro, and have your brain transferred into it? There's a fifty percent chance the operation will kill you and a one hundred percent guarantee it kills—whatever individual the clone might have been. No Betan med center would touch a job like that—clones have full civil rights there. House Bharaputra will."

"Ugh," said Ethan, revolted. "On Athos, cloning yourself is considered a sin."

She raised her eyebrows. "Oh, yeah? What sin?"

"Vanity."

"Didn't know that was a sin—oh, well. The point is, if somebody offered House Bharaputra enough money, they'd have cheerfully filled your boxes with—dead newts, for instance. Or eight-foottall bio-engineered super-soldiers, or anything else that was asked for." She fell silent, sipping her beer.

"So what do we do next?" he prodded bravely.

She frowned. "I'm thinking. I didn't exactly plan this Okita scenario in advance, y'know. I don't have orders for active interference in the affair—I was just supposed to observe. Professionally speaking, I suppose I shouldn't have rescued you. I should have just watched and sent off a regretful report on the radius of your splatter to Admiral Naismith."

"Will he, ah, be annoyed with you?" Ethan inquired nervously, with a skewed paranoid flash of her admiral sternly ordering her to restore the original balance by sending him to join Okita.

"Naw. He has unprofessional moments himself. Terribly impractical, it's going to kill him one of these days. Though so far he seems able to make things come out all right by sheer force of will." She speared the last tidbit on the platter, finished her beer, and rose. "So. Next I watch Millisor some more. If he has more back-up team than what I've spotted so far, his search for you and Okita should smoke them out. You can lie low in here. Don't leave the room."

Imprisoned again, although more comfortably. "But what about my clothes, my luggage, my room..."—his Economy Cabin, unoccupied, ticking up his bill nonetheless—"my mission!"

"You absolutely must not go near your room!" She sighed. "It's eight months till your return ship to Athos, right? Tell you what— you help me with my mission, I'll help you with yours. You do what I tell you, you might even live to complete it."

"Always assuming," said Ethan, chapped, "that Ghem-colonel Millisor doesn't outbid House Bharaputra or Admiral Naismith for your services."

She shrugged on her jacket, a lumpy thing with lots of pockets that seemed to have a deal more swing than accounted for by the weight of the fabric. "You can get one thing straight right now, Athosian. There are some things money can't buy."

"What, mercenary?"

She paused at the door, her lips curving up despite her sparking eyes. "Unprofessional moments."

The first day of his semi-voluntary incarceration passed sleeping off the exhaustion, terror, and biochemical cocktails of the preceding twenty-four hours. He came to muzzy consciousness once just as Commander Quinn was tiptoeing out of the room, but sank back. The second time he awoke, much later, he found her asleep stretched out on the floor dressed in uniform trousers and shirt, her jacket hung ready-to-hand. Her eyes slitted open to follow him as he staggered to the bathroom.

He found on the second day that Commander Quinn did not lock him in during the long hours of her absences. He dithered in the hallway for twenty minutes, upon discovering this, trying to evolve some rational program for his freedom besides being immediately gobbled up by Millisor, who was by now doubtless tearing the Station apart looking for him. The whir of a cleaning robot rounding the corner sent him spinning back into the room, heart palpitating. Maybe it wouldn't hurt to let the mercenary woman protect him a little longer.

By the third day he had recovered enough of his native tone of mind to begin serious worrying about his predicament, although not yet enough physical energy to try doing anything about it. Belatedly, he began boning up on galactic history through the comconsole library.

By the end of the next day he was becoming painfully aware of the inadequacy of a cultural education that consisted of two very general galactic histories, a history of Cetaganda, and a fiction holovid titled "Love's Savage Star" that he had stumbled onto and been too stunned to switch off. Life with women did not just induce strange behavior, it appeared; it induced *very* strange behavior. How long before the emanations from Commander Quinn would make him start acting like that? Would ripping open her jacket to expose her mammary hypertrophy really cause her to fixate upon him like a newly hatched chick on its mother hen? Or would she carve him to ribbons with her vibra-knife before the hormones or whatever they were cut in?

He shuddered and cursed the study time he'd wasted on timidity during the two month voyage to Kline Station. Innocence might be bliss, but ignorance was demonstrably hell; if his soul was to be offered up on the altar of necessity, by God the Father Athos should have the full worth of it. He read on.

The opposite of nirvana in his spiritual descent, Ethan decided, was tizzy; and by the sixth day he had achieved it.

"What the hell is Millisor doing out there?" he demanded of Commander Quinn during one of her brief stop-ins.

"He's not doing as much as I'd hoped," she admitted. She slumped in her chair, winding a curl of her dark hair around and around her finger. "He hasn't reported you or Okita missing to the Station authorities. He hasn't revealed hidden reserves of personnel. He's made no move to leave the Station. The time he's spending maintaining his cover identity suggests he's digging in for a long stay. Last week I'd thought he was just waiting for the return ship from Athos that you came on, but now it's clear there's something more. Something even more important than an AWOL subordinate."

Ethan paced, his voice rising. "How long am I going to have to stay in here?"

She shrugged. "Until something breaks, I suppose." She smiled sourly. "Something might, although not for our side. Millisor and

Rau and Setti have been searching the Station themselves, real quiet-like—they keep coming back to this one corridor near Ecobranch. I couldn't figure out why, at first. Now, Okita's clothes scanned clean of bugs, but just to be sure I mailed 'em off to Admiral Naismith. So I knew it couldn't be that. I finally got hold of the technical specs for that section. The damned protein-culture vats are behind that corridor wall. I think Okita may have had some sort of inorganic code-response-only tracer implanted internally. Some poor sod is going to break a tooth on it in his Chicken Kiev any day now. I just hope to the gods it won't be a transient who will sue the Station... So much for the perfect crime." She heaved a sigh. "Millisor hasn't figured it out yet, though—he's still eating meat."

Ethan was getting mortally tired of salads himself. And of this room and of the tension, indecision, and helplessness. And of Commander Quinn and the casual way she ordered him around.

"I have only your say-so that the Station authorities can't help me," he broke out suddenly. "*I* didn't shoot Okita. *I* haven't done anything! I don't even have an argument with Millisor—it's you who seem to be carrying on a private war with him. He'd never have thought I was a secret agent in the first place if Rau hadn't found your bug. It's you who've been getting me in deeper and deeper, to serve your spying."

"He'd have picked you up in any case," she observed.

"Yes, but all I needed was to convince Millisor that Athos didn't have his stuff. His interrogation might have done that, if your interference hadn't aroused his suspicions. Hell, he'd be welcome to come inspect our Rep Centers if he wants."

She raised her eyebrows, a gesture Ethan found increasingly irritating. "You really think you could negotiate that with him? Personally, I'd rather import a new plague bacillus."

"At least he's male," Ethan snapped.

She laughed; Ethan's temper rose to the boiling point. "How long are you going to keep me locked up in here?" he demanded again.

She paused, visibly. Her eyes widened, narrowed; she tamped out her smile. "You're not locked up," she pointed out mildly. "You can leave any time. At your own risk, of course. I shall be saddened, but I shall survive."

He slowed in his frenetic pacing. "You're bluffing. You can't let me go. I've learned too much."

Her feet came down from the desktop and she stopped twisting her hair. She stared at him with a discomforting expressionlessness, like someone calculating the narrowness of slice necessary to prepare a biological specimen for slide mounting. When she spoke again, her voice grated like gravel. "I should say you haven't learned bloody enough."

"You don't want me to tell the Station authorities about Okita, do you? That puts your neck on the line with your own people—"

"Oh, hardly my neck. They would of course have a shit fit if they found out what we did with the body—to which I might point out you were a willing accessory. Contamination is a much more serious charge than mere murder. Nearly up there with arson."

"So? What can they do, deport me? That's not a punishment, that's a *reward!*"

Her eyes slitted, concealing their sharpening light. "If you leave, Athosian, don't expect to come bleating back to me for protection. I have no use for quitters, quislings—or queers."

He supposed she was insulting him. He took it as intended. "Well, I have no use for a sly, tricky, arrogant, overbearing—woman!" he sputtered.

She spread her hand invitingly toward the door, pursing her lips. Ethan realized he had just had the last word. His credit chit was in his pocket, his shoes were on his feet. Nostrils flaring, he marched out the door, head held high. His back crawled in expectation of a stunner beam, or worse. None came.

It was very, very quiet in the corridor when the airseal doors had hissed shut. Had the last word really been what he'd wanted? And yet—he'd rather face Millisor, Rau, and Okita's ghost together than crawl back into his prison and apologize to Quinn.

Determination. Decision. Action. That was the way to solve problems. Not running away and hiding. He would seek out and confront Millisor face-to-face. He stomped off down the corridor.

By the time he reached the mallway exit from the hostel he was walking normally and he had revised his plan to the more sane and sensible one of calling Millisor from the safe distance of a public comconsole. He could be tricky himself. He would not approach his own hostel. If necessary, he might even abandon his personal gear and purchase a ticket off-Station—to Beta Colony?—at the last moment before boarding, thus escaping the whole crowd of insane secret agents. By the time he got back to Kline Station, they might even have chased each other off to some other part of the galaxy.

He removed himself a couple of levels from Quinn's hostel and found a comconsole booth.

"I wish to reach a transient, Ghem-colonel Luyst Millisor," he told the computer. He spelled the name out carefully. His voice, he noted with self-approval, scarcely quavered.

No such individual is registered at Kline Station, the holoscreen flashed back.

"Er... Has he checked out?" Gone, and Commander Quinn stringing him along all this time...?

No such individual registered within the past 12-month cycle, the holoscreen murmured brightly.

"Um, um—how about a Captain Rau?"

No such individual...

"Setti?"

No such individual...

He stopped short of mentioning Okita and stood blankly. Then it came to him; Millisor was the man's real name. But here on Kline Station he was doubtless using an assumed one, with forged identity cards to match. Ethan had not the first clue what the alias might be. Dead end.

At a loss, he wandered down the mall. He could, he supposed, just return to his room and let Millisor find *him*, but whether he'd get a chance to negotiate or even get a word out before being scragged by Okita's vengeful comrades was a very moot point.

The variegated passers-by scarcely ruffled his self-absorption, but two approaching faces were extraordinary. A pair of plainly dressed men of average height had brilliant designs painted upon their faces, completely masking their skin. Dark red was the base color of one, slashed with orange, black, white, and green in an intricate pattern, obviously meaningful. The other was chiefly brilliant blue, with yellow, white, and black swirls outlining and echoing eyes, nose, and mouth. They were deep in conversation with each other. Ethan stared covertly, fascinated and delighted.

It wasn't until they passed nearly shoulder to shoulder with him that Ethan's eye teased out the features beneath the markings. He suddenly realized that he did know what the face paint meant, from his recent reading. They were marks of rank for Cetagandan Ghem lords.

Captain Rau looked up at the same moment squarely into Ethan's face. Rau's mouth opened, his eyes widening in the blue mask, his hand reaching swiftly for a pouch on his belt. Ethan, after a second of confounded paralysis, ran.

There was a shout behind him. A God-the-Father *nerve disruptor* bolt crackled past his head. Ethan glanced back over his shoulder. Rau had only missed, it appeared, because Millisor had knocked the lethal weapon upward. They were yelling at each other even as they began pursuit. Ethan now remembered clearly just how terrifying the Cetagandans could be.

Ethan dove head first into an Up lift-tube and swam as frantically as any salmon through its languid field, hand over hand down the emergency grips. Jostled rising passengers swore at him in surprise.

He exited on another level, ran, took another lift, changed again, and again, with many a panicked backward glance. Here across a crowded shop, there through a deserted construction zone— AUTHORIZED PERSONNEL ONLY—twist, turn, double and dive. He crossed out of Transients' Lounge somewhere, for gadgets on the walls that had long lists of instructions and prohibitions beside them in the tourist ghetto here were nearly anonymous.

He went to ground at last in an equipment closet and lay gasping for breath on the floor. He seemed to have lost his pursuers. He had certainly lost himself.

CHAPTER SEVEN

He sat in a sour huddle for an hour after he caught his breath and his heart stopped hammering. So, running away and hiding was no way to solve problems? Any action was better than rotting in Quinn's cell-like hostel room? He meditated glumly on just how fast one could re-evaluate one's moral position in the flash and crackle from the silvered bell-muzzle of a nerve disruptor. He stared into the closet's dimness. At least Quinn's prison had had a bathroom.

He would have to go to the Station authorities, now. There was no going back to Quinn, she'd made that clear, and no illusion left of his ability to negotiate a separate peace with the Cetagandan crazies. He beat his head gently on the wall a few times in token of his self-esteem, unfolded from his crouch, and began to search his hidey hole.

A locker full of Stationer work coveralls made him suddenly conscious of his own downsider apparel, followed by another and more horrid thought; had Quinn planted another bug on him? She'd certainly had plenty of opportunity. He stripped to the skin and traded his Athosian clothes for some red coveralls and boots that were only a little too large. The boots chafed his feet, but he dared not retain even his socks. He only needed the camouflage long enough to sneak to—make that, locate and sneak to—the nearest Station Security post. It wasn't stealing; he would give the coveralls back at the first opportunity.

He slipped out of the closet and took a left down the empty corridor, trying to imitate the rolling purposeful stride of a Stationer

while fixing the closet's number in his memory so that he might retrieve his clothes later. He passed two women in blue coveralls floating a loaded pallet, but they were obviously in a hurry. Ethan couldn't
nerve himself to stop them for directions. A Stationer such as his red
suit proclaimed him to be would have known the way. It was bound
to seem peculiar to them even without his accent.

He was just beginning to seriously question his original assumption that if he didn't know where he was, neither would his pursuers,
when a scream, a thud, and a rattling crash snapped his attention to
the cross-corridor just ahead. Two float pallets had collided. Crying
and swearing mingled with a clatter of plastic boxes cascading from
one pallet and an ear-splitting, screeching twitter. Balls of yellow feathers exploded from a spilled box into the air, darting, swerving, and
ricocheting off the walls.

A woman was screaming—"The gravity! The gravity!" Ethan
recognized the voice with a start. It was the bony green-and-blue-
uniformed ecotech, Helda, from the Assimilation Station. She was
glaring at him, scarlet-faced. "The gravity! Wake up, you twit, they're
getting away!" She scrambled out from under the boxes and staggered
toward him, panting.

As Ethan struggled with his conscience whether or not to blow
his incognito by volunteering medical assistance—the other three
people involved all seemed to be moving, sitting up, and complaining at healthy volume—Helda yanked open a cover on the wall beside Ethan's head and turned a rheostat. The frantically fluttering song-
birds beat their wings in vain as they were sucked to the deck. Ethan's
knees nearly buckled as his weight more than doubled. He found
himself and the ecotech braced against each other.

"Oh, gods, you again," snarled Helda. "I might have known.
Are you on duty?"

"No," squeaked Ethan.

"Good. Then you can help me pick up these damned birds before they spread toxoplasmosis all over the Station."

Ethan recognized the disease, a mildly contagious, slow, subvi-
ral life-form that attacked RNA, and fell willingly to hands and knees

to crawl after her and pluck up the dozen or so hysterical birds pinned by their own weight. Only when the last bird was stuffed back into its box and the lid tied down with the ecotech's belt did she pay the least attention to the bitterly complaining human accident victims now lying flat on the deck and panting for breath. When she turned the gravity dial back to standard Ethan felt he might take off and fly himself, so great was the relief.

One of the victims sitting up shakily wore a pine-green and blue uniform like Helda's. Blood runneled down his face from a cut on his forehead. Ethan gauged it at a glance as spectacular but superficial. Clean pressure over the wound—not from his hands, he'd been handling the birds—would take care of it in a trice. The two white-faced teenagers from the other pallet, one male, one that Ethan's now-practiced eye identified immediately as female, clutched each other and stared at the blood in horror, obviously under the impression that they'd near-killed the man.

Ethan, holding his hands in loose fists to remind himself to touch nothing, put some gruff authority into his voice and directed the frightened boy to make a pad and stop the bleeding. The girl was crying that her wrist was broken, but Ethan would have bet Betan dollars it was merely sprained. Helda, holding her hands identically to Ethan's, elbowed open a comlink in the wall and called for help. Her first concern was for a decontamination team from her own department, her second for Station Security, and a distant third for a medtech for the injured.

Ethan blew out his breath in relief at his lucky break. Instead of his having to hunt for Station Security, it would be coming to him. He could fling himself upon Security's mercy and get unlost at the same time.

The decontamination team arrived first. Airseal doors cordoned off the area and the team began going over walls, floors, ceilings and vents with sonic scrubbers, x-ray sterilizers, and potent disinfectants.

"You'll have to deal with Security, Teki," Helda directed her assistant as she stepped into the sealed passenger pallet the decontamination team had produced. "See that they throw the book at those two joyriders."

The two teenagers paled still further, scarcely reassured by a secretive shake of his head directed at them by Teki.

"Well, come along," Helda snapped at Ethan.

"Huh? Uh…" Monosyllabic grunts might conceal his accent, but were lousy for eliciting information. Ethan dared a "Where to?"

"Quarantine, of course."

Quarantine? *For how long?* He must have mouthed the words aloud, for the decon man shooing him toward the float pallet said soothingly, "We're just going to scrub you down and give you a shot. If you've got a heavy date, you can call her from there. We'll vouch for you."

Ethan wanted to disabuse the decon man of this last dreadful misapprehension, but the ecotech's presence inhibited him. He allowed himself to be chivvied into the pallet. He seated himself across from the woman with a fixed smile.

The canopy closed and sealed, shutting off all sound from the exterior. Ethan pressed his face longingly to the transparent surface as the pallet rose and drifted past the two arriving security patrolmen in their orange and black uniforms. He doubted they could hear him if he screamed.

"Don't touch your face," Helda reminded him absently, glancing back for one last look at the disaster scene. It seemed to be under control now, the decon team having taken charge of her float pallet of birds and reopened the airseal doors.

Ethan displayed his closed fists in token of his understanding.

"You do seem to have grasped sterile technique," Helda admitted grudgingly, settling back and glowering at him. "For a while there I thought Docks and Locks was now hiring the mentally handicapped."

Ethan shrugged. Silence fell. Silence lengthened. He cleared his throat. "What was that?" he asked gruffly, with a jerk of his chin back to indicate the recent accident.

"Couple of stupid kids playing starfighter with a float pallet. Their parents will hear from me. You want speed, take a tube car. Float pallets are for work. Or do you mean the birds?"

"Birds."

"Condemned cargo. You should have heard the freighter captain scream when we impounded them. As if he had a civil right to spread disease all over the galaxy. Although it could have been worse." She sighed. "It could have been beef again."

"Beef?" croaked Ethan.

She snorted. "A whole bleeding herd of live beef, being transported somewhere for breeding. Crawling with microvermin. I had to cut them in half to fit them in the disposer. Worst mess you ever saw. We broke *them* down to atoms, you can bet. The owners sued the Station." Her eyes glinted. "They lost." She added after a moment, "I hate messes."

Ethan shrugged again, hoping the gesture would be taken for sympathy. This frightening female was the last person on the Station he wished to surrender to, bar Millisor. He trusted devoutly that Ecobranch did not dispose of diseased human transients in the same cavalier fashion.

"Did Docks and Locks clear up that trash dump in Bay Thirteen yet?" she inquired suddenly.

"Er, ah…" Ethan cleared his throat.

She frowned. "*What* is the matter with you? Do you have a cold?"

Ethan wouldn't have dared admit to harboring viruses. "Strained my voice yesterday," he muttered.

"Oh." She settled back like a disappointed bird dog. The monologue having now fallen officially to her, she stared around for another topic of conversation. "Now *that's* a disgusting sight." She jerked her thumb to the side; Ethan saw nothing but a couple of passing Stationers. "You wonder how someone can stand to let herself go like that."

"What?" muttered Ethan, totally bewildered.

"That fat girl."

Ethan looked back over his shoulder. The obesity in question was so clinically mild as to be nearly invisible to his eye, given the extra padding of the female build.

"Biochemistry," Ethan suggested in placation.

"Ha. That's just an excuse for lack of self-discipline. She prob-ably gorges at night on fancy imported downsider food." Helda brooded a moment. "Revolting stuff. You don't know *where* it's been. Now, *I* never eat anything but clean vat lean and salads—none of those high-fat, gooey dressings, either—" a lengthy dissertation upon her diet and digestion more than filled the time until the float pallet stopped at their destination.

Ethan waited until she'd exited before unpeeling himself from the farthest corner of his seat. He poked his head cautiously out.

The quarantine processing area had a hospitalish smell that pierced him with homesickness for Sevarin. A distressed lump rose in his throat, which he swallowed back down.

"This way, sir." A male ecotech in a sterile gown motioned him ahead. A couple more techs promptly began going over the passenger pallet with x-ray sterilizers. Ethan was directed down a corridor from the off-loading zone to a sort of locker room, the gowned tech fol-lowing behind sweeping up his invisible septic footprints with a sonic scrubber.

The tech gave him a brief, accurate lecture on how to take a de-contamination shower and absconded with his red suit and boots muttering, "No underwear? Some people!"

Ethan's IDs and credit chit were in the red coveralls' pocket. Ethan nearly cried. But there was no help for it. He showered thor-oughly, dried, scratched his itching nose at last, then hovered naked and alone about the chamber for what seemed a very long time. He was just meditating on the pros and cons of running howling nude back down the corridor when the gowned tech returned.

"Hello." The tech dropped his folded coveralls and boots on a bench, pressed a hypospray against his arm, said, "See Records on your way out. It's the other way," and wandered off. "Goodbye."

Ethan pounced on the clothes. His wallet was still in the pocket, or at any rate back in the pocket. He sighed relief, dressed, squared his shoulders in preparation for full confession, and at a guess from the tech's cryptic speech went on down the corridor in the direction opposite his entry.

He was just thinking himself lost again when he saw an open arched door and beyond it a room with a manned computer interface. The young man from the bird pallet, Teki, now pale and interesting with a white plastic bandage across his forehead, arrived at the doorway at the same time as Ethan. He paused rather breathlessly and with a bright nod let Ethan enter first. The bony Helda stood by the counter within, tapping one foot, with her arms folded.

She fixed Teki with a cold look. "It's about time you got off that comconsole. I thought I told you to tell your girlfriend not to call you at work."

"It wasn't Sara," said Teki righteously. "It was a relative. With a *business* message." Sensibly re-directing Helda's attention, he seized on Ethan. "Look, here's our helper."

Ethan swallowed and approached, wondering how to begin. He wished the woman weren't there.

"Good-oh," said the green-and-blue-uniformed man running the computer interface. "Just let me have your card, please." He held out his hand.

He wanted some standard Stationer ID, Ethan supposed. He took a deep breath, nerved himself, and glanced up at the frowning woman. His confession became an "Er, ah—don't have it with me…"

Her frown deepened. "You're supposed to have it with you at all times, Docks-and-Locks."

"Off duty," Ethan offered desperately. "My other coveralls." If he could just get away from this terrible female, he'd go straight to Security….

She inhaled.

Teki cut in. "Aw, c'mon, Helda, give the guy a break. He did help us out with those blasted tweety-birds." Winking, he took Ethan by the arm and towed him toward the chamber's other exit. "Just go get it and bring it back, all right?"

The woman said, "Well!" but the counterman nodded.

"Don't mind Helda," whispered the young man to Ethan as he pushed him past the inner door, through a UV-and-filtered-air lock, and out a final airseal. "She drives everybody crazy. That fat kid of hers emigrated Downside just to get away from her. I don't suppose she said thanks for the help?"

Ethan shook his head.

"Well, *I* thank you." He nodded cheerfully; the airseal doors hissed closed on his smile.

"Help," said Ethan in a tiny voice. He turned around. He was in another standard Station corridor, identical to a thousand others. He squeezed his eyes shut briefly in spiritual pain, sighed, and started walking.

Two hours later he was still walking, certain he was circling. Station Security posts, frequent and highly visible in Transients' Lounge, disappeared here in the Stationers' own areas. Or maybe, like the equipment in the walls, they were merely cryptically marked and he was walking right past them. Ethan swore softly under his breath as another blister rubbed up by his ill-fitting boots popped.

Glancing down a cross-corridor, he gave a joyous start. The stuff on the walls had labels, lists, and locks again. He turned that way. A few more junctions, another door, and he found himself in a public mallway. Not far along it, beside a fountain, shimmered a directory.

"You are here," he muttered, tracing through the holovid. Colored light licked over his finger. Nearest security post, there: he looked up to match the map with a mirrored booth on the balcony at the farthest end of the mall. Just one level below this mallway was his own hostel. Quinn's hostel was over a bit, up two. He wondered anxiously where the one in which the Cetagandans had questioned him was. Not far away enough, he was sure. He steeled himself and hobbled up the mall, glancing out of the corner of his eye for men in bright face paint or women in crisp gray-and-white uniforms.

KLINE STATION SECURITY, glowed the legend atop the booth. The mirroring was one-way. From inside there was a fine view overlooking the mall, Ethan found upon entering. Banks of monitors and com links filled the little room. A security person sat, feet up, eating little fried morsels of something from a bag and gazing idly down at the colorful concourse.

A security *woman*, Ethan corrected himself with an inward moan. Young and dark-haired, in her orange-and-black quasi-military uniform she bore a faint, generic resemblance to Commander Quinn.

He cleared his throat. "Uh, excuse me... Are you on duty?"

She smiled. "Alas, yes. From the time I put on this uniform to the time I take it off at the end of my shift, plus whenever they beep me after. But I get off at twenty-four-hundred," she added encouragingly. "Would you care for a newt nugget?"

"Uh, no—no, thank you," Ethan replied. He smiled back in nervous uncertainty. Her smile became blinding. He tried again. "Did you hear anything about a fellow firing a nerve disruptor in one of the mallways this morning?"

"Gods, yes! Is it gossip in Docks and Locks already?"

"Oh..." Ethan realized where some of the disjointedness in this conversation was coming from; the red coveralls were misleading her. "I'm not a Stationer."

"I can tell by your accent," she agreed cordially. She sat up and rested her chin on his hand. Her eyes positively twinkled. "Earning your way across the galaxy as a migrant worker, are you? Or did you get stranded?"

"Uh, neither..." Ethan continued smiling, since she did. Was this some expected part of exchanges between the sexes? Neither Quinn nor the ecotech had used such intense facial signals, but Quinn admitted herself atypical and the ecotech was definitely weird. His mouth was beginning to hurt. "But about that shooting..."

"Oh, have you talked to anybody that was there?" Some of her glowing manner fell away and she sat up more alertly. "We're looking for more witnesses."

Caution asserted itself. "Uh—why?"

"It's the charge. Of course the fellow claims he fired by accident, showing off the weapon to his friend. But the tipster who called in the incident claimed he shot at a man, who ran away. Well, the tipster vanished and the rest of the so-called witnesses were the usual lot—full of contagious drama, but when you pin 'em down they always turn out to have been facing the other way or zipping their boot or something at the actual moment the disruptor went off." She sighed. "Now, if it's proved the fellow with the disruptor was firing *at* someone, he gets deported, but if it was an accident all we can do is confiscate the illegal weapon, fine him, and let him go. Which we'll have to do in another twelve hours if this intent-to-harm business can't be substantiated."

Rau under arrest? Ethan's smile became beatific. "What about his friend?"

"Vouches for him, of course. He shook down clean, so there was nothing to be done with *him*."

Millisor on the loose, if he understood the security woman correctly. Ethan's smile faded. And Setti, whom Ethan had never seen and would not recognize if he walked right into him. Ethan took a breath. "My name is Urquhart."

"Mine's Lara," said the security woman.

"That's nice," said Ethan automatically. "But—"

"It was my grandmother's name," the security woman confided. "I think family names give such a nice sense of continuity, don't you? Unless you happen to get stuck with something like Sterilla, which happened to an unfortunate friend of mine. She shortens it to Illa."

"Uh—that wasn't exactly what I meant."

She tilted her head, chipper. "Which wasn't?"

"I beg your pardon?"

"What thing that you said wasn't what you meant?"

"Er..."

"—quhart," she finished. "It's a nice name, I don't think you should be shy about it. Or did you get teased about it as a kid or something?"

He stood with his mouth open, awash. But before the conversational thread could become more raveled, another, older security woman shot down the lift-tube that connected the booth to an upper level. She exited the tube with an authoritative thump.

"No socializing on duty, Corporal, may I remind you—again," she called over her shoulder as she went to a locker. "Wrap it up, we've got a call."

The security girl made a moue at her superior's back and whispered to Ethan, "Twenty-four-hundred, all right?" She came to her feet, and something like attention, as her officer pulled a pair of sidearms in holsters from the wall cabinet. "Serious, ma'am?"

"We're wanted for a search cordon, levels C7 and 8. A prisoner just vanished from Detention."

"Escaped?"

"They didn't say escaped. They said, vanished." The officer's mouth twisted dryly. "When Echelon insists on weasel-words, I get suspicious. The prisoner was that dirt sucker they pried loose from the nerve disruptor this morning. Now, I had a look at his weapon. Best military issue and not new." She buckled on her heavy-duty stunner and handed its twin to her corporal.

"Yeah, so? Army surplus." The corporal straightened her uniform, checked her face in a small mirror, then checked her weapon with equal care.

"Yeah, not so. I'll bet you Betan dollars to anything you choose he's another gods-please-damn unregistered military espionage agent."

"Not that plague again. Is it just one, or a bunch?"

"I hope it's not a bunch. That's the worst. Unpredictable, violent, don't care about the law, don't care about *public safety* for the gods' sakes, and after you half break your neck handling them with gloves you still get reprimanded at some embassy's request and all your carefully amassed case evidence gets tossed into the vacuum—" She turned to make shooing motions at Ethan. "Out, out, we've got to lock up here." She added to her corporal, "You stick tight by me, you hear? No heroics."

"Yes, ma'am."

And Ethan found himself locked out on the balcony as Station Security, in a pair, hurried out of sight. The corporal glanced back over her shoulder at his tentative raised hand and "Ah—ah…" and gave him a friendly little wave of her fingers.

Over three corridors. Up two levels. Through the maze within a maze of Quinn's hostel. The familiar door. Ethan moistened his lips and knocked.

And knocked again.

And stood…

The door hissed open. His relief was swallowed by surprise as a cleaning robot dodged around him. The room beyond was as anonymous and pristine as if never occupied.

"Where'd she go?" he wailed, rhetorically to relieve his feelings.

But the cleaning robot paused. "Please rephrase your question, sir or madam," it spoke from a grille in its maroon plastic housing.

He turned to it eagerly. "Commander Quinn—the person who had this room—where did she go?"

"The previous occupant checked out at eleven-hundred hours, sir or madam. The previous occupant left no forwarding address with this hostel, sir or madam."

Eleven-hundred? She must have gone within minutes of the time he'd stormed out, Ethan calculated. "Oh, God the Father…"

"Sir or madam," chirped the robot politely, "please rephrase your question."

"I wasn't talking to you," said Ethan, running his hands through his hair. He felt like tearing it out in clumps.

The robot hovered. "Do you require anything else, sir or madam?"

"No—no…"

The robot whirred away up the corridor.

Down two levels. Over three corridors. The security team had not yet returned. Their booth was still locked.

Ethan plunked down beside the fountain and waited. This time he would really turn himself in, for sure. If Rau had got himself on the wrong side of the law by firing at Ethan, Ethan must therefore be on the right side, correct? He had nothing to fear from Security.

Of course, if they couldn't keep Rau the arrestee in their secure area, how likely was it they could keep Rau the assassin out? Ethan studiously ignored this whisper from his logic as a fear planted by Quinn. Security was his best chance. Indeed, now that he had irrevocably offended Quinn, Security was his only chance.

"Dr. Urquhart?" A hand fell on Ethan's shoulder.

Ethan jumped half a meter and whirled. "Who wants t'know?" he demanded hoarsely.

A blond young man fell back a pace in consternation. He was of middle height, wire-muscled and slight, dressed in an unfamiliar downsider fashion: a sleeveless knit shirt, loose trousers bunched at the ankles into the tops of comfortable-looking boots of some butter-soft leather. "Excuse me. If you're Dr. Ethan Urquhart of Athos, I've been looking all over for you."

"Why?"

"I hoped you might help me. Please, sir, don't go—" He held out a hand as Ethan flinched away. "You don't know me, but I'm very interested in Athos. My name is Terrence Cee."

CHAPTER EIGHT

After a moment's stunned silence Ethan sputtered, "What do you want of Athos?"

"Refuge, sir," said the young man. "For I'm surely a refugee." Tension rendered his smile false and anxious. He grew more urgent as Ethan backed away slightly. "The census courier's manifest listed one of your titles as ambassador-at-large. You can give me political asylum, can't you?"

"I—I—" Ethan stammered. "That was just something the Population Council threw in at the last minute, because no one was sure what I'd find out here. I'm not really a diplomat, I'm a doctor." He stared at the young man, who stared back with a kind of beaten hunger. The automatic part of Ethan totted up the symptoms of fatigue Cee presented: gray in the hollows of his skin, bloodshot sclera, a barely observable tremula in his smooth corded hands. A horrid realization shook Ethan. "Look, uh—you aren't by chance asking me to protect you from Ghem-colonel Millisor, are you?"

Cee nodded.

"Oh—oh, no. You don't understand. It's just me, out here. I don't have an embassy or anything like that. I mean, real embassies have security guards, soldiers, a whole intelligence corps—"

Cee's smile twisted. "Does the man who arranged Okita's last accident really need them?"

Ethan stood with his mouth open, his utter dismay robbing him of reply.

101

Cee went on. "There are many of them—Millisor can command the resources of Cetaganda against me—and I'm alone. The only one left. The sole survivor. Alone, it isn't a question whether they'll kill me, only how soon." His beautifully structured hands opened in pleading. "I was sure I'd eluded them and it was safe to double back. Only to find Millisor—the fearless vampire hunter himself!"—the young man's mouth thinned in bitterness—"squatting across the last gateway. I beg you, sir. Grant me asylum."

Ethan cleared his throat nervously. "Ah—just what do you mean by 'vampire hunter'?"

"It's how he views himself." Cee shrugged. "To him all his crimes are heroics, for the good of Cetaganda, because somebody has to do the dirty work—his exact thought, that. He's proud to do it. But he doesn't have to nerve himself to do the dirty work on me. He hates and fears me worse than any hell, in his secretive little soul—ha! As if his secrets were more vital or vile than anyone else's. As if I gave a damn for his secrets, or his soul."

Wanly, Ethan recognized the seasick symptoms of talk at cross-purposes again. He stretched for some bottom to this floating conversation. "What are you?"

The young man drew back, his face suddenly shuttered with suspicion. "Asylum. Asylum first and then you can have it all."

"Huh?"

The suspicion turned to despair before Ethan's eyes. The excitement that hope had lent Cee evaporated, leaving a bleak dryness. "I understand. You see me as *they* do. A medical monstrosity, put together from graveyard bits, cooked in a vat. Well"—he inhaled resolution—"so be it. But I'll have vengeance on Ghem-captain Rau, at least, before my death. That much I swear to Janine."

Ethan seized upon the one intelligible item in all this and with as much dignity he could muster said, "If by a 'vat' you are referring to a uterine replicator, I'll have you know I was incubated in a uterine replicator myself and it is every bit as good as any other method of generation. Better. So I'll thank you not to insult my origins, or my life's work."

Some of the same floating confusion that Ethan was sure must be in his own face crossed Cee's. Why not. Misery, Ethan thought with acid satisfaction, loves company.

The young man—boy, really, for take away the aging effects of exhaustion upon him and he was surely younger than Janos—seemed about to speak, then shook his head and turned away.

Necessity, thought Ethan frantically, is the uterine replicator of invention. "Wait!" he cried. "I grant you the asylum of Athos!" He might as well have promised the remission of Cee's sins as well, since he had about as much power to effect one as the other. But Cee turned back anyway, hope flaring again in his blue eyes, hot like a gas jet. "Only," Ethan went on, "you have to tell me where you took the ovarian cultures the Population Council ordered from Bharaputra Laboratories."

It was Terrence Cee's turn to stand in open-mouthed dismay now. "Didn't Athos receive them?"

"No."

The breath hissed from the blond man's mouth as though he had been struck in the stomach. "Millisor! He must have got them! But no—but how—he could not conceal—"

Ethan cleared his throat gently. "Unless you think your Colonel Millisor would spend seven hours interrogating me—quite unpleasantly—as to their whereabouts for a practical joke, I don't think so."

It was actually quite refreshing to see somebody else look as agitated as he felt, Ethan thought. Cee turned to his new protector, his arms spread wide in bewilderment.

"But Dr. Urquhart—if you don't have them and I don't have them and Millisor doesn't have them—where'd they go?"

Ethan thought he finally understood Elli Quinn's stated dislike of being on the damned defensive. He'd had a belly full of it himself. Dump enough shit on it, he thought savagely, and even the fragile seed of resolution in his timid heart might blossom into something greater. He smiled pleasantly at the blond young man. Cee really did look like a shorter, thinner Janos. It was the coloration that did it.

But Cee's mouth held no hint of the petulance that sometimes marred Janos's when it set in anger or weariness.

"Suppose," suggested Ethan, "we pool our information and find out?"

Cee gazed up at him—he was several centimeters shorter than Ethan—and asked, "Are you truly Athos's senior intelligence agent?"

"In a sense," murmured Athos's only agent of any description, "yes."

Cee nodded. "It would be a pleasure, sir." He took a deep breath. "I must have some purified tyramine, then. I used the last of my supply on Millisor three days ago."

Tyramine was an amino acid precursor of any number of endogenous brain chemicals, but Ethan had never heard of it as a truth drug. "I beg your pardon?"

"For my telepathy," said Cee impatiently.

The floor seemed to drop away under Ethan. Far, far away. "The whole psionics hypothesis was definitively disproved hundreds of years ago," he heard his own voice say distantly. "There is no such thing as mental telepathy."

Terrence Cee touched his forehead in a gesture that reminded Ethan of a patient describing a migraine.

"There is now," he said simply.

Ethan stood blinded by the dawning of a new age. "We are standing," he croaked at last, "in the middle of a bleeding public mallway in one of the most closely monitored environments in the galaxy. Before Colonel Millisor leaps out of a lift-tube, don't you think we'd better, uh, find some quieter place to talk?"

"Oh. Oh, yes, of course, sir. Is your safe house nearby?"

"Er... Is yours?"

The young man grimaced. "As long as my cover identity holds."

Ethan gestured invitingly and Cee led off. Safe house, Ethan decided, must be a generic espionage term for any hideout, for Cee took him not to a home but to a cheap hostel reserved for transients with

Stationer work permits. Here were housed clerks, housekeepers, porters, and other lower-echelon employees of the service sector whose function Ethan could only guess at, such as the two women in bright clothing and gaudy make-up almost Cetagandan in its unnatural coloration, who started to accost Cee and himself and shouted some unintelligible insult after them when they brushed hastily by.

Cee's quarters were a near-clone of Ethan's own neglected Economy Cabin, plain and cramped. Ethan wondered rather fearfully if Cee were reading his mind right now—apparently not, for the Cetagandan expatriate gave no sign of realizing his mistake yet.

"I take it," said Ethan, "that your powers are intermittent."

"Yes," replied Cee. "If my escape to Athos had gone as I'd originally planned, I meant never to use them again. I suppose your government will demand my services as the price of its protection, now."

"I—I don't know," answered Ethan honestly. "But if you truly possess such a talent, it would seem a shame not to use it. I mean, one can see the applications right away."

"Can't one, though," muttered Cee bitterly.

"Look at pediatric medicine—what a diagnostic aid for pre-verbal patients! Babies who can't answer, Where does it hurt? What does it feel like? Or for stroke victims or those paralyzed in accidents who have lost all ability to communicate, trapped in their bodies. God the Father"—Ethan's enthusiasm mounted—"you could be an absolute savior!"

Terrence Cee sat down rather heavily. His eyes widened in wonder, narrowed in suspicion. "I'm more often regarded as a menace. No one I've met who knew my secret ever suggested any use for me but espionage."

"Well—were they espionage agents themselves?"

"Now that you mention it—yes, for the most part."

"So, there you are. They see you as what they would be, given your gift."

Cee gave him a very odd look and smiled slowly. "Sir, I hope you're right." His posture became less closed, some part of the tension uncoiling in his lean muscles, but his blue eyes remained intent upon Ethan. "Do you realize that I am not a human being, Dr. Urquhart? I'm an artificial genetic construct, a composite from a dozen sources, with a sensory organ squatting like a spider in my brain that no human being ever had. I have no father and no mother. I wasn't born, I was made. And that doesn't horrify you?"

"Well, er—where did the men who made you get all your other genes? From other people, surely?" asked Ethan.

"Oh, yes. Carefully selected strains, all politically purified." Wormwood could not have set Cee's mouth in a tighter line.

"So," said Ethan, "if you count back, let me see, four generations, *every* human being is a composite from as many as sixteen different sources. They're called ancestors, but it comes to the same thing. Your mix was just marginally less random, that's all. Now, I do know genetics. With the exception of that new organ you claim, I can flat guarantee the 'just marginally.' That is not the test of your humanity."

"So what is the test of humanity?"

"Well—you have free will, obviously, or you could not be opposing your creators. Therefore you are not an automaton, but a child of God the Father, answerable to Him according to your abilities," Ethan catechized.

If Ethan had sprouted wings and flapped up to the ceiling Cee could not be staring at him in more shaken astonishment. It seemed as though these perfectly obvious facts had never before been presented to him.

Cee strained forward. "What am I to you, then, if not a monster?"

Ethan scratched his chin reflectively. "We all remain children of the Father, however we may otherwise be orphaned. You are my brother, of course."

"Of course…?" echoed Cee. His legs and arms drew in, making his body a tight ball. Tears leaked between his squeezed eyelids. He scrubbed his face roughly on his trouser knee, smearing the tears' reflective sheen across his flushed face. "Damn it," he whispered, "I'm the ultimate weapon, the super agent. I survived it all. How can you make me weep now?" Suddenly savage, he added, "If I find out you're lying to me, I swear I will kill you."

In another man's mouth they might have seemed empty words. Coming from Cee's ragged edginess, the threat was stomach-knotting. "You're obviously extremely tired," Ethan, alarmed, offered in solace. Cee had not yet quite regained his self-control, though he was clearly trying, breathing as carefully as a yogi. Ethan hunted around the room and handed him a tissue. "And I'd think looking at the world through Millisor's eyes, if that's what you've been doing lately, would be something of a strain."

"You've got that straight," choked Cee. "I've had to go in and out of his mind since this thing"—he made the migraine gesture again—"got fully developed in my head when I was thirteen years old."

"Ick," said Ethan, in heartfelt candor. "Well, that's it, then."

Cee emitted a surprised laugh that did more for his self-control than the breathing exercise had. "How can you know?"

"I don't know anything about how your telepathy works, but I've met the man." Ethan rubbed his lips thoughtfully. "How old are you?" he asked suddenly.

"Nineteen."

There was no adolescent defiance in the reply. Cee was merely stating a fact, as if his youth had never been an object in any test put to him. The insight chilled Ethan, like sighting the tip of an iceberg. "Ah—I don't suppose you'd care to tell me a little more about yourself? Speaking as your Immigration Officer, as it were."

The work had been based on a natural mutation of the pineal gland, Terrence Cee explained. How the migrant witch-woman, deformed, impoverished, and quite mad, had first caught the attention of Dr. Faz Jahar, Cee did not know. But she had been swept from her slum hovel into the university laboratory of the alert young medico. Jahar knew somebody who knew somebody who knew a high-ranking army Ghem lord and could make him look and listen; and so Jahar tapped a researcher's dream, unlimited secret government funding. The madwoman vanished into classified oblivion and was never seen alive again. To be sure, none of her previous acquaintances ever inquired after her.

Cee's recitation was cool and distant now, on-track, as something practiced too many times and over-trained. Ethan was not sure if the previous breakdown or current excess of Cee's self-control was more unnerving.

The telepathy complex was refined in vitro, twenty generations in five years. The first three human experiments to have it spliced into their chromosomes died before they ever outgrew their uterine replicators. Four more died in infancy and early childhood of inoperable brain cancers, three of some subtler failure to thrive.

"Is this disturbing you?" Cee, glancing up, inquired of Ethan.

Ethan, greenish-white and curled into a corner, said, "No…go on."

The specifications of the matrix genetic blueprints—Ethan would have called them children—were made more rigid. Jahar tried again. L-X-10-Terran-C was the first survivor. His early test results proved ambiguous, disappointing. Funding was cut. But Jahar, after so much human sacrifice, refused to give up.

"I suppose," said Cee, "Faz Jahar was as much of a parent as I ever had. He believed in me—no. He believed in his own work, within me. When the nurses and the extra technicians were dropped out of his budget, he tutored me himself. He even tutored Janine."

"Who is Janine?" asked Ethan after a moment, as Cee fell silent.

"J-9-X-Ceta-G was—my sister, if you will," said Cee at last. His inward gaze did not meet Ethan's eyes. "Although we shared few genes besides those for the pineal receptor organ. She was the only other survivor among Jahar's early creations. Or perhaps she was my wife. I'm not sure if Jahar intended her from the beginning as a co-progenitor of his new model human, or if she was merely an experimental trifle—he encouraged sex between us, as we grew older—but she was never trained as an intelligence agent. Millisor always thought of her as a sort of potential brood-mare for some nest of spylets—he had these secret, sexually-charged fantasies about her…." Ethan was relieved when Cee broke off, sparing him a guided tour of Millisor's questionable sexuality.

Dr. Faz Jahar's fortunes took an abrupt upward turn when Terrence Cee hit puberty. Completion of his brain growth and change in his biochemical balance at last activated the frustratingly quiescent organ. Cee's telepathic abilities became demonstrable, reliable, repeatable.

There were limitations. The organ could only be kicked into a state of electrical receptivity upon the ingestion of high doses of the amino acid tyramine. Receptivity faded as Cee's body metabolized the excess and returned him to his original biochemical balance. Telepathic range was limited to a few hundred meters at best. Reception was blocked by any barrier that interfered with the electrical signals emitted by the target brains.

Some minds could be experienced more clearly than others, some could barely be picked up at all even when Cee was actually touching his target's body. This seemed to be a problem of fit, or match, between sender and receiver, for some minds that registered as no more than a formless, mushy sense of life to Terrence came through in hallucinatory clarity—subvocalization, sensory input, the stream of conscious thought, and all—to Janine and vice versa.

Too many individuals within target range created interference with each other. "Like being at a party where everything is too loud," said Cee, "and straining to pick out one conversation."

Dr. Jahar had primed Terrence Cee all his short life for his destiny in service to Cetaganda and at first Cee had been content, even proud, to fulfill it. The first hairline cracks in his resolve came as he became familiar with the true minds of the hard-edged security personnel who surrounded the project. "Their insides didn't match their outsides," explained Cee. "The worst ones were so far gone in their corruptions, they didn't even smell it anymore."

The cracks propagated with each new experimental assignment in counter-intelligence.

"Millisor's deadliest mistake," Cee said thoughtfully, "was having us probe the minds of suspected intellectual dissidents while he interrogated them on their loyalty. I never knew people like them were possible, before."

Cee began military training with carefully selected private tutors. There was talk of using him as a field agent, on safe assignments or ones vital enough to justify risking his expensive person. There was no talk at all of ever admitting him to the Ghem-comrades, the tightly-knit society of men who controlled the officer corps and the military junta that in turn controlled the planet of Cetaganda, its conquests, and its client outposts.

Cee's telepathy gave him no secret window into the subconscious minds of his subjects. The only memories he could probe were those the subjects were presently calling to mind. This made using Cee for mere surveillance, in the hopes of catching something valuable on the fly-by, rather wasteful of the telepath's time. Organized interrogations were much more efficient. The interrogations Cee attended became wider in scope and often much uglier.

"I understand completely," said Ethan with a small shiver.

It was Janine, perhaps, who first began thinking of their creators as their captors. The dream of flight, never spoken aloud, fed back and forth between them during the rare occasions when both their powers were activated at the same time. Both began siphoning off and hoarding their tyramine tablets. Escape plans were laid, debated, and honed in utter silence.

The death of Dr. Faz Jahar was an accident. Cee became quite passionate trying to convince Ethan, who hadn't questioned the point, of the truth of this. Perhaps the escape might have gone better if they hadn't tried to destroy the laboratory and bring the four new children with them. It had complicated things. But Janine had insisted that none be left behind. When she and Terrence were made to sit in more frequently on more intensive interrogations of political prisoners, Cee gave up arguing that part of the plan with her.

If only Jahar hadn't tried to save his notes and gene cultures, he wouldn't have gone up with the bomb. If only the little children hadn't panicked and cried out, the guard might not have spotted them; if only they hadn't tried to run, he might not have fired. If only Terrence and Janine had chosen a different route, a different planet, a different city, different identities, in which to lose themselves.

The coolness of Cee's recitation froze altogether, his voice going flat, drained of emotion and self. He might have been denouncing the past decisions of some figure of ancient history, instead of his own, except that he began to rock, unconsciously, in cadence with his words. Ethan found his foot tapping along and stilled it.

If only he had not left the apartment that afternoon to pick a little money off the spacers at cards down by the shuttleport docks and get groceries. If only he had arrived back a little earlier and Captain Rau a little later. If only Janine had not gambled her life against Captain Rau's nerve disruptor to warn him. If only. If only. If only.

Cee discovered the altered consciousness of the berserker within himself in the battle to keep her body, every cell harboring the genetic secret, from falling back into Millisor's hands. It was a full day before Cee was able to get her corpse cryogenically frozen, much too long to beat brain-death even if there had been no disruptor damage.

He hoped anyway. All his will was focused now on the single obsession of making as much money as he could as quickly as possible. Terrence Cee, who had embraced a near-honest poverty for the sake of Janine's scruples while she lived, now plumbed the twisted uses of his power to their limits to amass the wealth needed to serve her corpse. Enough for the passage of a man and a heavy cryo-carton to the laboratories of Jackson's Whole where, it was whispered, enough money could buy *anything*.

But even a great deal of money could not buy life back from that death. Alternatives were gently suggested. Would the honored customer perhaps wish a clone made of his wife? A copy could be produced which even the most expert could not tell from the original. He would not even have to wait seventeen years for the copy to grow to maturity; things could be speeded up amazingly. The copy's personality could even be recreated with a surprising degree of verisimilitude, for the right price—perhaps even improved upon, were there aspects of the original not quite to the honored customer's taste. The clone herself would not know the difference.

"All I needed to get her back," said Cee, "was a mountain of money and the ability to convince myself that lies were truth." He paused. "I had the money."

Cee was silent for a long time. Ethan stirred uneasily, embarrassed as a stranger in the presence of death.

"Not to be pushy or anything," he prodded at last, "but I trust you were about to explain the connection of all this with the order for four hundred and fifty live human ovarian cultures Athos sent to Bharaputra Laboratories?" He smiled winningly, hoping that Terrence Cee was not about to clam up just before the pay-off.

Cee glanced sharply at Ethan, rubbing his forehead and temples in unconscious frustration. In a little while he answered, "Athos's order came into the genetics section of Bharaputra Labs while I was going around and around with them about Janine. I'd never heard of the planet before. It sounded so strange and distant to me—I thought, if only I could get there, maybe I could lose Millisor and my past forever. After Janine's remains were"—he swallowed painfully, his eyes flinching away from Ethan's—"were cremated, I left Jackson's Whole and started on a roundabout route designed to bury my trail. I lined up a job here to give me a cover identity while I waited for the next ship to Athos.

"I got here five days ago. Out of pure habit, I checked the transients' register for Cetagandan nationals. And found Millisor had been set up here for three months as an art and artifacts broker. I couldn't imagine how I'd spotted him before he spotted me, until I maneuvered close enough to read him. He'd pulled everyone off transient surveillance to hunt for you and Okita. They're at least a week behind in covering the exits and with one man short they're going to be a long time catching up. I believe I owe you more than one thank you, Doctor. What did you do with Okita, anyway?"

Ethan refused to be diverted. "What did you have Bharaputra Laboratories do to Athos's order?" He experimented with giving Cee a stern and fishy stare.

Cee moistened his lips. "Nothing. Millisor just thinks I did. I'm sorry it got him all wound up."

"I'm not quite as dense as I appear," said Ethan gently. Cee made a vague I-never-suggested-it gesture. "I happen to have independent information that Bharaputra's top genetics team spent two months assembling an order that could have been put together in a week." He glanced around at the tiny, sparse room. "I also note that you appear to be minus a mountain of money." Ethan gentled his voice still further. "Did you have them make an ovarian culture from your *wife's* remains, instead of having her cloned, when you realized cloning could not bring back what was essential in her? And then bribe them to slip the culture into our order, meaning to follow it on to Athos?"

Cee twitched. His mouth opened; he finally whispered, "Yes, sir."

"Complete with the gene complex for this pineal mutation?"

"Yes, sir. Unaltered." Cee stared at the floor. "She liked children. She was beginning to dare to want them, when we thought we were safe, before Rau caught up with us the final time. It was the last thing—the last thing I could do for *her*. Anything else would have merely been for myself. Can you see that, sir?"

Ethan, moved, nodded. At that moment he would have cheerfully decked any Athosian fundamentalist who dared to argue that Cee's tragic fixation upon his forbidden female could have no honor in it. He trembled at his own radical emotion. And yet, something did not add up. He almost had it...

The door buzzer blatted.

They both jumped. Cee's hand checked his jacket for some hidden weapon. Ethan merely paled.

"Does anyone know you're here?" Cee asked.

Ethan shook his head. But he had promised this young man the protection of Athos, such as it was. "I'll answer it," he volunteered. "You, er—cover me," he added as Cee started to object. Cee nodded and slipped to one side.

The door hissed open.

"Good evening, Ambassador Urquhart." Elli Quinn, framed in the aperture, beamed at him. "I heard the Athosian Embassy might be in the market for security guards—soldiers—an intelligence corps. Look no further, Quinn is here, all three in one. I'm offering a special discount on daring rescues to any customer who places his order before midnight. It's five minutes till," she added after a moment. "You going to invite me in?"

CHAPTER NINE

"You again," groaned Ethan. He gave Commander Quinn a malignant glower as her exact words—his exact words—registered. "Where'd you plant the bug, Quinn?"

"On your credit chit," she answered promptly. "It was the one item you slept with." She rocked on her toes, cocking her head to peer around Ethan's shoulder. "Won't you introduce me to your new friend? Pretty please?"

Ethan bleated under his breath.

"Exactly," Quinn nodded. "And I must say you're the best stalking-goat I ever ran. The way troubles flock to you is just astonishing."

"I thought you had no use for—ah—queers," said Ethan coldly.

She grinned evilly. "Well, now, don't take that too much to heart. To tell the truth, I was starting to wonder just how I was ever going to shift you out from under my bed. I was really very pleased with your initiative."

Ethan's lip curled, but until she took her booted foot off the door groove the safety seals would refuse to close. He stepped aside with what grace he could choke up.

Terrence Cee's right hand smoothed his jacket, tensely. "Is she a friend?"

"No," said Ethan curtly.

"Yes." Commander Quinn nodded vigorously, turning her best smile on the new target.

115

Cee, Ethan noted irritably, showed the same silly startle reflex that all galactic males displayed upon their first encounter with Commander Quinn; but to Ethan's relief he seemed to recover far more quickly, his eyes jumping from her face to her holster to her boots and other likely weapons check-points. Quinn's eyes mapped Cee's inventory of her against Cee himself and crinkled smugly in the knowledge of where to look for *his* weapons. Ethan sighed. Was the mercenary woman always destined to be one step ahead of them?

The door seals hissed shut. Quinn seated herself with her hands resting demurely on her knees, away from whatever arsenal she carried. "Tell this nice young man who I am, Ambassador Doctor Urquhart."

"Why?" Ethan grumped.

"Oh, c'mon. You owe me a favor, after all."

"What!" Ethan inhaled in preparation for fully expressing his outrage, but Quinn went on.

"Sure. If I hadn't primed my cousin Teki to ease you on out of quarantine you'd still be hung up in there with no ID, legal prisoner of the hand-washers. And you and Mr. Cee here would never have met."

Ethan's jaw snapped shut. "Introduce yourself," he finally fumed.

She gave him a gracious nod and turned to Cee, her studied ease not quite concealing an intent excitement. "My name is Elli Quinn. I hold the rank of Commander in the Dendarii Free Mercenary Fleet and the post of a field agent in the Fleet intelligence section. My orders were to observe Ghem-colonel Millisor and his group and discover their mission. Thanks largely to Ambassador Urquhart here, I have finally done so." Her eyes sparked satisfaction.

Terrence Cee stared at them both in new suspicion. It made Ethan boil, after all his careful work to coax Cee's damaged spirit to trust him a little.

"Who are you working for?" asked Cee.

"Admiral Miles Naismith commands me."

Cee brushed this aside impatiently. "Who is *he* working for, then?"

Ethan wondered why this question had never occurred to him.

Commander Quinn cleared her throat. "One of the reasons, of course, for hiring a mercenary agent instead of using your own in-house people is precisely so that if the mercenary is captured, he cannot reveal where all his reports went."

"In other words, you don't know."

"That's right."

Cee's eyes narrowed. "I can think of another reason for hiring a mercenary. What if you want to do an in-house check of your own people? How can I be sure you're not working for the Cetagandans yourself?"

Ethan gasped at this horrific, logical idea.

"In other words, might Colonel Millisor's superiors just be evaluating him for his next promotion?" Quinn's smile grew quizzical. "I hope not, because they would be awfully unhappy with that last report of mine." By which vagueness Ethan gathered that she had no intention of publicly reclaiming Okita as her kill. This generosity failed to fill him with gratitude.

"—the only guarantee I can offer you is the same one I'm relying on myself. I don't think Admiral Naismith would accept a contract from the Cetagandans."

"Mercenaries get rich by taking their contracts from the highest bidder," said Cee. "They don't care who."

"Ah—hm. Not precisely. Mercenaries get rich by winning with the least possible loss. To win, it helps if you can command the best possible people. And the very best do care who. True, there are moral zombies and outright psychos in the business—but not on Admiral Naismith's staff."

Ethan barely restrained himself from quibbling with this last assertion.

Well-launched, she continued, forgetting her carefully non-threatening posture and rising to pace about in all her nervous concentration. "Mr. Cee, I wish to offer you a commission in the Dendarii Free Mercenary Fleet. Based on your telepathic gift alone— if proved—I can personally guarantee you a tech/spec lieutenancy on the Intelligence Staff. Maybe something more, given your experience, but I'm sure I can deliver a lieutenancy. If you were indeed bred and born for military intelligence, why not make that destiny your own? No secret power structures like the Ghem lords make or break you in the Dendarii. You rise on merit alone. And however strange you think yourself, there you will find comrades who are stranger still—"

"I'll bet," muttered Ethan.

"—live births, replicator births, genetically altered marginal habitat people—one of our best ship captains is a genetic hermaphrodite."

She wheeled, she gestured; she would swoop down like a hawk if she could, Ethan felt, and carry off his new charge.

"I might point out, Commander Quinn, that Mr. Cee asked for the protection of *Athos*."

She didn't even bother to be sarcastic. "Yes, there you are," she said quickly. "If it's Millisor you fear, what better place to find protection than in the middle of an army?"

Furthermore, Ethan thought, Commander Quinn was unfairly good-looking when she was flushed with excitement…. He peeked fearfully at Cee and was relieved to find him looking cold and unmoved. If that pitch had been aimed with such passion at him, he might be ready to run out and sign up himself. Did the Dendarii need ship's surgeons?

"I presume," Cee said dryly, "they would wish to debrief me first."

"Well"— she shrugged—"sure."

"Under drugs, no doubt."

"Ah—well, it is mandatory for all Intelligence volunteers. In spite of all good conscious intent, it's possible to be a plant and not know it."

"Interrogation with all the trimmings, in short."

She looked more cautious. "Well, we have all the trimmings in stock, of course. If needed."

"To be used. If needed."

"Not on our *own* people."

"Lady"—he touched his forehead—"when this thing is activated I *am* the other people."

Some of her energy drained away in doubt for the first time. "Ah. Hm."

"And if I choose not to go with you—what will you do then, Commander Quinn?"

"Oh—well…" She looked, Ethan thought, exactly like a cat pretending not to stalk a mouse. "You're not off Kline Station yet. Millisor's still out there. I might be able to do you a favor or two yet—"

Was this a threat or a bribe?

"In return, you might care to give me some more information about Millisor and Cetagandan Intelligence. Just so I have *something* to take back to Admiral Naismith."

Ethan pictured a cat proudly depositing a dead mouse on its owner's pillow.

Cee must have been picturing something similar, for he inquired sardonically, "Would my dead body do?"

"Admiral Naismith," Quinn assured him, "wouldn't like that *nearly* so well."

Cee snorted. "What do you blindlings know of men's real minds? What can any of you really tell? When I look at you blind like this, what can I know?"

Quinn hesitated in real thought. "Well, that's the way we must judge people all the time," she offered slowly. "We measure actions, as well as words and appearances. We make imaginative guesses. We place faith, if you will." She nodded toward Ethan, who, prodded by honest conscience, nodded back even though he had no wish to prop any argument of hers.

Cee paced. "Both actions and lies may be compelled, against the real will. By fear, or other things. I know." He turned, turned again. "I must know. I must *know*." He stopped, fixed them both with a stare like a man trying to penetrate black midnight. "Get me some tyramine. Then we'll talk. When I can know what you *really* are."

Ethan wondered if the dismay in his own face matched Quinn's. They looked at each other, not needing telepathy to picture the other's thoughts: Quinn, doubtless stuffed with secret Dendarii intelligence procedures; himself, well—Cee was bound to find out eventually what a mistake he'd make seeking protection from Ethan. Perhaps it had better not be the hard way. Ethan sighed regret for the demise of his flatteringly exalted image in Cee's eyes. But a fool is twice a fool who tries to conceal it. "All right by me," he conceded mournfully.

Quinn was chewing her lip, abstracted. "That's obsolete," she muttered, "and so's that and they have to have changed that by now—and Millisor knows all *that* already. And all the rest is purely personal." She looked up. "All right."

Cee appeared nonplused. "You agree?"

Quinn's mouth quirked. "The first time the Ambassador and I have agreed on anything, I think?" She raised her eyebrows at Ethan, who muttered, "Humph."

"Do you have access to purified tyramine?" Cee demanded of them. "On hand?"

"Oh, any pharmacy would stock it," Ethan said. "It has some clinical uses in—"

"There's a problem with going to a pharmacy," Cee began grimly, when Quinn burst out in a tone of sudden enlightenment. "Oh. *Oh.*"

"Oh, what?" asked Ethan.

"Now I understand why Millisor went to such trouble to penetrate the commercial computer network, but didn't bother trying to get into the military one. I didn't see how he could have possibly got 'em mixed up." The satisfaction of a puzzle solved glowed attractively in her dark eyes.

"Huh?" said Ethan.

"It's a trap, right?" said Quinn.

Cee nodded confirmation.

She explained to Ethan, "Millisor has the commercial computer network flagged. I bet if anybody on Kline Station purchases purified tyramine, whistles go off in Millisor's listening post and up pops Rau or Setti or somebody—cautiously, on account of there are sure to be false alarms—and—oh, yes. Very neat." She nodded professional approval.

She sat a moment, absently scratching one perfect front tooth with a fingernail. An ex-nail biter, Ethan diagnosed. "I may have a way around that," she murmured.

Ethan had never manned an espionage listening post before and he found the gadgetry fascinating. Terrence Cee seemed coolly familiar with the principles if not the particular models. The Dendarii apparently went in heavily for micro-miniaturization along Betan lines. Only the need to interface with gross human eyes and fingers bloated the control pad, propped open on the table between Cee and Ethan, to the size of a small notebook.

The view displayed by the little holovid plate of the Station arcade where Quinn now stood tended to jump rather disorientingly with movements of her head, since the vid pick-up surfaces were concealed in her tiny bead earrings. But with concentration and a little practice Ethan found himself absorbed in the display with almost the illusion of being an eyewitness to the scene half the Station away. Cee's darkened hostel room faded from his consciousness, although Cee himself, intent beside Ethan, remained a distracting presence.

"Nothing can go wrong, if you do exactly what I tell you and don't try to ad lib," Quinn was explaining to her cousin Teki, who was looking smart in a fresh pine-green and sky-blue uniform. The white bandage on Teki's forehead from yesterday's float pallet accident had been replaced by a clear permeable plastic one. Ethan noted with approval no sign of redness or swelling around the neatly sealed cut. "Remember, it's the *absence* of a signal that calls for an abort," Quinn went on. "I'll be nearby in case of emergencies, but try not to look at me. If you don't see me wave from the balcony, just turn right around and take the stuff back and tell them you wanted the other, the, um…"

"Tryptophan," Ethan muttered, "for sleep."

"Tryptophan," Quinn continued, "for sleep. Then just go home. Don't try to look for me. I'll get in touch with you later."

"Elli, has this got something to do with that fellow you were so hot to spring from Quarantine yesterday?" said Teki. "You promised you'd explain it later."

"It's not later enough yet."

"It's got something to do with the Dendarii Mercenaries, doesn't it?"

"I'm on leave."

Teki grinned. "You in love, then? At least he's an improvement over the crazy dwarf."

"Admiral Naismith," said Quinn stiffly, "is not a dwarf. He's nearly five feet tall. And I am not 'in love' with him, you low-minded twit; I merely admire his brilliance." The view jiggled as she bounced on her heels. "Professionally."

Teki hooted, but cautiously. "All right, so if this isn't something for the dwarf, what is it? You're not smuggling drugs or some damned thing, are you? I don't mind doing you a favor, but I'm not risking my job even for you, coz."

"You're on the side of the angels, I assure you," Quinn told him impatiently. "And if you don't want to be late for your precious job, it's time to shove off."

"Oh, all right." Teki shrugged good-naturedly. "But I demand the whole fairy-tale later, you hear?" He turned to saunter off up the arcade, adding a last word over his shoulder. "But if it's all so legal, moral, and non-fattening, why do you keep saying, 'Nothing can go wrong'?"

"Because nothing *can* go wrong." Quinn invoked the phrase like a charm under her breath and waved him off.

In a few minutes she sauntered after him. Ethan and Cee were treated to a leisurely window-shopping tour of the arcade. Only an occasional, offhand pan around reassured them that the cousin was still in sight. Teki entered the pharmaceutical dispensary. Quinn moved up, adjusting the directional audio pick-up in her hair clip, pausing to mull over a display of medications against nausea due to weightlessness.

"Hm," the pharmacist was saying. "We don't get much call for that one…" He tapped out a code on his computer interface. "Half-gram or one-gram tablets, sir?"

"Uh—one-gram, I guess," answered Teki.

"Coming up," the man replied. There was a long pause. The sound of more tapping; a muttered curse from the pharmacist. The sound of a fist pounding lightly on the casing of the control panel. A plaintive beep from the computer. More tapping, in a repeat of the previous pattern.

"Millisor's trap at work?" Ethan whispered to Cee.

"Almost certainly. Time delay," Cee muttered back.

"I'm sorry, sir," said the pharmacist to Teki. "There seems to be a glitch. If you'll have a seat, I'll retrieve your order manually. It will just be a few minutes."

Quinn dared a look toward the counter. The pharmacist pulled out a thick index book, blew off a fine layer of dust, and thumbing through the thin pages exited by a rear door.

Teki sighed and flopped down on a padded bench. He glanced up at Quinn; her gaze immediately broke away from the dispensing counter to focus in apparent fascination upon a rack of contraceptives. Ethan flushed in embarrassment and stole a glance at Cee, whose concentration appeared unruffled. Ethan returned his gaze straightly to the holovid. The galactic man was no doubt used to these things, having by his own admission lived intimately with a woman for several years. He probably saw nothing wrong. Personally, Ethan wished Quinn would go back to the spacesick pills.

"Rats," breathed Quinn. "That was quick."

Another dizzying glance, up at the new customer hastily entering the dispensary. Average height, blandly dressed, compact as a bomb—Rau.

Rau slowed down abruptly, cased the counter, spotted Teki, and drifted down the display aisle breathing deeply and quietly. He fetched up on the opposite side of the contraceptive rack from Quinn. She must have given him one of her dazzling smiles, for a startled answering smile was jerked involuntarily from his lips before he retreated across the room and away from her distracting face.

The pharmacist returned at last and fed Teki's credit card to the computer which, working properly now, tasted it and gave it back with a demure burp. Teki gathered up his package and left. Rau was not more than four paces behind him.

Teki wandered slowly down the arcade, with many a furtive glance toward the empty balcony on the far end. He finally seated himself by the standard fountain-and-green-plants display in the middle and waited a good long time. Rau seated himself nearby, pulled out a hand-viewer, and began to read. Quinn window-shopped interminably.

Teki glanced at the balcony, checked his chronometer in frustration, and stared down the arcade at Quinn, who took no apparent notice of him. After a few more minutes of fuming foot-tapping, Teki got up and started to leave.

"Oh, sir," called Rau, smiling. "You forgot your package!" He held it up invitingly.

"Gods fly away with you, Teki!" Quinn whispered fiercely under her breath. "I said no ad libs!"

"Oh. Er—thank you." Teki took the package back from death's polite hand and stood a moment blinking indecisively. Rau nodded and returned to his hand-viewer. Teki sighed aggrievedly and trudged back up the arcade to the dispensary.

"Excuse me," Teki called to the pharmacist. "But is it tyramine or tryptophan that's the sleep aid?"

"Tryptophan," said the pharmacist.

"Oh, I'm sorry. It was the tryptophan I wanted."

There was a slightly murderous silence. Then, "Quite, sir," said the pharmacist coldly. "Right away."

"It wasn't a total loss," said Quinn, pulling out her earrings and attaching them carefully to their holders in the monitor case. "At least I confirmed that Rau is hiding out in Millisor's listening post. But I'd kinda figured that anyway."

She added the hair clip, sealed the case, and slipped it into her jacket. Hooking a chair under herself with one foot, she sat with her elbows on Terrence Cee's little foldout table. "I suppose they'll follow Teki around for the next week, now. So much the better, I like to see my adversaries overworked. Just so he doesn't try to call me, nothing can go wrong."

Nothing can go right, either, thought Ethan with a sideways look at Terrence Cee's face. Cee had been almost hopeful when the tyramine seemed within their grasp. Now he was closed and cold and suspicious once again.

Quite aside from his own ill-advised pledge to protect Cee, Ethan could not walk away from this frenetic tangle as long as Millisor remained a threat to Athos. And whatever their separate ends might be, Cee's and Quinn's and his own, the untangling would surely take all their combined resources.

"I suppose I could try to steal some," said Quinn unenthusiastically, evidently also conscious of Cee's renewed frigidity. "Although Kline Station is not the easiest place for that sort of tactic..." She trailed off in thought.

"Is there any particular reason it has to be purified tyramine?" Ethan asked suddenly. "Or do you just need so many milligrams of tyramine in your bloodstream, period?"

"I don't know," said Cee. "We always just used the tablets."

Ethan's eyes narrowed. He rummaged the little wall-desk nearby for a note panel and began to tap out a list.

"What now?" asked Quinn, craning her neck.

"A prescription, by God the Father," said Ethan, tapping on in growing excitement. "Tyramine occurs naturally in some foods, you know. If you choose a menu with a high concentration of it—Millisor can't possibly have every food outlet on the Station bugged—nothing illegal about going grocery shopping, is there? You'll probably have to hit the import shops for a lot of this. I don't think much of it is room service console standard fare."

Quinn took the list and read it, her eyebrows rising. "All of this stuff?"

"As much as you can get."

"You're the doctor." She shrugged, getting to her feet. Her smile grew lopsided. "I think Mr. Cee is going to need one."

Two hours of strained silence later, Quinn returned to Cee's hostel room lugging two large bags.

"Party time, gentlemen," she called, dumping the bags on the table. "What a feast."

Cee quailed visibly at the mass of edibles.

"It—seems rather a lot," remarked Ethan.

"You didn't say how much," Quinn pointed out. "But he only has to eat and drink until he switches on." She lined up claret, burgundy, champagne, sherry, and dark and light beer bulbs in a soldierly row. "Or passes out." Around the liquids in an artistic fan she placed yellow cheese from Escobar, hard white cheese from Sergyar, two kinds of pickled herring, a dozen chocolate bars, sweet and dill pickles. "Or throws up," she concluded.

The hot fried chicken liver cubes alone were native produce from the Kline Station culture vats. Ethan thought of Okita and gulped. He picked up a few items and blanched at the price tags.

Quinn caught his grimace and sighed. "Yes, you were right about having to hit the import shops. Do you have any idea how this is going to look on my expense account?" She bowed Terrence Cee toward the smorgasbord. "Bon appetit."

She kicked off her boots and lay down on Cee's bed with her hands locked behind her neck and an expression of great interest on her face. Ethan pulled the plastic seal off a liter squeeze bottle of claret and helpfully offered up the cups and utensils the room service console produced.

Cee grimaced doubtfully and sat down at the table. "Are you sure this will work, Dr. Urquhart?"

"No," said Ethan frankly. "But it seems like a pretty safe experiment."

An audible snicker drifted from the bed. "Isn't science wonderful?" said Quinn.

CHAPTER TEN

For courtesy's sake Ethan shared the wine, although he gave the chicken livers, pickles, and chocolate a pass. The claret was rotgut despite its price, although the burgundy was not bad and the champagne—for dessert—was quite tasty. A slightly gluey disembodiment warned Ethan that courtesy had gone far enough. He wondered how Cee, still dutifully nibbling and sipping across the table, was holding up.

"Can you feel anything yet?" Ethan inquired of him anxiously. "Can I get you anything? More cheese? Another cup?"

"A spacesick sack?" asked Quinn helpfully. Ethan glared at her, but Cee merely waved away the offers, shaking his head.

"Nothing yet," he said. His hand unconsciously rubbed his neck. Ethan diagnosed incipient headache. "Dr. Urquhart, are you quite sure that no part of the shipment of ovarian cultures Athos received could have been what Bharaputra sent?"

Ethan felt he'd answered that question a thousand times. "I unpacked it myself and saw the other boxes later. They weren't even cultures, just raw dead ovaries."

"Janine—"

"If her, um, donation was cultured for egg cell production—"

"It was. They all were."

"Then it wasn't there. None were."

"I saw them packed myself," said Cee. "I watched them loaded at the shuttleport docks on Jackson's Whole."

127

"That narrows down the time and place they could have been switched, a little," observed Quinn. "It had to have been on Kline Station, during the two months in warehouse. That only leaves, ah, four hundred and twenty-six suspect ships to trace." She sighed. "A task, unfortunately, quite beyond my means."

Cee swirled burgundy in a plastic cup and drank again. "Beyond your means, or simply of no interest to you?"

"Well—all right, both. I mean, if I really wanted to trace it, I'd let Millisor do the legwork and just follow him. But the shipment is only of interest because of that one gene complex in one culture which, if I understand things correctly, you also contain. A pound of your flesh would serve my purposes just as well—better. Or a gram, or a tube of blood cells…" She trailed off, inviting Cee to pick up on the hint.

Cee sidestepped. "I can't wait for Millisor to trace it. As soon as his team catches up on their backlog, they'll find me here on Kline Station."

"You have a little margin yet," she pointed out. "I'll wager they're going to waste quite a few man-hours following poor innocent Teki around while he does the housework. Maybe it'll bore them to death," she hoped, "sparing me the bother of completing a certain odious task I promised House Bharaputra."

Cee glanced at Ethan. "Doesn't Athos want the shipment back?"

"We'd written it off. Although retrieving it would save purchasing another, I'm afraid it would be a false economy if Millisor followed it to Athos with an army at his back and genocide on his mind. He's so obsessed with this idea that Athos must have it—I'd actually like to see him find the damned thing, just to be sure Athos was rid of him." Ethan gave Cee an apologetic shrug. "Sorry."

Cee smiled sadly. "Never apologize for honesty, Dr. Urquhart." He went on more urgently. "But don't you see, the gene complex *cannot* be allowed to fall back into their hands. Next time they'll be more careful to make their telepaths true slaves. And then there will be no limits to the corruptions of their use."

"Can they really make men without free will?" said Ethan, chilled. The old catch phrase 'Abomination in the eyes of God the Father' seemed illuminated with real and disquieting meaning. "I must say I don't like that idea, followed to its logical conclusion. Machines made of flesh...."

Quinn spoke lazily from the bed in a tone, Ethan was becoming aware, that concealed fast-moving thought. "Seems to me the genie's out of the bottle anyway, whether Millisor gets the stuff back or not. Millisor thinks in terms of counter-intelligence from a lifetime of habit. He's only going through so much exercise to be sure nobody *else* gets it. Now that Cetaganda knows it can be done, they'll duplicate the research in time. Twenty-five years, fifty years, whatever it takes. By then maybe there had better be a race of free telepaths to oppose them." Her eyes probed Cee as if already locating a good spot for a biopsy.

"And what makes you think your Admiral Naismith's employer would be any improvement over the Cetagandans?" asked Cee bitterly.

She cleared her throat. The telepath had been reading her mind ever since he'd started asking questions, Ethan realized, and she already knew it. "So, send a duplicate tissue sample of yourself to every government in the galaxy if you like." She grinned wolfishly. "Millisor would have a stroke, giving you your revenge and getting Athos off the hook at the same time. I *like* efficiency."

"To make a hundred races of slaves?" asked Cee. "A hundred mutant minorities, all feared and hated and controlled by whatever ruthless force seems necessary to their uneasy captors? And hunted to their deaths when that control fails?"

Ethan had never found himself clinging to a cusp of human history before. The trouble with the position, he found, was that in whatever direction you looked there fell away a glassy, uncontrollable slide down to a strange future you would then have to live in. He had never wanted to pray more, nor been less sure that it would do any good.

Cee shook his head, drank again. "For myself, I'm done with it. No more. I'd have walked into the fire three years ago, but for Janine."

"Ah," said Quinn. "Janine."

Cee looked up with piercing eyes. Not nearly drunk, Ethan thought. "You want a pound of flesh, mercenary? That's the price that will buy it. Find me Janine."

Quinn pursed her lips. "Mixed in, you say, with the rest of Athos's mail-order brides. Tricky." She wound a strand of hair around her finger. "You realize, of course, that my mission here is finished. I've done my job. And I could stun you where you sit, take my tissue sample, and be gone before you came to."

Cee stirred uneasily. "So?"

"So, just so you realize that."

"What do you want of me?" Cee demanded. Anger edged his voice. "To trust you?"

Her lips thinned. "You don't trust anybody. You never had to. Yet you demand that others trust you."

"Oh," said Cee, looking suddenly enlightened. "That."

"You breathe one word of *that*"—she smiled through clenched teeth—"and I'll arrange an accident for you like Okita never dreamed of."

"Your Admiral's personal secrets are of no interest to me," said Cee stiffly. "They're hardly relevant to this situation anyway."

"They're relevant to me," Quinn muttered, but she gave him a small nod, conditional acceptance of this assurance of privacy.

Every sin that Ethan had ever committed or contemplated rose unbidden to his mind. He took Quinn's unspoken point. So, evidently, did Cee, for he turned the subject by turning to Ethan.

Ethan suddenly felt terribly naked. Everything that he least wanted to be caught thinking about seemed to race through his consciousness. Cee's marvelous physical attractiveness, for example, the nervous intelligent leanness of him, the electric blue eyes—Ethan damned his own weakness for blonds and yanked his thoughts back from a slide to the sexual. Watching himself be mentally undressed in Ethan's thoughts would hardly impress Cee with Ethan's cool diplomatic medical professionalism. Ethan envied Quinn's bland, unfailing control.

But it could be worse. He could think about just how gossamer-thin was the shield of Athos's protection he had supposedly thrown over Cee, on the basis of which the telepath had revealed so damagingly much. How betrayed was Cee going to feel when he discovered that the asylum of Athos consisted of Ethan's wits, period? Ethan reddened, utterly ashamed, and stared at the floor.

He was going to lose Cee to Quinn and the glamour of the Dendarii Mercenaries before he even had a chance to tell him about Athos—the beautiful seas, the pleasant cities, the ordered communes and the patchwork terraformed farmlands, and beyond them the vast wild desolate wastes with their fascinating extremes of climate and people—the saintly, if grubby, contemplative hermits, the outlaw Outlanders... Ethan pictured himself taking Cee sailing on the South Province coast, checking the underwater fences of his father's fish farm—did Cetaganda have oceans?—salt sweat and salt water, hot hard work and cold beer and blue shrimp afterward.

Cee shivered, as a man forcing himself awake from some bright but dangerous narcotic dream. "There are oceans on Cetaganda," he whispered, "but I never saw them. My whole life was corridors."

Ethan's red went to scarlet. He felt as transparent as glass.

Quinn, watching him, emitted a sour chuckle of perfect understanding. "I predict your talent will not make you popular at parties, Cee."

Cee appeared to pull himself back on track by force of will. Ethan was relieved.

"If you can give me asylum, Dr. Urquhart, why not Janine's seed as well? And if you can't protect her, how do you figure to..."

Ethan was not relieved. But lies were pointless now. "I haven't even figured out how to get my own tail out of this mess yet," he admitted ruefully, "let alone yours." He eyed Quinn. "But I'm not quitting."

A wave of her index finger indicated a touché. "I might point out, gentlemen, that before any of us can do anything at all about that genetic shipment we must first find the damned thing. Now, there seems to be a missing element in this equation. Let's try to narrow it down. If none of us nor Millisor has it, who else might?"

"Anyone who found out what it was," answered Cee. "Rival planetary governments. Criminal organizations. Free mercenary fleets."

"Watch who you put in the same breath, Cee," Quinn muttered.

"House Bharaputra must have known," said Ethan.

Quinn smiled with half her mouth. "And they fit two categories out of the three, being both a government and a criminal organization.... Ahem. Pardon my prejudices. Yes. Certain individuals in House Bharaputra did know what it was. They all became smoking corpses. I fear that House Bharaputra no longer knows what it hatched. Internal evidence: Bharaputra didn't exactly take me into their entire confidence, but I submit that if they'd known, my assignment would have been to return Millisor and company to them alive for questioning and not, as explicitly requested, dead." She caught Cee's eye. "You doubtless knew their minds better than I. Does my reasoning hold?"

"Yes," Cee admitted reluctantly.

"We're going in circles," Ethan observed.

Quinn twisted her hair. "Yeah."

"What about some individual entrepreneur," suggested Ethan, "stumbling on the knowledge by accident. A ship's crewman, say…"

"Aargh," groaned Quinn, "I said to narrow the range of possibilities, not widen them! Data. Data." She swung to her feet, studied Cee. "You done for now, Mr. Cee?"

Cee was hunched over, his hands pressing his head. "Yes, go. No more now."

Ethan was concerned. "Are you experiencing pain? Does it have a localized pattern?"

"Yes, never mind, it's always like this." Cee stumbled to his bed, rolled over, curled up.

"Where are you going?" Ethan asked Quinn.

"First, to empty my regular information traps; second, to try a little oblique interrogation of the warehouse personnel. Although what the human supervisor of an automated system is likely to remember after five to seven months about one shipment out of thousands… Oh, well. It's a loose end I can nail down. You may as well stay here. It's as safe as anyplace." A jerk of her head implied, *And you can keep an eye on our friend in the bed.*

Ethan ordered up three-fourths of a gram of salicylates and some B-vitamins from the room service console and pressed them on the pale telepath. Cee took them and rolled back up with a never-mind-me gesture that failed to reassure Ethan. But Cee's clenched glazed stupor at last relaxed into sleep.

Ethan watched over him, chafing anew at his own helplessness. He had nothing to offer, nothing half so clever as Quinn's bags of tricks. Nothing but an insistent conviction that they all had hold of the problem by the wrong end.

Quinn's return woke Ethan, asleep on the floor. He creaked to his feet and let her in, rubbing sand out of his eyes. It was time for another shave, too; maybe he could borrow some depilatory from Cee.

"How did it go? What did you find out?" he asked.

She shrugged. "Millisor continues to maintain his cover routine. Rau's back at the listening post. I could call in an anonymous tip to Station Security where to look for him, but if he slipped out of Detention again I'd just have to track him down someplace new. And the warehouse supervisor can drink premium aquavit by the liter and talk for hours without remembering anything." She smothered a slightly aromatic belch herself.

Cee awoke to their voices and sat up on the edge of his bed. "Oh," he muttered and lay back down rather more carefully, blinking. After a moment he sat up again. "What time is it?"

"Nineteen-hundred hours," said Quinn.

"Oh, hell." Cee jerked to his feet. "I've got to get to work."

"Should you go out at all?" asked Ethan anxiously.

Quinn frowned judiciously. "He'd probably better maintain his cover for the time being. It's worked so far."

"I'd better maintain my income," said Cee, "if I'm ever to buy a ticket off this vacuum-packed rat warren."

"I'll buy you a ticket," offered Quinn.

"Going your way," said Cee.

"Well, naturally."

Cee shook his head and stumbled to the bathroom.

Quinn dialed orange juice and coffee from the room service console. Ethan, scooting around the table to reserve a place for Cee, accepted both gratefully.

Quinn sipped from an insulated bulb of shimmering black liquid. "Well, my shift was a bust, Doctor, but how about yours? Did Cee say anything new?"

This was mere polite conversation, Ethan gauged. She had probably recorded every snore they'd emitted.

"We slept, mostly." Ethan drank. The coffee was hot and vile, some cheap synthetic. Ethan considered that it was being charged to Cee and made no comment. "But I've been thinking about the problem of tracking the shipment. It seems to me we've been going at it wrong way round. Look at the internal evidence of what actually arrived on Athos."

"Trash, you said, to fill up the boxes."

"Yes, but—"

A peeping noise, as from a captive baby chick, sounded from Quinn's rumpled gray and white jacket. She patted the pockets, muttering, "What the hell—oh gods, Teki, I told you not to call me at work…" She pulled out a small beeper and checked a glowing numeric readout.

"What is that?" asked Ethan.

"My emergency call-back signal. A very few people have the code. Supposedly not traceable, but Millisor has some equipment that— hm, that's not Teki's console number."

She swung around in her chair to Terrence Cee's comconsole. "Don't talk, Doctor, and stay out of range of the vid pick-up."

The face of a perky auburn-haired young woman wearing blue Stationer coveralls appeared over the holovid plate.

"Oh." Quinn sounded relieved. "It's you, Sara." She smiled.

Sara did not smile. "Hello, Elli. Is Teki with you?"

A tiny spurt of coffee shot out the bulb's mouthpiece as Quinn's hand convulsively tightened. Her smile became fixed. "With me? Did he say he was going to see me?"

Sara's eyes narrowed. "Don't play games with me, Elli. You can tell him I was at the Blue Fern Bistro on time. And I'm not going to wait more than three hours for any guy, even one wearing a spiffy green and blue uniform." She frowned at Quinn's gray-and-whites. "I'm not as taken with uniforms as he is. I'm going ho—out. I'm going out and you can tell him that a party doesn't need him to get started." Her hand moved toward the cut-off control.

"Wait, Sara! Don't cut me off! Teki's not with me, honest!" Quinn, who'd seemed about to climb into the vid, relaxed slightly as the girl's hand hesitated. "What's this all about? I last saw Teki just before his work shift. I know he got to Ecobranch all right. Was he supposed to meet you after?"

"He said he was going to take me to dinner and to the null-gee ballet, for my birthday. It started an hour ago." The girl sniffed, anger masking distress. "At first I thought he was working late, but I called and they said he left on time."

Quinn glanced at her chronometer. "I see." Her hands flexed, gripping the desk edge. "Have you called his home, or any of his other friends yet?"

"I called everywhere. Your father gave me your number." The girl frowned again in renewed suspicion.

"Ah." Quinn's fingers drummed on her stunner holster, now refilled with a shiny lightweight civilian model. "Ah." Ethan, jolted by the thought of Quinn having a father, struggled to pay attention.

Quinn's eyes snapped up to the girl in the vid. Her voice became lower in register, with a clipped hard edge. *This one*, Ethan thought involuntarily, *really has commanded in combat.* "Have you called Station Security?"

"Station Security!" The girl recoiled. "Elli, what for?"

"Call them now and tell them everything you've told me. File a missing person report on Teki."

"For a fellow who's late for a date? Elli, they'll laugh at me. You're laughing at me, aren't you?" she said uncertainly.

"I'm dead serious. Ask to speak with Captain Arata. Tell him Commander Quinn sent you. He won't laugh."

"But, Elli—"

"Do it now! I have to go. I'll check back with you as soon as I can."

The girl's image dissolved in sparkling snow. Invective hissed under Quinn's breath.

"What's going on?" asked Cee, emerging from the bathroom fastening the wrists of his green coveralls.

"I think Millisor has picked up Teki for questioning," said Quinn. "In which case my cover has just gone up in smoke. Damn it! There was no logical reason for Millisor to do that! Is he thinking with his gonads now? That's not like him."

"The logic of desperation, maybe," said Cee. "He was very upset by the disappearance of Okita. Even more upset by Dr. Urquhart's reappearance. He, um—had some very strange theories about Dr. Urquhart."

"On the basis of which," said Ethan, "you went to a great deal of trouble to find me. I'm sorry I'm not the super-agent you were expecting."

Cee gave him a rather odd look. "Don't be."

"I meant to push Millisor off-balance." Quinn bit through a fingernail with an audible snap. "But not that far off. I gave them no reason to take Teki. Or I wouldn't have, if he'd done what I told him and turned around immediately—I knew better than to involve a non-professional. Why didn't I listen to myself? Poor Teki won't know what hit him."

"You didn't have any such scruples about involving me," remarked Ethan, miffed.

"You were involved already. And besides, I didn't use to baby-sit you when you were a toddler. And besides…"—she paused, shoot-

ing him a look strangely akin to the one Cee had just given him—
"you underestimate yourself," she finished.

"Where are you going?" asked Ethan in alarm as she stalked toward the door.

"I'm going to—" she began determinedly. Her hand, reaching
for the door control, hesitated and fell back. "I'm going to think this
through."

She turned and began to pace. "Why are they holding him so long?"
she asked. Ethan was not quite sure if the question was addressed to
him, Cee, or the air. "They could've drained him of everything he knew
in fifteen minutes. Let him wake up on a tube car thinking he'd dozed
off on the way home and no one the wiser, not even me."

"They found out everything I knew in fifteen minutes," Ethan
pointed out, "but that didn't stop them."

"Yes, but their suspicions were aroused, sorry, you were quite
right, by finding my bug on you. I deliberately put nothing on Teki
so that couldn't happen again. Besides, they can check Teki in Kline
Station records back to his conception. You were a man without a
past, or at least with an inaccessible one, leaving lots of room for
paranoid fantasies to grow."

"As a result of which it took them seven hours to convince themselves they were right the first time," said Ethan.

Cee spoke. "And since Okita's disappearance they think you
are an agent who successfully resisted seven hours of interrogation.
They may be even less willing to take 'I don't know' for an answer
now."

"In that case," said Quinn grimly, "the sooner I get Teki out of
there the better."

"Excuse me," said Ethan, "but out of where?"

"Odds are, Millisor's quarters. Where you were questioned. Their
quiet room, the one I've never been able to bug." She ran her hands
wildly through her hair. "How the hell am I going to do this? A fron-
tal assault on a defended cube in the middle of a pack of innocent
civilians in the delicate mechanical environment of a space station…?
Doesn't sound too efficient."

"How did you rescue Dr. Urquhart?" asked Cee.

"I waited—patiently—for him to come out. I waited a long time for the best opportunity."

"Quite a long time, yes," Ethan agreed cordially. They exchanged tight smiles.

She paced back and forth like a frenzied tigress. "I'm being stampeded. I know I am. I can feel it. Millisor is reaching out for me through Teki. And Millisor's a man with no inhibitions about applying leverage. Q.E.D.—Quinn Eats Dirt. Gods. Don't panic, Quinn. What would Admiral Naismith do in the same situation?" She stood still, facing the wall.

Ethan envisioned diving Dendarii starfighters, waves of space-armored assault troops, ominous lumbering high-energy weapons platforms jockeying for position.

"Never do yourself," muttered Quinn, "what you can con an expert into doing for you. That's what he'd say. Tactical judo from the space magician himself." Her straight back held the dynamism of zen meditation. When she turned her face was radiant with jubilation. "Yes, that's exactly what he'd do! Sneaky little dwarf, I love you!" She saluted an invisible presence and dove for the comconsole.

Cee glanced dismayed inquiry at Ethan, who shrugged helplessly.

The image of an alert-looking clerk in pine green and sky blue materialized above the vid plate. "Ecobranch Epidemiology Hotline. May I help you?" the clerk intoned politely.

"I'd like to report a suspected disease vector," said Quinn in her most brusque, no-nonsense manner.

The clerk arranged a report panel at her elbow, poised her fingers over it. "Human or animal?"

"Human."

"Transient or Stationer?"

"Transient. But he may even now be transmitting it to a Stationer."

The clerk looked even more seriously interested. "And the disease?"

"Alpha-S-D-plasmid-three."

The clerk's tapping hand paused. "Alpha-S-D-plasmid-*two* is a sexually transmitted soft tissue necrosis that originated on Varusa Tertius. Is that what you mean?"

Quinn shook her head. "This is a new and much more virulent mutant strain of Varusan Crotch-rot. They haven't even bioengineered the counter-virus last I heard. Hadn't you people heard of it yet? You're fortunate."

The clerk's eyebrows rose. "No, ma'am." She tapped furiously and made several adjustments to her recording equipment. "And the name of the suspected vector?"

"Ghem-lord Harman Dal, a Cetagandan art and artifacts broker. He has a new agency in Transients' Lounge, just licensed a few weeks ago. He comes in contact with a lot of people."

Harman Dal, Ethan gathered, was Millisor's alias.

"Oh, dear," said the clerk. "We're certainly glad to get this report. Ah…" the clerk paused, groping for phrasing. "And how did you come to know about this individual's disease?"

Quinn's stern gaze broke from the clerk's face to her own feet, to distant corners of the room, to her twisting hands. She positively shuffled. She'd have blushed if she'd had a chance to hold her breath long enough. "How would you think?" she muttered to her belt buckle.

"Oh." The clerk did blush. "Oh. Well, in that case we are extremely grateful that you chose to come forward. I assure you all such epidemiological matters are handled in the strictest confidence. You must see one of our own quarantine physicians at once—"

"Absolutely," agreed Quinn, feigning nervous eagerness. "Can I come down now? But—but I'm terribly afraid that if you don't hurry, Dal is going to put three patients on your hands instead of just two."

"I assure you, ma'am, our department is adept at handling delicate situations. Please place your ID so the machine can read it—"

Quinn did so, promised again to report directly to Quarantine, was reassured of anonymity and gratitude, and broke off.

"There, Teki," she sighed. "Help is on the way. I've signed my real name to a criminal act, but the price was right."

"Being sick is against the law here?" asked Ethan, startled.

"No, but lodging a false report of a disease vector definitely is. When you see all the machinery it sets in motion you'll realize why they discourage practical jokers. But I'd rather face criminal charges than plasma fire any day. I'll put the fine on my expense account."

Cee's face bore awed delight. "Will Admiral Naismith approve?"

"He may give me a medal." Quinn winked at him, cheerful again. "Now. Ecobranch may get more resistance from their new patient than they expect. Best they get a little low-profile back-up, eh? Can you handle a stunner, Mr. Cee?"

"Yes, Commander."

Ethan waved a hesitant hand. "I had Athosian Army basic training," he heard himself volunteering insanely.

CHAPTER ELEVEN

In the event, it was Ethan and not Cee whom Quinn chose to accompany her person on what she dubbed "the second wave of this assault." She left the telepath stationed by the lift tubes at the end of Millisor's transient hostel corridor, arming him with the second stunner of her matching pair.

"Stay out of sight and pick off anybody who bolts," she instructed him, "and don't be shy about firing. With a stunner you can always apologize for mistakes later."

Ethan lifted an eyebrow at this as he turned to pace her down the corridor.

"All right, almost always," she muttered, glancing back over her shoulder to check Cee's concealment in the confusion of potted plants, mirrors, and angled conversation niches that formed the decor of the lift tube foyer. Millisor's chosen hostel was clearly meant for a class of traveler beyond Ethan's budget.

About this time Ethan realized a fatal flaw in the attack plan. "You didn't give me a stunner," he whispered urgently to Quinn.

"I only had two," she murmured back impatiently. "Here. Take my medkit. You can be the medic."

"What am I supposed to do, hit Rau over the head with it?"

She grinned briefly. "If you get the chance, sure. Meantime Teki's going to be needing an antidote to whatever they've pumped him full of. You'll probably be wanting the fast-penta antagonist. It's right in there next to the fast-penta. Unless things have gone really ugly, in which case I leave it up to your medical expertise."

"Oh," said Ethan, mollified. It almost made sense.

He was just opening his mouth with a newly marshaled objection when Quinn bundled him into the limited and inadequate concealment of a door niche. Coming down the corridor from the opposite end, toward the bulk freight lift, were three silhouettes leading a sealed passenger pallet with the Ecobranch logo of a stylized fern and water blazoned on the front. Passing into the soft, luxurious light—Ethan sensed someone had done some careful psychological studies of the response of the human brain to selected optical wavelengths—the three figures resolved into a burly Station Security man and two ecotechs, one male, one female.

One bony, angular female whose very walk—stalk—radiated all the personal warmth and charm of a hatchet....

"God the Father," squeaked Ethan, "It's Horrible Helda—"

"Don't *panic*," Quinn hissed at him, pushing him back into the niche. It was scarcely twenty centimeters deep, not enough to hide one person, let alone two. "Just turn your back and pretend to be doing something normal and they'll scarcely notice you. Here, turn around, put your hand on the wall beside my head"—she arranged him hastily—"lean in, keep your voice down—"

"What am I pretending to be doing?"

"Cuddling. Now shut up and let me listen. And don't look at me like that or I'll start giggling. Though a few well-placed giggles might add conviction..."

Doing something normal? Ethan had never felt more abnormal in his life. His shoulder blades crawled in expectation of some lethal outburst from Millisor's room, just across the hall. It didn't help that he couldn't see what was coming. Quinn, of course, had a fine view, with the added bonus that her face was partly concealed by Ethan's arm and her body shielded from stray shots by his.

"Only one security troop for their back-up?" Quinn muttered, eyes glinting between fluttering eyelashes. "Glad we came."

A muffled peeping sound broke from her jacket. Her hand dove to wring it to silence. She lifted her beeper just far enough out to eye the numeric readout. Her lip curled.

"What is it?" whispered Ethan in her ear.

"That bastard Millisor's room comconsole number," she murmured back sweetly, curling her other hand realistically around the back of Ethan's neck. "So, he squeezed my code out of Teki. Probably wants me to call him up so he can make threats at me. Let him sweat."

Ethan, growing desperate, pressed artistically close to her, oozing around to one side and winning himself a better view.

Ecotech Helda stabbed the door buzzer to Millisor's room and checked a report panel in her hand. "Ghem-lord Harman Dal? Transient Dal?"

There was no response.

"Is he home?" asked the other ecotech.

For answer Helda pointed to a sealed panel in the wall. Ethan guessed its colored lights must encode some sort of life-support usage reading, for the other ecotech said, "Ah. And with company, too. Maybe this is for real,"

Helda buzzed again. "Transient Dal, this is Kline Station Biocontrol Warden Helda. I require you to open this door at once or find yourself in violation of Biocontrol Regulations one-seventy-six-b and two-a."

"At least give him time to get his pants on," the other ecotech said. "I mean, this has gotta be embarrassing."

"Let him be embarrassed," said Helda shortly. "The dirtsucker deserves it, bringing his filthy—" She struck the buzzer again.

At the third no-response she pulled a device from her jacket and held it over the door locking mechanism. The device's lights twinkled; nothing happened.

"Gods," said the other ecotech, startled, "they've blocked the emergency override circuits!"

"Now *that's* a violation of fire safety regulations," said the burly security man happily and tapped out a quick note on his report panel.

At a look of inquiry from the other ecotech he explained his sudden good cheer. "You Biocontrol guys may be able to barge over every Transient civil rights guarantee on hearsay evidence but *I* gotta have documented justification or my tail goes on the line." He sighed envy.

"Dal, unblock this door at once!" Helda yelled furiously into the intercom.

"We could cut off his food service from down below," suggested the other ecotech. "He'd have to come out eventually."

Helda ground her teeth. "I'm not waiting that long for some infected dirt-sucker to decide to get cooperative with me." She moved to a sealed locked panel a little farther down the wall marked FIRE CONTROL: AUTHORIZED PERSONNEL ONLY and stuck her ID card in its read-slot. Its transparent doors hissed obediently apart. They wouldn't have dared do otherwise, Ethan thought. She pressed a complex series of bright keypads.

A muffled hissing roar and faint cries penetrated from the sealed door to Millisor's room. Helda smiled satisfaction.

"What's she doing?" Ethan whispered in Quinn's shell-like ear.

Quinn was grinning ferociously. "Fire control. Downside, you have automatic sprinkler systems that fling water on fires. Very inefficient. Here we seal the room and pump out the air. Real fast. No oxygen, no oxidation. Millisor either wasn't smart enough or wasn't stupid enough to sabotage the fire control vents."

"Er...isn't that rather hard on anyone trapped inside?"

"Normally there's an alarm to evacuate the room first. Helda overrode it."

The unlocking device pressed over the door mechanism by the other ecotech twinkled and beeped. Frantic pounding came from the interior.

"Now Millisor wants to open it and can't, because of the pressure differential," Quinn whispered.

After a good long pause Helda reversed the airflow. The doorseals parted with an audible pop and whoosh. Millisor and Rau, noses bleeding, stumbled gasping into the corridor, swallowing and working their jaws in an effort to equalize inner-ear pressure.

"Helda didn't even give the poor fellows a chance to tell her about their hostage," Quinn smirked. "*Efficient* lady…"

Millisor finally got his breath. "Are you insane?" he snarled at the three Stationer officials. He focused on the security man. "My diplomatic immunity—"

The security man jerked his thumb at Helda. "She's in charge here."

"Where is your warrant?" cried Millisor angrily. "This space is legally paid for and possessed, and furthermore I hold a Class IV diplomatic waiver. You have no right to restrict or impede my movements for anything except a major felony charge—"

Ethan could not tell if the bluster was feigned or real, Harman Dal or Ghem-colonel Millisor talking.

"The rights you cite are for transients versus Security," said Helda sharply. "A biocontrol emergency abrogates them all. Now step into the float pallet."

Ethan and Quinn had been playing the part of goggling bystanders. About this time Rau's eye fell on them; a hand on his superior's arm stemmed the next argument. Millisor's head swiveled and his mouth shut with a snap. There was something chilling about so much rage being so abruptly controlled. Not quenched, but banished from the surface, conserved for some future moment. Thought boiled in Millisor's eyes.

"Hey," the security man said, sticking his head into the recently evacuated room, "there's a third guy in here. Tied to a chair, naked."

"That's disgusting," said Helda. She treated Millisor to a withering glare.

The glare failed its intended effect, bouncing off Millisor's furious introspection. Rau stirred nervously. His hand twitched toward his jacket, but both Millisor and Quinn shook their heads at him, each from their different perspective.

"He's bleeding," said the security man, advancing into the room and, with a glance back at Millisor and Rau, meditatively loosing his stunner in its holster.

"It's the nose," called Helda. "Always makes it look like a slaughter, but I guarantee you nobody ever died of a bloody nose."

"My friend here is a doctor," Quinn chirped, inserting herself into the group with a quick wriggle. "Can we help?"

"Oh, yes," called the security man, sounding relieved.

Quinn grabbed Ethan by the hand and thrust him past her into the room, never taking her smiling gaze off Millisor and Rau. Her stunner had found its way into her other hand, somehow. The security man glanced back at her and nodded gratefully. Helda grudgingly snapped on plastic gloves and followed to view the scene of debauch for herself.

Ethan approached Millisor's trussed prey anxiously. The security man knelt beside the chair and poked tentatively at the wires binding Teki's ankles. They had cut through; his skin oozed blood. Teki's clothes were laid out on the bed in the familiar search array. Wires also bound his wrists and the skin puffed up redly along their tight lines. Blood from his nose masked his lower face. Teki's head lolled, but his eyes were open and smiling, unnaturally bright. He giggled as the security man touched his ankle. The security man jumped back in startlement, eyed him with growing grimness, and pulled out his report panel with the air of a swordsman unsheathing his steel. "I don't like the looks of this," he stated.

Helda, coming up behind Ethan, stopped short. "By all the gods! Teki! I always thought you were an idiot, but this goes beyond all—"

"I'm off-shift," said Teki in a small, dignified voice. "I don't hafta put up with you off-shift, Helda." He twitched against his bonds, starting a new trickle of blood across his feet.

Helda's voice stumbled to silence as she got a better view. But not for long. *What is this?*

"Is he drugged, Doctor?" asked the security man as Ethan knelt beside Teki. "What with? Was this a, a private act that got out of hand, or something chargeable?" His thick fingers poised hopefully over his report panel.

"Drugged and tortured," said Ethan shortly, opening Quinn's medkit. "Kidnapped, too." There was a vibra-scalpel. A touch and the ankle wires parted with a ping.

"Raped?"

"I doubt it."

Helda, closing in, turned her head at the sound of Ethan's voice and stared at him. "You're no doctor," she gasped. "You're that moron from Docks and Locks again. My department wants a word with you!"

Teki yelped with laughter, causing Ethan to drop the sterile sponge he'd been applying to his ankle. "Joke's on you, Helda! He really is a doctor." He leaned toward Ethan, nearly tipping the chair, and confided conspiratorially, "Don't let on you're an Athosian, or she'll pop an artery. She hates Athos." He nodded happily, then, exhausted, let his head loll sideways again.

Helda recoiled. "An Athosian? *Is* this some kind of joke?" She glared anew at Ethan.

Ethan, absorbed in his work, jerked his head at Teki. "Ask him, he's the one full of truth serum." Teki's pulse was racing, his extremities cold, but he was not quite shocky. Ethan released the wrists. Reassuringly, Teki did not fall over, but sat up on his own. "But for your information, madam, I am indeed Dr. Ethan Urquhart of Athos. *Ambassador* Doctor Urquhart, on a special mission for the Population Council."

He hadn't really expected to impress her, but to his surprise she drew back whitely. "Oh?" she said in a neutral tone.

"Don't tell her that, Doc," Teki urged anew. "Ever since her son sneaked off to Athos nobody dares to mention the place. She can't even nag him long-distance there—their censorship guys send back any vids from a woman. She can't get at him at *all*." Teki dissolved in giggles. "I bet he's happy as a clam."

Ethan cringed at the thought of getting drawn into some family squabble. The security man looked equally dubious, but asked, "How old was the boy?"

"Thirty-two," Teki snickered.

"Oh." The security man lost interest.

"Do you possess an antidote to that—so-called truth serum, *Doctor?*" Helda inquired frostily. "If so I suggest you administer it and we'll sort the rest of this out down in Quarantine."

Ethan slowed. His words fell from him one by one, like drops of cold honey. "Where you possess dictatorial powers and where you…" He looked up to catch her frigid, frightened eyes. Time stopped. "You…"

Time sprang forward. "Quinn!" Ethan bellowed.

At her prompt appearance, herding Millisor and Rau before her with jabs from her stunner, Ethan jumped to his feet. He felt like running around in tight circles, or tearing his hair out in great clumps, or grabbing her by her gray-and-white jacket and shaking her until her teeth rattled. His clenched hands beat the air. His words tumbled over one another in his excitement.

"I kept trying to tell you, but you never stopped to listen. Pretend you're the agent, or whatever, on Kline Station trying to grab Athos's shipment. You make an impromptu decision to replace the frozen tissues with substitute material. We know it's impromptu, because if it had been planned you could have brought real cultures with you and nobody would ever have known a switch had been made, right? Where, where, in God the Father's name even on Kline Station, are you going to come up with four-hundred-and-fifty human ovaries? Not even four-hundred-fifty. Three hundred eighty-eight and six cows' ovaries. I don't think even you could pull 'em out of your jacket, Commander Quinn."

Quinn opened her mouth, closed it, and looked extremely thoughtful. "Go on, Doctor."

Millisor had dropped his Harman Dal act and, oblivious now to Quinn's stunner, stood with his attention rapt on Ethan. Rau watched his leader anxiously for some signal to action. The other ecotech looked bewildered; the security man, although his eyebrows were up in equal puzzlement, was absorbing every word.

Ethan gabbled on. "Forget the four hundred twenty-six suspect ships. Trace backwards from one ship, the census courier to Athos. Method, motive, and opportunity, by God! Who has ready access to every corner and cubbyhole on Kline Station, who could pass in and out of a guarded transfer warehouse with no question asked? Who has access to human cadavers every day? Cadavers from which a few grams of selected tissues will never be missed, because the bodies are biochemically destroyed immediately after the theft? But not quite enough cadavers, eh Helda, before it was time for the census courier to leave for Athos? Hence the cow ovaries, thrown in out of desperation to make up the numbers, and the short-changed boxes and the empty box." Ethan paused, panting.

"You're insane," choked Helda. Her face had gone from white to red to white again. Millisor's stunned eyes devoured her. Quinn looked like a woman taken by a beatific vision. The security's man's fingers were locked on his report panel in a sort of overloaded paralysis.

"Not as crazy as you are," said Ethan. "What did you hope to accomplish?"

"Redundant question," snapped Millisor. "We know what she accomplished. Forget the window-dressing and find out where—" A sharp gesture from Quinn's stunner reminded him that his status had been reversed from interrogator to prisoner.

"You're all coming to Quarantine—"

"It's over, Helda," said Ethan. "I bet if I look around your Assimilation Station I'll even find a shrink-wrap sealer."

"Oh, yes," chorused Teki helpfully. "We use it to seal suspected contaminants, to store them for later analysis. It's under the wet bench. I sealed my shoes up once, on a slow day. I tried to seal water, to make balloons to drop down the lift tubes, but it didn't work—"

"Shut *up*, Teki!" snarled Helda desperately.

"It's not as bad as what Vernon did with the white mice—"

"Stop," growled Millisor in exasperation out of the corner of his mouth. Teki subsided and sat blinking.

Ethan spread his hands and asked Helda more gently and urgently, "Why? I have to understand."

The concentrated venom in her posture broke into speech almost despite her will. "Why? You even need to ask why? It was to cut you motherless unnatural bastards off, that's why. I meant to get the next shipment too, if there was one, and the next and the next, until—" She was choking now. On her rage? No, Ethan realized, his buoyant intellectual triumph turning sickly-sour in his stomach: on tears. "Until I'd hooked Simmi out of there and he came to his senses and came home and got a real woman, I swear I wouldn't criticize a hair on her head this time, I'll never be allowed to even see my own grandchildren on that dreadful dirty planet..." She turned her back and stood stiff-legged, defiant but for her hands over her red, smeared face, ugly and helpless and snorting.

Ethan thought he understood how a propaganda-stuffed young soldier must feel the first time in combat, stumbling by some sudden chance over his enemy's human face. He had gloried for a red moment in his power to break her. Now he stood foolishly with the pieces in his hands. Not at all heroic.

"Ye gods," muttered the security man, in awe touched with glee, "I have to arrest an eco-cop...?"

Teki giggled. The other ecotech, clearly taken aback by Helda's confession, looked as though he didn't know whether to argue or try to become invisible.

"But what did you do with the *other?*" Millisor rocked forward, teeth clenched.

"Other what?" Helda sniffed.

"The frozen human ovarian cultures you took out of the boxes for Athos," Millisor ground out, carefully, like a man speaking in words of one syllable to a mutant.

"Oh. I threw them out."

The veins stood out on the Cetagandan's forehead. Ethan could name each one. Millisor seemed to be having trouble breathing. "Idiot bitch," he panted. "Idiot bitch, do you know what you've done...?"

Quinn's laughter rang over them all like morning bells. "Admiral Naismith will love it!"

The Ghem-colonel's steel self-control broke at last. "Idiot bitch!" he screamed and launched himself toward Helda, clawed hands outstretched. Both Quinn's and the security man's stunner beams caught him in a neat cross-fire and he crashed as trees do.

Rau just stood shaking his head and muttering over and over, "Shit. Shit. Shit…"

"Attempted assault," the security man paused to croon over his report panel, "on a Biocontrol Warden carrying out her duties…"

Rau sidled toward the door.

"Don't forget breaking Detention," Quinn added helpfully. "This here's the fellow," she gestured at Rau, "that you were all looking for who evaporated out of C-9 the other day. And I bet if you search this room you'll find all sorts of military goodies that Kline Station Customs never authorized."

"Quarantine first," said the other ecotech, after a nervous glance at his still emotionally incapacitated superior.

"But surely Ambassador Urquhart will wish to lay charges for the admitted theft and destruction of Athosian property," suggested Quinn. "Who's going to arrest whom?"

"We're *all* gonna go to Quarantine, where I can make you all hold still till I get to the bottom of this," said the security man firmly. "People who disappear out of C-9 will find that slipping Quarantine is quite another matter."

"Too true," murmured Quinn.

Rau's lip rippled silently as another pair of heavily armed security officers appeared in the doorway, cutting off retreat. The room seemed suddenly crowded. Ethan hadn't seen the burly security man call for reinforcements, but it must have been some time earlier. His estimation of the slow-seeming man went up a notch.

"Yes, sir?" said one of the new officers.

"Took you long enough," said the security man. "Search that one"—he pointed to Rau—"and then you can help us run 'em all to Quarantine. These three are accused of vectoring communicable disease. That one's been fingered as the jailbreak from C-9. This one's accused of theft by that one, who appears to be wearing a Station code-uniform to which he is not entitled, and who also claims that one over there was kidnapped. I'll have a printout as long as I am tall of charges for the one out cold on the floor when he wakes up. Those three are all gonna need first aid—"

Ethan, reminded, slipped up to Teki and pressed the hypospray of fast-penta antagonist into his arm. He felt almost sorry for the young man as his foolish grin was rapidly replaced by the expression of a man with a terminal hangover. The security team in the meanwhile were shaking all sorts of glittering mysterious objects out of the un-resisting Rau.

"—and the pretty lady in the gray outfit who seems to know so much about everybody else's business, I'm holding as a material wit-ness," the security man concluded. "Ah—where is she?"

CHAPTER TWELVE

In Quarantine, Rau followed the supine form of his still-stunned superior off for whatever short-arm inspection Biocontrol demanded without a word. He had said nothing, in fact, since they'd left the hostel room under heavy guard, but had remained close to Millisor with a sort of grim loyalty, like a dog refusing to leave its encoffined master.

Ethan wasn't sure what tests were required for detecting Alpha-S-D-plasmid-2—or its mythical mutation-3—but from the dour look on Rau's face he suspected they were rather invasive. He'd have felt better if Rau had shown the least sign of possessing a sense of humor. The light in Rau's eyes as he glanced back one last time at Ethan was like reflections off knife blades.

Ethan was in turn carried off to an office for a long, long talk with Security in the persons of the burly arresting officer and a female officer who was apparently his administrative superior. Part way through they were joined by a third security man, introduced as Captain Arata, a neurasthenic Eurasian type with lank black hair, pale skin, and eyes like needles, who said little and listened much.

Ethan's first impulse to tell all and throw himself upon their mercy was blunted almost at once by the problem of Okita. He managed not to mention Okita. Cetaganda's psionics breakthrough was modified, under the wilting effect of those three pairs of Stationer eyes, to the vaguer news that "a culture in Athos's ovarian shipment had been doctored on Jackson's Whole with some altered ge-

153

netic material stolen from Cetaganda." Ethan avoided touching on Cee altogether. It would have made things so complicated.

"Then," said the security woman, "Ecotech Helda actually did Athos a favor, albeit unintentionally. She saved your gene pool from contamination, in fact."

She was, Ethan realized, obliquely pressing him to drop charges against Helda, to save Kline Station from public embarrassment. He thought of the quantities of trade that passed through their supposedly secure switching warehouses. The realization that they were sweating as hard as he was felt wonderfully invigorating and he took the offensive instantly.

Security became extremely polite. The half-dozen or so little charges the burly officer had worked up against Ethan were matched against Ethan's ambassadorial status and somehow made to evaporate. No vandalism like Helda's, they assured him, would ever be permitted to happen again. Ecotech Helda was of a sufficient age to take an early retirement, with no questions asked. Ambassador Urquhart need not concern himself with Ghem-lord Harman Dal, or Colonel Millisor as Ethan named him; he and his assistants were definitely slated for deportation on the first ship available, for the proven felony of kidnapping.

"By the way, Mr. Ambassador," Captain Arata put in, "do you have any idea where the Ghem-lord's third and fourth employees are?"

"You mean you haven't arrested Setti yet?" asked Ethan.

"We're working on it," said Arata. His cool, controlled face gave Ethan no clue as to what that meant.

"You'd better ask Colonel Millisor when he wakes up, then. As for the other one—ah—you'd better ask Commander Quinn."

"And just where is Commander Quinn, Mr. Ambassador?"

Ethan sighed. "On her way back to the Dendarii Mercenaries, probably." With her draftee Cee in tow, no doubt. How long would the rootless young man survive, cut off from his own dreams? Longer than he would live if Millisor caught up with him, Ethan had to admit in all honesty. Let it go. Let it go.

Arata sighed too. "Slippery witch," he muttered. "We'll see about that. She still owes me some information."

And then Ethan was free to go. Thank you for your kind assistance, Mr. Ambassador. If there is any little thing Kline Station can do to help make your stay more pleasant, please ask. They made no further mention of Helda; he made no further mention of Helda. Have a nice day, Mr. Ambassador.

In the corridor leading to the exit locks Ethan paused. "Come to think of it, Captain Arata, there is a favor you can do me."

"Yes, sir?"

"Colonel Millisor is under guard, right? If he's awake, would it be possible for me to speak briefly to him?"

Arata gave him a look of sharp speculation. "I'll check, sir."

Ethan accompanied the security captain out of the administrative section and through two more sterility-locks. There they found a gowned ecotech just exiting a glassed-in room. The ecotech killed a lighted "Do Not Enter" sign on the room's door and began peeling out of his protective garb. An armed security guard, within, passed out a similar set of garments rolled up in a wad, which the ecotech tossed in the general direction of a laundry receptacle.

"What's the status of your patient?" Captain Arata inquired.

The ecotech took in Arata's rank insignia. "Alert and oriented. Some residual tremors from stunner trauma, headache likewise. He has chronically elevated blood pressure, stress-induced gastritis, a liver showing pre-cirrhotic degeneration, and a slightly enlarged prostate that will probably have to be watched over the next few years. In short, his health is normal for a man of his age. What he does *not* have is Alpha-S-D-plasmid-two, -three, -twenty-nine, or any other number. He doesn't have so much as a head cold. Somebody was jerking us around, Captain, with that vector report and I hope you'll find out who. I don't have time for this sort of nonsense."

"We're working on it," said Captain Arata.

Ethan followed Arata into the now-unsealed room. Arata motioned the guard to a station outside the door and himself took up a stance of polite but firm parade rest just within. It was probably not worthwhile requesting him to wait out of earshot, Ethan reflected; the room was undoubtedly monitored.

Ethan approached the bed on which Millisor, dressed in an ordinary patient gown, lay—restrained, Ethan noted with relief—and edged closer. Millisor made no move. His hands lay relaxed, as if having tested his bonds once was sufficient for his logic. He watched Ethan with cool calculation. It all made Ethan feel a dreadful coward, like some gawker poking at a trussed-up predator that braver hunters had captured.

"Uh, good afternoon, Colonel Millisor," Ethan began inanely.

"Good afternoon, Dr. Urquhart." Millisor returned an ironic nod of his head like an abbreviated bow. He seemed drained now of personal animosity—professional, like Quinn. Of course, he'd exhibited no personal animosity when he'd ordered Ethan's execution, either.

"I, uh—just wanted to be absolutely and finally sure, before you left, that you clearly understood that Athos does not have, and never at any time did have, the shipment of genetic material from Jackson's Whole," Ethan said.

"The probabilities would now seem to lean that way," agreed Millisor. "I doubt everything, you see."

Ethan thought this over. "Encountering the truth must be horribly confusing for you, then."

Millisor's lips twitched dryly. "Fortunately, it happens very seldom." His gaze narrowed. "So, what do you think of Terrence Cee, now that you've met him?"

Ethan jumped guiltily. "Who?"

"Come, Doctor. I know he's here. I can feel the shape of him in the tactical situation. Did you find him attractive, Athosian? Many people do. I have often wondered if his, ah, gift, truly only worked one way."

It was a nasty thought, particularly as Ethan had found Cee very attractive indeed. He jittered. Millisor was now staring with covert interest at Arata, alert for reactions on the security officer's part to the new turn in the conversation. Ethan hurried to cut off any unnecessary extension of Millisor's secret hit list. "I haven't discussed Mr. Cee with—with anyone. Just in case you were wondering."

Millisor's eyebrows rose in disbelief. "As a favor to me?"

"As a favor to them," Ethan corrected.

Millisor accepted this with a little provisional nod. "But Cee is on Kline Station. Where, Doctor?"

Ethan shook his head. "I truly do not know. If you choose not to believe that, it's your problem."

"Then your pet mercenary knows. It comes to the same thing. Where is she?"

"She's not mine!" Ethan denied, horrified. "I don't have anything to do with Commander Quinn. She's on her own. You have a problem with her, you take it up with her, not me."

Arata, without moving a muscle, became more intent.

"On the contrary," said Millisor, "she has all my admiration. Much that I could not account for now is entirely clear. I wouldn't mind hiring her myself."

"Uh—I don't think she's available."

"All mercenaries have price tags. Maybe not money alone. Rank, power, pleasure."

"No," said Ethan firmly. "She seems to be in love with her C.O. I've seen the phenomenon in Athos's army—hero-worship of certain senior officers by their juniors—some seniors abuse their advantage, others don't. I don't know which category her admiral falls in, but in either case I don't think you can match the bid."

Arata nodded silent agreement, looking faintly bleak.

"I too know the phenomenon," sighed the Ghem-lord. "Well. That's too bad." A chill seemed to waft from the man in the bed which made Ethan wonder if his defense of Quinn's honor had perhaps been untimely. But Millisor was safely immobilized.

"I confess, Doctor, you puzzle me," Millisor went on. "If you and Cee were not co-conspirators, then you could only have been his victim. I fail to see your advantage in continuing to protect the man after what he tried to do to Athos."

"He didn't try to do anything to Athos, except immigrate there. Hardly a crime. From what I've seen of the galaxy so far, it made perfectly good sense. I can hardly wait to go home myself."

Millisor's eyebrows rose nearly to his hairline, one of the few gestures currently available to him. "By God! I begin to believe you really are as naive a fool as your face proclaims you, Doctor! I thought you knew what had been done to your shipment."

"Yes, so he put his wife in it. A little necrophiliac, maybe. Considering his upbringing, the only wonder is that the man isn't a lot stranger still."

Millisor actually laughed out loud. Ethan felt no urge to chuckle along. He regarded the Ghem-lord uneasily.

Millisor sighed. "Let me present you with two facts. Obsolete facts, since that idiot Stationer female committed her mindless act of sabotage. One. The gene-complex, ah, in question"—he glanced at Arata—"was recessive and would not appear in phenotype until found in both halves of the genotype. Two. Every single one of the cultures bound for Athos had had the complex spliced into them. Think it through, Doctor."

Ethan did.

In the first generation, the ovarian cultures would contribute their recessive, hidden alleles to the children—and at the rate the old cultures were dying off, very soon all the children—born on Athos. But not until the second generation reached puberty would the functional telepathic organ appear in its statistical one-half of the population, from breeding back to the double-recessive cultures. In the third generation, half the remaining population would pass from latent to functional and so on, the telepathic majority edging out the non-telepathic minority in perpetual half-increments.

But by then even the non-telepaths would bear the genes in their bodies, potential fathers of telepathic sons. The entire population would be permeated with the gene complex, too late, impossible to eradicate.

The question *Why Athos?* was answered at last. Of course Athos. Only Athos.

The audacity, the perfection, the beauty—and the enormity—of Cee's plot took Ethan's breath away. It all fit, with the overpowering self-evidence of a mathematical proof. It even accounted for Cee's missing mountain of money.

"Now who cannot recognize truth?" mocked Millisor softly.

"Oh," said Ethan, in a very small voice.

"The most insidious thing about the little monster is his charm," Millisor went on, watching Ethan closely. "We built him that way on purpose, not knowing then that the limits of his talent would render him unsuitable as a field agent. Although from the trouble he subsequently gave us we may have been wrong on that point as well. But do not mistake charm for virtue, Doctor. He is dangerous, utterly devoid of loyalty to the humanity from which he sprang, but of which he is not a part—"

Ethan wondered if that should be understood as Humanity = Cetaganda.

"—a virus of a man, who would make the whole universe over in his twisted image. Surely you of all men understand that lethal contagions demand vigorous counter-measures. But ours is the controlled violence of surgery. You must not swallow the virus's propaganda. We are not the butchers he would have you believe us to be."

Millisor's hands turned in their restraints, opened in pleading. "Help us. You must help us."

Ethan stared at Millisor's bonds, shaken. "I'm sorry…" God the Father, was he actually apologizing to Millisor? "No, Colonel. I remember Okita. I can understand a man being a killer, I think. But a *bored* killer?"

"Okita is only a tool. The surgeon's knife."

"Then your service has turned a man into a thing." An old quote drifted through Ethan's memory: *By their fruits you shall know them….*

Millisor's eyes narrowed; he did not pursue the argument, but rather, with a glance at Arata, inquired, "And just what did you do to Sergeant Okita, Dr. Urquhart?"

Ethan glanced at Arata, too, sorry he'd brought up the subject. "*I* didn't do anything to him. Maybe he met with an accident. Or perhaps he deserted." Or considering Okita's ultimate fate, perhaps "desserted" might be the better term… Ethan squelched that line of thought. "In any case, I can't help you. Even if I wanted to betray Cee to you—if that's what you're asking me to do—I really don't know where he is."

"Or where he is headed?" said Millisor suggestively.

Ethan shook his head. "Anywhere, for all I know. Anywhere but Athos, that is."

"Alas, yes," murmured Millisor. "Before, Cee was tied to that shipment. If I had the one, I had a string to the other. Now that the shipment is destroyed, a very poor second choice to our recovering it, he is entirely unleashed. Anywhere," Millisor sighed. "Anywhere…"

The Ghem-colonel, Ethan reminded himself firmly, was the one who was tied down. He had his feet under him; it was up to him to end this interview before the smooth spy plucked any more information from him.

Ethan paused in his strategic retreat out the door. "I will leave you with one last thought, though, Colonel. If you had made that pitch to me when we first met, instead of doing what you did, you might have convinced me and had it all."

Millisor's hands clenched and jerked against their bonds at last.

And so Ethan returned to his own hostel room, rented his first day on Kline Station and never occupied since. He thanked his spotty luck that he had paid for it in advance, for his personal effects were all as he had left them. He bathed, shaved, trimmed, changed back into his own clothes at last, and ate a light meal from the room service console.

He sighed over his coffee. Pushing two weeks—he would have to look up the date, having lost track—expended on this adventure, as Quinn's stalking-goat, as Millisor's moving target, Cee's pawn, anybody's pingpong ball, and what did he have to show for it? An education? Once he returned his red coveralls and boots, he would have no more tangible souvenir than the learning. He pulled out his credit chit and regarded it. Quinn's microscopic bug was presumably still on it somewhere. If he shouted into it, might he cause a feedback squeal in her left ear? But she was gone, with no word of farewell. Anyhow, people who talked to their credit cards would doubtless make their neighbors uneasy, even on Kline Station.

He lay down wearily, only to find his nerves still too strung up to allow sleep. Was it day, or night? On Kline Station, who could say? He wasn't sure if he missed Athos's diurnal rhythm or its weather more. He wanted rain, or a brisk polar front to blow the cobwebs out of his brains. He could turn up the air conditioning, but it would still smell the same.

After nearly an hour spent comparing all the things he should have said and done this last fortnight with the actual events, he gave up in disgust, dressed, and went out. If sleep was to elude him, he might at least be doing something useful with his time. Athos was paying an ungodly enough sum for it.

He strolled back to the Transients' Lounge level where the embassies and consuls were concentrated and began doing some serious shopping for legitimate biological supply houses. Most of the more technically advanced planets offered something. Beta Colony offered nineteen separate sources, from purely commercial ventures to a government-sponsored gene pool at Silica University stocked entirely by invited donations from talented and gifted citizens. As much as Ethan cringed at taking any more of Quinn's advice on anything, Beta Colony did seem to be the best destination. He would not be disappointed, the woman expediting the commercial directory interface assured him. He exited feeling he had done a good day's work at last and a little smug. He had dealt with the female expediter just as he would have dealt with a man. It could be done; wasn't hard at all.

He returned to his room for a quick snack, then sat down at his comconsole for a little comparison-shopping for the best price on a round-trip ticket to Beta Colony. The straightest route was via Escobar, giving him a chance to check out another potential source at no added cost to the Population Council. At least half the committee would be pleased with him, about as good odds as he was likely to obtain.

All his decisions made at last, his weariness washed over him. He lay down to rest for a minute.

Hours later, an insistent chiming from his comconsole hooked him to mushy consciousness. One foot was asleep, from lying at an odd angle with his shoes on, and it tingled numbly as he stumbled to press the "Receive" keypad.

Terrence Cee's face materialized over the holovid plate. "Dr. Urquhart?"

"Well. I didn't expect to hear from you again." Ethan rubbed sleep from his face. "I thought you'd have no further use for the asylum of Athos. You and Quinn both being the practical sort."

Cee winced, looking distinctly unhappy. "In fact, I'm about to leave," he said in a dull voice. "I wanted to see you one more time, to—to apologize. Can you meet me in Docking Bay C-Eight right away?"

"I suppose," said Ethan. "Are you off to the Dendarii Mercenaries with Quinn, then?"

"I can't talk any more now. I'm sorry." Cee's image turned to sparkling snow, then emptiness.

Quinn was hanging over Cee's shoulder, perhaps, inhibiting his frankness. Ethan suppressed an impulse to call Security and tell Captain Arata where to look for her. He and Quinn were even now, help averaging harm. His mystery was solved; she had the intelligence coup she wanted. Let it end so.

As he exited his hostel to the mall a man, who had been idly seated by the central pool feeding the goldfish with pellets from a credit-card-operated dispenser placed nearby, rose and approached him.

Ethan stifled an urge to run back up the mall in screaming paranoia. The man couldn't be Setti. He was altogether the wrong racial type for a Cetagandan: tall, dark-skinned with a high-bridged nose, and wearing a pink silk jacket gaudy with embroidery.

"Dr. Urquhart?" the man inquired politely.

Ethan kept some distance between them. If this was another damned spy of some sort, he swore he would put him head first into the pool.... "Yes?"

"I wonder if I might request a small service of you."

"Request away."

The man produced a small flat oblong from his jacket, a little holovid projector. "Should you see him again, I wish you would give this message capsule to Ghem-colonel Luyst Millisor. The message is activated by entering his military serial number."

Definitely the pool. "Colonel Millisor is under arrest by Kline Station Security. You want to get a message to him, go see them."

"Ah." The man smiled. "Perhaps I shall. Still, who can say what chances the turning of the great wheel may bring us? Take it anyway. If no opportunity arises to deliver it, throw it away." He tried to press the little oblong on Ethan, who foiled him by backing up. Rather than chase Ethan skipping backwards down the mall, the man paused, shaking his head. He laid the message capsule down on a bench Ethan had put between them. "I leave it to your discretion, sir." He bowed with a flourish of his hand reminiscent of a genuflection and turned to go.

"I'm not touching it," Ethan stated flatly. The man smiled over his shoulder as he stepped into a nearby lift tube. "I'll take it to Security!" Ethan shouted. The man cupped his hand to his ear and shook his head, rising up the crystal tube. "I'll—I'll—" Ethan swore under his breath as the pink apparition ascended out of sight.

Ethan circled the bench, watching the little oblong from the corner of his eye. With a wordless growl, he finally pocketed it. He would take it to Captain Arata, then, at the first opportunity and let him worry about it. He glanced at his chronometer and hurried on.

He had to take a tube-car to the docking bay, which was in a freight section on the opposite side of the station from Transients' Lounge. This time he had a map ready to hand and made no wrong turns.

The docking bay was extremely quiet. A single flex tube was activated, indicating a small ship on the other side, perhaps a fast courier hired especially for the occasion. In any case, not a commercial run lading other cargo. Quinn's expense account must be elastic indeed, Ethan reflected.

Terrence Cee, dressed in his green Stationer coveralls, sat wanly on a packing case, alone in the middle of the bay. He looked up as Ethan stepped out of a ramp corridor. "You came quickly, Dr. Urquhart."

Ethan glanced at the flex tube. "I figured you were catching a scheduled run of some sort. I didn't realize you'd be traveling in this much style."

"I thought perhaps you wouldn't come at all."

"Because—why? Because I'd found out the whole truth about that shipment?" Ethan shrugged. "I can't say I approve of what you tried to do. But given the obvious problems your—your race, I guess—would suffer as a minority anywhere else, I think I can understand why."

A melancholy smile lit Cee's face, then was gone. "You do? But of course. You would." He shook his head. "I should have said, I hoped you would not come."

Ethan followed the direction of his nod.

Quinn stood in the shadows by a girder. But she was an unusually frazzled-looking Quinn. Her crisp jacket was gone and she wore only a black T-shirt and her uniform trousers. Her boots were gone, too. And, Ethan realized as she moved into the light, her stunner holster was empty.

She moved because she was prodded by a man in the orange and black uniform of Kline Station Security. So they'd caught up with her at last. Ethan nearly chuckled. Watching her wriggle out of this one ought to be just fascinating....

His humor drained away as he caught a better look at the weapon with which the compact, bland-faced man was poking her spine. A lethal nerve disruptor. Altogether non-regulation for Security.

At the ring of footsteps Ethan turned his head the other way, to find Millisor and Rau walking toward them.

CHAPTER THIRTEEN

Ethan and Quinn were shoved together within the potential radius of fire from the bell-muzzle of the nerve disruptor, held in the tense hand of the man in the Security uniform. Cee was segregated from them under Rau's stunner. It needed nothing more than that to give Ethan a silent appreciation of their relative status.

Quinn looked even worse close up, with a split, swollen lip and white and shaking from either pain or the aftereffects of low stun. She seemed shorter without her boots. Cee stumbled like a corpse looking only for a place to lie down; congealed, cold, the blue light of his eyes extinguished.

"What happened?" Ethan whispered to Quinn. "How did *they* ever find you when Security couldn't?"

"I forgot the damned beeper," she hissed back through clenched teeth. "Should've shoved it down the first trash vent we passed. I knew it was compromised! But Cee was arguing with me and I was in a hurry and—oh, hell, what's the use…" She bit her lip in frustration, winced, and licked it tenderly. Her eyes returned again and again to their opponents, adding up the unfavorable odds, rejecting the sum and trying again with no better luck.

Millisor walked around them, smooth and smug. "So glad you could make it, Dr. Urquhart. We could have arranged accidents for you and the commander separately, but having you both together allows us a rather exquisite opportunity for—efficiency."

"Vengeance?" quavered Ethan. "But we never tried to kill you."

167

"Oh, no," Millisor protested. "Vengeance has nothing to do with it. You both simply know too much to live."

Rau grinned nastily. "Tell them the rest, Colonel," he urged.

"Ah, yes. With your sense of humor, Commander, you will particularly like this one. Observe, if you will, all those unused flex tubes on the outer wall. Sealed at both ends, they make a very private little compartment. Just the spot for a couple with rather odd tastes in adventure to arrange a tryst. How unfortunate that, in the sound sleep following their exertions—"

Rau waved his stunner cheerfully, by way of indicating just how that sound sleep was to be achieved.

"—the flex tube is vented into space in preparation for locking in the auto-conveyer from a freighter hold. Said freighter being due in this docking bay immediately after my courier departs. Shall we leave you two entirely nude, I wonder?" he mused, "or merely naked from the waist down, suggesting fumbling passionate hurry?"

"God the Father," Ethan moaned in horror, "the Population Council will think I was depraved enough to make love to a woman in a flex tube!"

"Gods forbid," Quinn, looking equally appalled, echoed under her breath, "that Admiral Naismith would think I was stupid enough to make love to anything in a flex tube!"

Terrence Cee's gaze roved over the docking bay, as if seeking death as desperately as Quinn's gaze sought escape. He made a little jerky motion; Rau's stunner instantly drew a bead on him.

"Dream on, mutant," Rau growled. "We aren't giving you a chance. One wrong move and you'll be carried aboard stunned." His lips drew back unpleasantly. "You don't want to miss the show your friends are going to put on for us, do you?"

Cee's hands clenched and unclenched, despair and rage struggling for ascendancy in him, both equally impotent. "I'm sorry, Doctor," he whispered. "They held a nerve disruptor to the commander's head and I knew they weren't bluffing. I thought maybe you wouldn't come, just for a call from me. I should have let them shoot her then. Sorry. Sorry..."

Quinn's lips turned sardonically upward, breaking to bleed again. "You don't have to apologize quite that fervently, Cee.... Your resisting wouldn't have saved him anyway."

"You don't have to apologize at all," said Ethan firmly. "I'd have done the same myself, in all probability."

The man with the nerve disruptor waved them apart and drove Ethan and Quinn to the outer wall and along it toward the bay's far end.

"Who is that guy, anyway?" Ethan asked Quinn with a jerk of his head. "Setti?"

"You guessed it. I should have shot him in the back when I had the chance and collected the other half of my bounty from House Bharaputra," Quinn replied in a disgusted undertone. She added thoughtfully, "If I jumped that goon, d'you think you could make it across the bay to one of those corridors before Rau stunned you?"

It was fifty meters or more across the cavernous chamber. "No," said Ethan frankly.

"How about a dash for the cover of that flex-tube?"

"Then what? Make faces at them till they walked over and shot me?"

"All right," she snarled impatiently, "you come up with a better idea."

Ethan's hands twitched in his pockets and encountered a little oblong. "Maybe we could buy some more time with this?" he said, pulling out the message capsule.

"What the hell's that?"

"It was the weirdest thing. On my way here this man came up to me in the mall and pushed it on me—he said it was a message for Millisor. It's activated by Millisor's military service number and I should give it to him if I saw him—"

Quinn froze, her hand clenched on his arm. "What color was he?"

"Huh?"

"The man, the man!"

"Pink. That is, he had this pink suit."

"Not the suit, the man!"

"Interesting—sort of a coffee-color. Extremely elegant. I wish I could've got some of those skin genes for Athos—"

"Hey," Setti began, moving toward them with a frown.

"Giveittome, giveittome," Quinn gabbled, grabbing the message capsule out of Ethan's hand. "Lessee. 672-191-, oh gods, is it 142 or 124?" Her shaking index finger jabbed at the tiny keypad, then agonized in hesitation. "421 and pray. Here, Setti!" Quinn cried, and tossed the message capsule at the startled Cetagandan, whose left hand snaked out in an easy, automatic catch. "Down!" she yelled in Ethan's ear, kicked his feet out from under him, and dropped atop his head.

There was a moment's puzzled silence. The tiny hum of a holovid forming its image sounded insect-thin.

"Aw, rats," Quinn groaned, her weight slumping on Ethan. "Wrong again."

Ethan, rather muffled, complained, "What the devil do you think you're—"

The shock wave blew them both ten meters across the docking bay floor, to fetch up in a tangle of arms and legs against the outer bulkhead. Except for the ringing in his ears, Ethan could not at first hear a thing. His bones seemed to reverberate like a struck gong and his vision darkened.

"Thought that had to be the case," Quinn muttered in shaky satisfaction. She stood up, fell down, stood up again and bounced off the wall, blinking rapidly, her hands feeling in front of her.

Alarms seemed to be shrieking like mad things all over the place. Emergency lights came on with a brilliant glare—Ethan was relieved to realize he hadn't been struck blind—and the distant booms of airseals shutting followed one another like dominos falling.

Closer, quieter, and much more ominous was a hissing, rising to a whistling, of air escaping around the nearest flex-tube seal, damaged in the explosion. Icy fog boiled in a cloud around it.

Even Ethan had the sense to start away from it, crawling on his hands and knees. The gravity wavered nauseatingly. A melted patch in the metal deck was just ceasing to bubble. Ethan skirted it. Of Setti there was no sign anywhere.

"By God," Ethan muttered dizzily, "she *is* good at getting rid of bodies...."

He looked up across an interminable metallic desert to see Terrence Cee, running like a deer, brought down in a flying tackle by Rau. Millisor, dashing up behind, took aim to give the telepath a swift kick in the head, thought better of it, and hopped to his other foot to deliver a blow to Cee's less-valuable solar plexus instead. Millisor and Rau each grabbed an arm, dragging Cee from his crouch toward the activated flex tube beyond which their ship waited.

Ethan staggered to his feet and began running toward them. He hadn't the least idea what he was going to do when he got there. Except stop them, somehow. That was the only clear imperative. "God the Father," he moaned, "there had better be a reward in heaven for this sort of thing..."

He had the advantage of a shorter angle to cross, against Millisor's and Rau's disadvantage of their writhing burden. Ethan found himself standing, legs spread apart, blocking the entrance to the flex tube. Perfectly positioned for a fast draw, barring the minor hitch of being weaponless. *Help*, he thought. "Stop!" he cried.

To his surprise, they did, cautious. Rau had lost his stunner somewhere, but Millisor pulled a vicious, glittering little needier from his jacket and took aim at Ethan's chest. Ethan pictured its tiny needles expanding on impact and whirling like razors through his abdomen. His autopsy would be the godawfullest mess...

Terrence Cee yanked away from Rau and spun to stand in front of Ethan, his arms spread wide in a futile gesture of protection. "No!"

"You think I have to keep you alive just because the cultures are gone, mutant?" Millisor, furious, cried at him. "Dead will do, by God!" He raised his weapon in both hands. "What the—" he lurched as his feet rose from the floor, his hands clutching out for lost balance.

Ethan grabbed Cee. His stomach seemed to be floating away independently of the rest of him. He looked around hysterically, to spot Quinn clinging to the far wall near one of the corridor entrances, the cover plate forcibly torn off an environmental engineering control panel beside her.

Millisor's body undulated in midair, compensating expertly for his unwanted spin, and he brought his weapon back to steady aim. Quinn, yelling helplessly, tore the cover plate the rest of the way off its cabinet and flung it toward them. It spun wickedly through the air, but it was obvious before it was halfway across the bay that it was going to miss Millisor. The Cetagandan's grip tightened on his needler trigger—

Millisor's body, haloed for a blinding instant like some burning martyr, convulsed in the booming blue crackle of a plasma bolt. Ethan's head jerked at the pungent stench of burnt meat and fabric and boiling plastics. He blinked red and purple afterimages of the dancing, dying silhouette of the Ghem-lord.

The needler spun away and Rau lost his grip on the floor in an aborted grab for it. The Cetagandan captain swam frantically in air, swiveling his head in urgent search for the source of this devastating new attack. Quinn's cover plate, rebounding off the far wall, winged by, nearly taking Ethan's head with it.

"There he is!" Cee, grappling in midair with Ethan, pointed with a shout at the catwalks and girders. A pink blur moved along them, aimed something at Rau. "No! He's my meat!" Cee cried. With a berserker yell, Cee launched himself off Ethan toward Rau. "Kill you, bastard!"

The only benefit Ethan could see coming from this insane outbreak of martial spirit was that he, Ethan, was pushed toward the outer bulkhead wall. He managed to catch a grip on a projection without breaking a wrist, halting his mindless momentum.

"No, Terrence! If somebody's firing at Cetagandans, the thing to do is get *out* of the way!" But this voice of reason whipped away in the wind. Wind? The air leak must be widening—explosive decompression at any moment, surely…

Cee's and Rau's struggling forms sank to the deck like a pebble dropping through oil, as Quinn gradually turned up a little gravity.

Ethan's own body stopped flapping like a flag in the breeze and he found himself hanging, though still lightly, entirely too far above the deck. He began to climb down hastily, before Quinn decided to try something like Helda's trick with the birds.

Rau threw the smaller, lighter Cee bouncing and skidding along the deck and whirled to dash for his ship's flex tube. Two steps, and he flared, melted, and burned like a wax image in a brilliant plasma cross-fire, coming from not one but two sources among the girders. He fell with a meaty thunk and, horribly, lived a moment more, writhing and screaming soundlessly through fleshless black jaws. Cee, on hands and knees, watched open-mouthed, as though himself dismayed by the completeness of his vicarious revenge.

Ethan started across the deck toward the telepath. On the Station side of the bay, two men swung out of the network of girders and catwalks. One was the pink apparition from the mallway; a second was another dark-skinned man dressed in shimmering brown in a similar highly-decorated style. They closed on Quinn, who, so far from welcoming her rescuers, started back up the wall like a busy spider.

Each of the dark men grabbed an ankle and yanked her down, careless of what her head struck on the way. An attempted karate kick on her part was foiled by brown-silk and turned into what would have been a nasty fall in higher gravity and still didn't look exactly pleasant. Pink-suit pinioned her arms from behind and brown-silk took the fight out of her with a breath-stopping blow to her stomach.

One on each side, they hustled her away up the corridor ramp toward the emergency exit as pressure-suited Stationer damage control squads began to pour into the chamber from several other entrances.

"They're—they're snatching Quinn!" Ethan cried to Cee. "Who are they? What are they?" He danced from foot to foot in an agony of bewilderment, pulling Cee up.

Cee squinted after them. "Jackson's Whole? Bharaputrans, here? We've got to go after her!"

"Preferably while there's still air to breathe—"

Clinging to each other, they proceeded in a sort of bounding hobble as rapidly as they could across the docking bay and up the ramp.

At the emergency airseal they had to wait for terrifying seconds, working their jaws to protect their ears against the now rapidly decreasing air pressure, while the trio ahead of them cycled through and vacated the personnel lock that permitted escape from blocked chambers. Jabbing at the control button in a panicked tattoo, or even leaning on it, did nothing to hasten the process, Ethan found; the door opened only when it was damned good and ready.

They fell through and had to wait again while pressure equalized and Quinn's assailants gained a lengthening head start. Ethan gasped in relief. He had been entirely mistaken about Stationer air; it smelled just great, better than any air he'd ever had.

"How the devil," Ethan panted to Cee as they waited, "did Millisor and Rau ever get out of Quarantine? I thought even a virus couldn't escape it."

"Setti sprang them," Cee panted back. "He came in either along with, or pretending to be, the guard taking them to their deportation dock, I'm not sure which. They walked right out the door. All the documentation and IDs perfect, of course. I don't think even Quinn realizes how far into the Station computer network they'd penetrated in the time they were here."

The emergency airseal lock hissed open at last and Ethan and Cee staggered up the corridor in hot pursuit of a quarry now out of sight. They bumped to a halt at the first cross-corridor.

Cee, his arm flung out, turned in a circle a couple of times like a damaged clockwork mechanism. "That way," he pointed to their left.

"You sure?"

"No."

They galloped down it anyway. At the next cross-corridor they were rewarded by the sound of a familiar alto voice, raised in protest, wafting from the right. They followed on, to come out in a stark freight lift-tube foyer.

The man in chocolate-brown silk had Quinn shoved up facing a wall, her arms twisted behind her. Her toes stretched and sought the floor, without success.

"Come on, Commander," the man in pink was saying, "We haven't got time for this. Where is it?"

"Wouldn't dream of keeping you," she replied in a rather smeary voice, as her face was being squashed sideways into the wall. "Ow! Hadn't you better run off to your embassy before Security gets here? They'll be all over the place after that bomb blast."

The man in pink whirled, raising his plasma gun, as Ethan and Cee skidded into the foyer. "Wait," Cee said, his hand restraining Ethan's arm.

"Friends!" Quinn shrieked, twitching. "Friends, friends, don't fire, we're all friends here!"

"We are?" Ethan, winded and dizzy, dubiously absorbed the tableau before him.

"Mercenaries who take money for contracts they can't carry out don't have friends," growled brown-silk. "At least, not for long."

"I was *working* on it," argued Quinn. "You goons have no appreciation of subtlety. Besides, you can litter the place with corpses and run off to the protection of your House consul. No skin off you if you're deported and declared persona non grata on Kline Station forever. Not only do I have to play by different rules, but I wanna be able to come back here someday. Let's try for a little finesse, huh?"

"You've had nearly six months for finesse. Baron Luigi wants the House's money back," said pink-silk. "That's the only subtlety I have to appreciate."

Brown-silk lifted Quinn a few more centimeters.

"Ow, ow, all right, no problem!" yammered Quinn. "Your credit chit is in my right inner jacket pocket. Help yourselves."

"And just where is your jacket?"

"Millisor took it off me. It's back in the docking bay. Ow, no, honest!"

There was a disgusted pause. "It *could* be the truth," mused pink-silk.

"Docking bay's crawling with Station Security by now," brown-silk pointed out. "It could be a trick."

"Look, fellas, let's be reasonable about this, huh?" said Quinn. "Luigi's deal was half in advance and half on delivery. Now, I already took care of Okita. That's one-quarter right there."

"We have only your word for that. I haven't seen a body," said pink-silk.

"Finesse, Gen'ral, finesse."

"Major," pink-silk corrected automatically.

"And it was I who took out Setti in the docking bay just now. That's half. Seems to me we're even."

"With our bomb," said brown-silk.

"You gonna argue with results? Look, are we allies, or not?"

"Not," said brown-silk and elevated her slightly more.

Voices and a clatter of boots and equipment, echoed down the corridor from the direction of the docking bay. Pink-silk shoved his plasma arc into a holster out of sight under his embroidered jacket. "Time's up."

"Are you going to let this slide?" demanded brown-silk.

Pink-silk shrugged. "Call it even at half-pay. You right-handed or left-handed, Quinn?"

"Right-handed."

"Take the Baron's interest out of her left arm and let's go."

Brown-silk, quite deliberately, let Quinn drop, achieved an arm-bar and popped her left elbow. The muffled cartilaginous crack was quite audible. Quinn made no other sound. Again, Cee restrained Ethan's forward lurch. The pair of Bharaputrans stepped delicately into the nearest lift-tube and sank from sight.

"Damn, I thought they'd never leave," Quinn sighed. "The last thing I need is for Security to catch up with those guys and start comparing notes." She slithered greenly to a seat on the floor, her back propped against the wall. "I want to go back to combat duty. I don't think I like this Intelligence stuff as well as Admiral Naismith said I would."

Ethan cleared his throat. "You, ah—need a doctor, Commander?"

She grinned wanly. "Yeah. Do you?"

"Yeah." Ethan sat down rather heavily beside her. His ears still rang and the chamber walls seemed to pulsate. He mulled over her comment. "This isn't by chance your first Intelligence assignment, is it?"

"Yep."

"Just my luck." The floor beckoned; never had friction plating looked so soft and inviting.

"Security's coming," she observed. She glanced up at Cee, hovering in anxious but helpless solicitude. "What do you say we do them a favor and simplify the scenario for them? Get gone, Mr. Cee. If you walk and don't run, those green coveralls will carry you right past 'em. Go to work or something."

"I—I…" Terrence Cee spread his hands. "What can I ever do to repay you? Either of you?"

She winked. "Never fear, I'll think of something. Meantime, I haven't seen any telepaths around here today. Have you, Doctor?"

"Not a one," agreed Ethan blandly.

Terrence Cee shook his head in frustration, glanced up the corridor, and faded into the Up lift-tube.

When Security finally arrived, they arrested Quinn.

CHAPTER FOURTEEN

Ethan stepped through the weapons detector without eliciting a beep or blink of false accusation and breathed more easily. Kline Station Security Detention was a stark, intimidating environment, gleaming and efficient, without any of the usual Stationer attempts to soften the ambience with plants or artistic displays. The effect was doubtless designed; it certainly worked. Ethan felt guilty just visiting the Minimum Security block.

"Commander Quinn is in Number Two Detention Infirmary, Ambassador Urquhart," the guard assigned to be his guide informed him. "This way, please."

Up some lift-tubes, down some corridors. Station life, Ethan decided, must exert powerful evolutionary pressures to develop a good sense of direction. Not to mention sensitivity to subtleties of status. Color blindness could prove a mortal handicap here. The Security uniforms, as all other work uniforms, were color coded, and furthermore the proportion of orange to black varied with rank. The ordinary guard wore orange picked out with black; he paused to give a snappy salute, casually returned, to a white-haired man whose sleek black uniform was barely highlighted with orange piping. One might study the entire Station hierarchy in nuances of hue.

Captain Arata, who was just now exiting the Infirmary as Ethan and his guide approached, wore mostly black, with broad orange bands on collar and sleeves and an orange stripe down his trouser legs. He also wore a frustrated frown.

"Ah, Ambassador Urquhart." The frown was put away and replaced with a slightly ironic smile. "Come to visit our star boarder, have you? You needn't have troubled; she'll be a free woman shortly. Her credit check passed—astonishingly enough—her fines are paid, and she waits only for her medical release."

"That's all right, Captain—it's no trouble," said Ethan. "I just wanted to ask her a question."

"As did I," sighed Arata. "Several. I trust you will have better luck getting answers. These past few weeks, when I wanted a date, all she wanted to do was trade information under the counter. Now I want information and what do I get? A date." He brightened slightly. "We will doubtless talk shop. If I worm any more out of her, maybe I'll be able to charge our night out to the department." He nodded at Ethan; an inviting silence fell.

"Good luck," said Ethan, cordially unhelpful. He had handled the Security post-mortem of yesterday's terrifying affair in the docking bay by climbing onto his ambassadorial status and referring all questions ruthlessly to the ever-inventive Quinn. She had stitched truth to lies to produce a fabulous beast of a story that nevertheless held up on every checkable point. In her version, for example, Millisor and Rau had been attempting to kidnap her, to program her as a double agent to penetrate the Dendarii Mercenaries for Cetagandan Intelligence. The Bharaputrans were accused of all the crimes they had in fact committed and a few they hadn't—Okita who? Most of Security's energies were now diverted to the Consulate where the Bharaputran hit squad was still holed up, negotiating the terms of their deportation. Terrence Cee had vanished utterly from the scenario. Ethan wouldn't have dared add or subtract a word.

"How unfortunate," Arata murmured, permitting a little of the needle-sharpness to flash in his eyes, "that *I* require a court order to use fast-penta."

Ethan smiled blandly. "Quite." They bowed each other farewell.

The guard turned Ethan over to the infirmary doctor. Except for the coded locks on the doors, Quinn's cell might have been any hospital room. Any Stationer hospital room, that is. Ethan was beginning to miss openable windows, taken for granted on Athos, with a starved passion.

Not wishing to state his real mission straight off, Ethan began with that thought.

"How do you feel about windows that open?" he asked Quinn. "Downside, I mean."

"Paranoid," she answered promptly. "I keep looking around for things to seal them up with. Aren't you going to ask how I am?"

"You're fine," Ethan said absently, "except for the dislocated elbow and the contusions. I asked the doctor. Oral analgesics and no violent exercise for a few days."

In fact, she looked well. Her color was good and her movements, except for the immobilized left arm, were only a little stiff. She sat up on, rather than in, her bed. She had escaped her patient gown, itself a uniform of sickness, and was back in her gray-and-whites, although minus the jacket and with slippers in place of boots.

"Suits me." Her eyes crinkled. "And how do you feel about women now, Dr. Urquhart?"

"Oh—" he paused, "somewhat the way you feel about windows, I'm afraid. Did you ever get used to windows, or learn to enjoy them?"

"Rather. But then, I've been accused of being a thrill-seeker." Her grin tilted. "I'll never forget my first trip downside, after I'd signed on with the Dendarii Mercenaries—the Oseran Mercenaries, they were back then, before Admiral Naismith took over. I'd dreamed all my life of experiencing a real planetary climate. Mountain mists, ocean breezes, that sort of thing. The directory said the planet's climate was 'temperate', which I took as a synonym for mild. We landed for emergency re-supply in the middle of a bloody blizzard. It was a year before I volunteered for downside duty again."

"I can imagine." Ethan laughed, relaxing a little, and sat down.

Her head tilted to match her smile. "Yes, so you can. One of your more surprising charms, coming from your background. Being able to make an effort of the imagination, that is, and see through a different person's eyes."

Ethan shrugged, embarrassed. "I've always liked learning new things, finding out how things work. Molecular biology was the best. Curiosity is not a theological virtue, though."

"Mm, true. Are there carnal virtues?"

Ethan puzzled over this unusual thought. "I—don't know. It seems like there ought to be. Perhaps they're called something else. I'm sure there are no new virtues under the sun—or new vices, either." Before Quinn could point out that they were under no sun—for surely the distant cinder Kline Station orbited could not be so called—Ethan hurried on. "Speaking of things carnal—I, uh—that is, before you go back to the Dendarii Mercenaries, I wanted to ask you if—um—I have what you may think a rather unusual request. If it doesn't offend you?" he inquired nervously.

He had her entire attention, her head cocked, eyes bright, a smile pressed out straight. "Before you say what it is, how can I tell? But I believe I've heard it all, so go on, by all means."

He was closer to the door than she; besides, she had one hand tied behind her back, so to speak, and there was a guard outside to defend him. How much trouble could he possibly get into? He took a breath.

"I plan to go on to complete my mission of collecting new ovarian cultures for Athos. Probably to Beta Colony, as you recommended, and the government gene repository that stocks the donations from its outstanding citizens—their seed catalog sounded quite attractive."

She nodded judicious approval, her eyes full of amused expectation.

"However," Ethan went on, "there's no reason I can't begin now. Speaking of outstanding or, um, extraordinary sources. What I mean is, um—would you care to donate an ovary to Athos, Commander Quinn?"

There was a moment's dumbfounded silence. "By the gods," she said in a rather weak voice, "I *hadn't* heard it all."

"The operation is quite painless," Ethan assured her earnestly. "Kline Station has quite nice tissue culturing facilities, too—I've spent the morning checking them out. It's not a common request, but it's quite within their capabilities. And you did say you'd help me with my mission if I helped you with yours."

"I did? Oh. So I did…"

An anxious new thought struck Ethan. "You do have one to spare, don't you? I'd understood women all had two ovaries, in analogue to male testes. You haven't donated before, or had an accident—combat or something—I'm not asking for your only one, am I?"

"No, I'm still fully equipped with all my original parts." She laughed; Ethan was subtly reassured. "I was just a little taken aback. That—that wasn't the proposition I was expecting, is all. Excuse me. I fear I am become incurably low-minded."

"You can't help that, I'm sure," Ethan said tolerantly. "Being female and all that."

She opened her mouth, closed it, and shook her head. "Not touching that one with a stick," she muttered cryptically. "Well," she took a breath, let it run out, "well…" She cocked her head at him. "And just who would make use of my, um, donation?"

"Anyone who chose," Ethan answered. "In time, the culture would be divided and a subculture placed on file in each Reproduction Center on Athos. This time next year, you could have a hundred sons. As soon as I get my designated alternate problems straightened out, I rather fancied—I, uh"—Ethan found himself turning inexplicably red under her level gaze—"I rather fancied having all my sons from the same culture, you see. I'll have earned four sons altogether by then. I never had a double-brother, from the same culture as me. The practice seems to give a family a certain attractive unity. Diversity in unity, as it were…" He became conscious that he was babbling and ran down.

"A hundred sons," she mused. "But no daughters?"

"Well—no. No daughters. Not on Athos." He added timidly, "Are daughters as important to a woman as sons are to a man?"

"There is a certain—ease, in the thought," she admitted. "There is no room for either daughters or sons in my line of work, however."

"Well, there you are."

"Well. There I am." The semi-permanent amusement lurking in her eyes had given way to a meditative seriousness. "I could never see them, could I? My hundred sons. They would never know who I was."

"Only a culture number. EQ-1. I—I might be able to push my Clearance Level A censorship status far enough to, say, send you a holocube someday, if—if that's something you would like. You could never come to Athos, nor send a message—at least, not under your own identity. You might fudge your sex and get it past the censors that way…" He'd been associating with Quinn and her rough-and-ready approach to authority too long, Ethan reflected, upon the ease with which this anti-social suggestion fell from his lips. He cleared his throat.

Her eyes glinted, amusement rampant again. "What a positively revolutionary idea."

"You know I'm not a revolutionary," Ethan replied with some dignity. He paused. "Although—I'm afraid home is going to look a little different, when I go back. I don't want to change out of all fit."

She glanced around the room and by implication beyond its walls to the surrounding Station, her former home. "Your instincts are sound, sir, although I suspect futile. Change is a function of time and experience, and time is implacable."

"An ovarian culture can defeat time for two hundred years—maybe longer now, as we refine our methods of caring for them. You could be having children long after your own death."

"I could have been dead yesterday. I could be dead this time next month, for that matter. Or this time next year."

"That's true of anybody."

"Yeah, but my odds are about six times worse than average. My insurance has it calculated to the third decimal place, y'know." She sighed. "Well. Here we are." Her lips curved. "And I thought Tav Arata was cheeky. Dr. Urquhart, you've topped them all."

Ethan's shoulders slumped with disappointment, as he saw his imagined string of dark-haired sons with mirror-bright eyes fading back into the realm of ungraspable dream. "I'm sorry. I didn't mean to give offense. I'll go." He began to rise.

"You give up too easily," she remarked to the air.

He sat back down hastily. His hands clasped each other between his knees, to keep his fingers from nervous drumming. He searched his mind for supplication. "The boys would be excellently cared for. Certainly mine would be. We screen our paternal applicants very carefully. A man who does not live up to his trust may have his sons repossessed, a shame and disgrace all strive to avoid."

"What's in it for me, though?"

Ethan thought this over carefully. "Nothing," he had to admit honestly at last. He had a sudden impulse to offer her money—a mercenary, after all—no. That felt all wrong, somehow, he could not say why. He slumped again.

"Nothing." She shook her head ruefully. "What woman could resist that appeal? Did I ever tell you that one of my other hobbies was banging my head against brick walls?"

He glanced at her forehead, startled, then realized this was a joke.

She nibbled her last unbitten fingernail, without biting through. "You sure Athos can take a hundred little Quinns?"

"More than that, in time. It might liven the place up…. Perhaps it would improve our military."

Quinn looked bemused indeed. "What can I say? Dr. Urquhart, you're on."

Ethan lit with joy.

Ethan met Quinn by pre-arrangement at a cafe in a small arcade near the Stationer edge of Transients' Lounge. She had arrived before him and sat sipping something blue from a small stemmed glass, which she lifted to him in toast as he threaded the tables toward her.

"How are you feeling?" he asked as he sat down beside her.

She rubbed the right side of her abdomen pensively. "Fine. You were quite correct, I didn't feel a thing. Still don't. Not even a scar to show for my charity." She sounded faintly disappointed.

"The ovary took the culturing treatment just fine," he assured her. "The cells are dividing nicely. It will be ready for freezing for transport in forty-eight hours. And then, I guess, I'm off to Beta Colony. When will you be leaving?" A faint speculation—hope?—that they might possibly be traveling on the same ship crossed his mind.

"I'm leaving tonight. Before I get into any more trouble with the Station authorities," she replied, dashing Ethan's nascent scenario of further conversations. He never had had time to ask her about all the planets she had undoubtedly seen in her military pilgrimages. "I also want to be long, long gone before any Cetagandan follow-up on Millisor's death arrives. Though it seems they are going to get directed back to Jackson's Whole—I wish them all joy of each other." She stretched, grinning, like a cat full of bird after a successful hunt and picking a few feathers from its teeth.

"I'd just as soon avoid meeting any more Cetagandans myself," said Ethan. "If I can."

"Shouldn't be too difficult. For your peace of mind, I might mention that before his death Ghem-colonel Millisor managed to send off a confirmation of Helda's destruction of the Bharaputran cultures to his superiors. I doubt the Cetagandans will show any further interest in Athos. Although Mr. Cee is another matter, since the same report also confirmed his presence here on Kline Station.

"But I've got a stack of reports myself that will give Admiral Naismith something to meditate on for months. I'm glad I don't have to decide what to do with it all. I lack but one item to make his day complete—and here it comes, I trust, now." She nodded past Ethan's shoulder and he turned in his seat.

Terrence Cee was making his way toward them. His green Stationer coveralls were inconspicuous enough, although his wiry blond intensity turned an older female head or two, Ethan noted.

He sat down with them, nodding at Quinn, smiling briefly at Ethan. "Good afternoon, Commander, Doctor."

Quinn smiled back. "Good afternoon, Mr. Cee. Can I buy you a drink? Burgundy, sherry, champagne, beer…"

"Tea," said Cee. "Just tea."

Quinn put the order on her credit card in the table's auto-waiter. The Station, it seemed, did not import all comforts. The real thing—

a pleasant aromatic black variety grown and processed on Kline Station—appeared promptly, steaming in a transparent mug. Ethan ordered some too, the business hiding the little discomfort Cee's presence induced in him. The telepath could have no further interest in Athos now, either.

Cee sipped; Quinn sipped. "Well," Quinn said. "Did you bring it?"

Cee nodded, sipped again, and laid three thin data discs and an insulated box perhaps half the size of Ethan's hand upon the table. They all disappeared into Quinn's jacket. At Ethan's look of inquiry, Quinn shrugged, "We all trade in flesh here, it seems," by which Ethan understood the box contained the promised tissue sample from the telepath.

"I thought Terrence was going back to the Dendarii Mercenaries with you," said Ethan, surprised.

"I've tried to talk him into it—by the way, the offer remains open, Mr. Cee."

Terrence Cee shook his head. "When Millisor was breathing down my neck, it seemed the only exit. You've given me a little space to make a choice, Commander Quinn—for which I thank you." A movement of his finger toward the packets secreted in her jacket indicated the tangible form of his thanks.

"I am too kind," Quinn sighed wryly. "If you change your mind later, you can still look us up, you know. Look for a heap of trouble with a squiggly-minded little man on top of it, and tell him Quinn sent you. He'll take you in."

"I'll remember," Cee promised noncommittally.

"Ah, well—I won't be traveling alone." Quinn smiled smugly. "I scrounged up another recruit to keep me company on the trip back. Interesting fellow—a migrant worker. He's knocked around all over the galaxy. You should meet him, Mr. Cee. He's about your height—skinny—blond, too." She lifted her stemmed glass in toast and tossed off the rest of her blue drink. "Confusion to the enemy."

"Thank you, Commander," Cee said sincerely.

"Where, ah—were you thinking of going now, if not the Dendarii Mercenaries?" Ethan asked him.

Cee spread his hands. "There are a multitude of choices. Too many, really, and all about equally meaningless...excuse me." He remembered to feign good cheer. "Some direction away from Cetaganda." He nodded toward Quinn's left jacket pocket. "I trust you won't have any trouble smuggling that package out. It should go into a proper freeze-box as soon as possible. A very small one, maybe. It might be better if a freeze-box does not appear on your luggage manifest."

She smiled slowly, scratching one tooth—her fingernails were all neatly filed down again—and murmured, "A very small one, or—hm. I think I may have an ideal solution to that little problem, Mr. Cee."

Ethan watched with interest as Quinn dropped the enormous white freezer transport box down upon the counter of Cold Storage Access 297-C. It banged, startling the attention of the counter girl dreaming over a holovid drama. The figures of the girl's private play vanished in smoke and she hastily removed an audio plug from her ear.

"Yes, ma'am?"

"I've come for my newts," said Quinn. She reached around and shoved her thumb-printed authorization into the read-slot in the counter's computer.

"Oh, yes, I remember you," said the girl. "A cubic meter in plastic. Do you want it quick-thawed?"

"Don't want it thawed at all, I'm shipping them frozen, thanks," said Quinn. "Eighty kilos of newts would be a little icky after four weeks' travel warm, I fear."

The girl wrinkled her nose. "I think they're icky at any temperature."

"I assure you, they will be appreciated in direct ratio to their distance from their source." Quinn grinned.

The corridor doors hissed open behind them. Ethan and Terrence Cee stepped out of the way as a float pallet entered piloted by a green-and-blue-uniformed ecotech and bearing half a dozen small sealed canisters.

"Oh, oh, priority," said the counter girl. "Excuse me, ma'am."

Ethan recognized the ecotech with a pleasant start; it was Teki, presumably from his workstation just around the corner. Teki recognized Quinn and Ethan at the same moment. Cee, not known to the ecotech, didn't register and stepped smoothly into the background.

"Ah, Teki!" said Quinn. "I was just about to step around and say goodbye. You're fully recovered from your little adventure of last week, I trust?"

Teki snorted. "Yeah, getting kidnapped and worked over by a gang of homicidal lunatics is my idea of a real fun time, sure. Thanks."

Quinn's mouth quirked. "Has Sara forgiven you for standing her up?"

Teki's eyes twinkled and he failed to suppress a slow smirk. "Well, yes—once she was finally convinced it wasn't a put-on, she got real, um, sympathetic." He attempted sternness. "But damn, I knew it had to be something for the dwarf! You can tell me now, can't you, Elli?"

"Sure. Just as soon as it gets declassified."

Teki groaned. "Not fair! You promised!"

She shrugged, helpless. He frowned grudgingly, then, palpably, let the grudge go: "Goodbye? You leaving soon?"

"In a few hours."

"Oh." Teki looked genuinely disappointed. He glanced at Ethan. "Afternoon, Mr. Ambassador. Say, I'm, uh—sorry about what Helda did to your stuff. Hope you won't take it as representative of our department. She's on medical leave—they're calling it a nervous breakdown. I'm acting head of Assimilation Station B now," he added with a bit of shy pride. He held out a green sleeve for inspection, circled by two blue bands in place of his previous one. "At least till she gets back." On closer look, Ethan found the second band to be but lightly tacked in place.

"It's all right," said Ethan. "You stitch that armband on good and tight—I'm assured her medical leave will be permanent."

"Oh, yeah?" Teki brightened still more. "Look, let me throw this shit out—" he gestured to the little canisters on his float pallet, "and I'll be with you—you all can come around to Station B for a couple of minutes, can't you?"

"Only a couple," warned Quinn. "I can't stay long, if I'm to make my ship."

Teki waved in a gesture of understanding. "Come on back," he invited, maneuvering his float pallet past the counter and through the airseal doors behind them that the counter girl had keyed open for him.

"Gotta wait for my stuff," Quinn excused herself, but Ethan, curious, trailed along. Cee drifted behind, inconspicuous and quiet, a lonely figure still, odd man out. Ethan smiled over his shoulder, trying to include him in the group.

"So tell me more about Helda," said Teki to Ethan. "Is it really true she mailed all that stolen tissue to Athos?"

Ethan nodded. "I'm still not sure what she hoped to accomplish. I don't think she even knew. Maybe it was just to have something in the shipping cartons to pass casual inspection—I mean, empty boxes would show obvious tampering. She managed to create a mystery almost in spite of herself."

Teki shook his head, as if still unable to believe it all.

"What is all this?" Ethan gestured toward the float pallet.

"Samples, of some contaminated stuff we confiscated and destroyed today—they go into cold storage, for proof later in case of lawsuits, or further outbreaks, or whatever."

They entered a chill white room featuring quantities of robotic equipment and an airlock; a chamber on the very skin of the Station, Ethan realized.

Teki tapped instructions rapidly into a control console, inserted a data disc, placed the canister into a high-tensile-strength plastic bag with a coded label, and attached the bag to a robotic device. The device rose and floated into the airlock, which hissed shut and began to cycle.

Teki touched a control on the wall and a panel slid back, revealing a small transparent barrier like the great ones in Transients' Lounge. Crowding projections of bits of the Station blocked most of the spectacular galactic view. It was the Station equivalent of a back alley, Ethan decided, except that it was brightly lit. Teki watched carefully as the robot exited the airlock and floated through the vacuum across a long grid of metal columns all tethered about with bags and boxes.

"It's like the universe's biggest closet," mused Teki. "Our own private storage locker. We really ought to clean house and destroy all the really old stuff that was thrown out there in Year One, but it's not like we're running out of room. Still, if I'm going to be an Assimilation Station head, I could organize something…responsibility…no more playing around…"

The ecotech's words became a buzzing drone in his ears as Ethan's attention was riveted on a collection of transparent plastic bags tethered a short way down the grid. Each bag seemed to contain a jumble of little white boxes of a familiar type. He had seen just such a little box readied for Quinn's donation at a Station biolab that morning. How many boxes? Hard to see, hard to count. More than twenty, surely. More than thirty. He could count the bags that contained them, though; there were nine.

"Thrown out," he whispered. "Thrown—*out?*"

The robot reached the end of a column and attached its burden thereto. Teki's attention was all on the working device; he moved off to monitor it as it cycled back through the airlock. Ethan reached back, grabbed Cee by the arm, bundled him forward, and pointed silently out the window.

Cee looked annoyed, then looked again. He stiffened, his lips parting. He stared as if his eyes might devour the distance and the barrier. The telepath began to swear under his breath, so softly that Ethan could hardly make out the words; his hands clenched, unclenched, and splayed against the transparency.

Ethan gripped Cee's arm harder. "Is it them?" he whispered. "Could it be?"

"I can make out the Bharaputra House logo on the labels," breathed Cee. "I saw them packed."

"She must have put them out here herself," muttered Ethan. "Left no record in the computer—I bet a search would list that bin as empty. She threw them *out*. She really literally did throw them *out. Out there.*"

"Could they still be all right?" asked Cee.

"Stone frozen—why not…?"

They stared at each other, wild in surmise.

"We've got to tell Quinn," Ethan began.

Cee's hands clamped down over Ethan's wrists. "No!" he hissed. "She has hers. Janine—those are mine."

"Or Athos's."

"No." Cee was trembling white, his eyes blazing like blue pinwheels. "Mine."

"The two," said Ethan carefully, "need not be mutually exclusive."

In the loaded silence that followed, Cee's face flared in an exaltation of hope.

CHAPTER FIFTEEN

Home. Ethan's eye teased him as he stared eagerly through the shuttle window. Could he make out the patchwork farmlands, name cities, rivers, roads yet? Cumulus clouds were scattered over the bays and islands off the South Province coast, dappling the bright morning with shade, obscuring his certainty. But yes, there was an island the shape of a crescent moon, there the silver thread of a small river where the coastline looped.

"My father's fish farm is in that bay there," he pointed out to Terrence Cee in the seat beside him. "Just behind that crescent-shaped outer island."

Cee's blond head craned. "Yes, I see."

"Sevarin is north and inland. The shuttleport where we'll be landing is at the capital, north one district from that. You can't see it yet."

Cee settled back in his seat, looking reflective. The first whispers of the upper atmosphere carried a hum from the shuttle's engines. A hymn, to Ethan's ears.

"Will you be getting a hero's welcome?" Cee asked Ethan.

"Oh, I doubt it. My mission was secret, after all. Not strictly, in the military sense you're familiar with, but done quietly, on account of not wanting to start a public panic or cause a crisis of confidence in the Rep Centers. Although I imagine some of the Population Council will be there. I'd like you to meet Dr. Desroches. And some of my family—I called my father from the space station, so I know he'll be waiting. I told him I was bringing a friend," Ethan added,

193

hoping to ease Cee's obvious nervousness. "He seemed quite pleased to hear it."

He was nervous himself. How *was* he going to explain Cee to Janos? He had run through several hundred practice introductions in his mind, during the two-month leg of their journey from Kline Station, until he had wearied of worrying. If Janos was going to be jealous, or hard-nosed about it, let him get down to work and earn his designated alternate status. It might be just the stimulus needed to kick him into action at last; given Janos's own personal proclivities, he was unlikely to believe that Cee had shown every sign of being a prime candidate for one of the Chaste Brotherhoods. Ethan sighed.

Cee regarded his hands meditatively and glanced up at Ethan. "And will they view you as a hero, or a traitor, in the end?"

Ethan surveyed the shuttle. His precious cargo, nine big white freezer cartons, was not consigned to the chances of the cargo hold, but strapped to the seats all around them. The only other passengers, the census statistician and his assistant and three members of the galactic census courier's crew heading for downside leave, hung together protectively at the far end, out of earshot.

"I wish I knew," said Ethan. "I pray about it daily. I haven't prayed on my knees since I was a kid, but on this I do. Don't know if it helps."

"You're not going to change your mind and switch back at the last minute? The last minute is coming up fast."

As fast as the ground below. They were dropping through the cloud layer now, white fog beading on the window and flaring off in the wind of their passage. Ethan thought of the other cargo, secreted in his personal luggage, compressed and concealed: the four hundred fifty ovarian cultures he had purchased on Beta Colony for the sake of assuring any possible future Cetagandan follow-up of his activities—and indeed, of assuring the Population Council itself—that the original Bharaputran cultures had never been found. Cee had helped him make the switch, hours and hours spent in the census courier's cargo hold changing labels, doctoring records. Or maybe it had been

Ethan helping Cee. They were both in it together now, anyway, to the neck and beyond.

Ethan shook his head. "It was a decision that somebody had to make. If not me, then the Population Council. There are only two choices in the long run that don't risk race war or genocide: all, or nothing. I am convinced you were right on that score. And the committee—well—I feared they would be constitutionally incapable of anything but a split decision. You're right in your perception—as always—I tremble at our future. But even in fear and trembling, I'm willing to reach for it. It ought to be—interesting."

If Ethan felt a spasm of guilt, it was for the four-hundred-and-fifty-first culture, EQ-1, whose container he held on his lap. If he were unable to complete his scheme, of all the sons born to Athos in the next generation, only his would not bear the hidden alleles, the recessive telepathy time-bomb. But his grandsons would get them, he assuaged his conscience. It would all average out in the long run. May he live to see it; may he live to nurture it.

"But you retained the chance to change your mind," Cee noted. A jerk of his chin in the direction of the cargo bay and Ethan's luggage indicated the cause of his unease.

"I'm afraid I'm hopelessly economical," Ethan apologized. "I should have been a housekeeper, I sometimes think. The Betan cultures were just too good to jettison into the vacuum. But if I get my old job back, or better still advance to head a Rep Center, there may be a chance—I'd like to try my hand at gene splicing the telepathy complex into the genuine Betan cultures and slipping them back into Athos's gene pool, if I can do it in secrecy. As soon as I become adept at the operation, this one too." He lifted EQ-1 from his lap, set it back carefully, his conscience quieted still further. "I did promise Commander Quinn a hundred sons. And as a Rep Center chief, I would have a seat on the Population Council. Maybe even a shot at the chairmanship, someday."

There was a small crowd in the Athosian shuttleport docking bay in spite of the close secrecy surrounding Ethan's mission. Most of them turned out to be representatives from the nine District Reproduction Centers, eager to carry off their new cultures. Ethan was nearly trampled in the rush for the freezer boxes. But the Chairman of the Population Council was there and Dr. Desroches and best of all Ethan's father.

"Did you have any trouble?" the chairman asked Ethan.

"Oh…"—Ethan clutched EQ-1—"nothing we couldn't handle…"

Desroches grinned. "Told you so," he murmured to the chairman.

Ethan and his father embraced, not once but several times, as if to assure each other of their continued vitality. Ethan's father was a tall, tanned, wind-wrinkled man; Ethan could smell the salt sea lingering even in his best clothes and inhaled pleasurable memories therefrom.

"You're so pale," Ethan's father complained, holding him at arm's length and looking him up and down. "God the Father, boy, it's like getting you back from the dead in more ways than one." His father embraced him again.

"Well, I've been indoors for a year." Ethan smiled. "Kline Station didn't have a sun to speak of, I was only on Escobar for a week, and Beta Colony had too much sun—nobody goes aboveground there unless they want to be fried. I'm healthier than I look, I assure you. In fact, I feel great. Uh—" he looked around surreptitiously one more time, "where's Janos?" Sudden fear shot through him at his father's grave look.

Ethan's father took a deep breath. "I'm sorry to have to tell you this, son—but we all agreed it would be better to tell you first thing…."

God the Father, thought Ethan, *Janos has gone and killed himself in my lightflyer…*

"Janos isn't here."

"I can see that." Ethan's heart seemed to rise and choke his words.

"He got kind of wild, after you left—nobody to be a restraining influence on him, Spiri says, though I take it as a man's duty to restrain himself and Janos was old enough to start playing a man's part—Spiri and I had a bit of an argument about it, in fact, though it's all settled now—"

The docking bay seemed to spin around Ethan's center of gravity, just below his stomach. "What *happened?*"

"Well—Janos ran off to the Outlands with his friend Nick about two months after you left. He says he's not coming back—no rules or restrictions out there, he says, nobody keeping score on you." Ethan's father snorted. "No future, either, but he doesn't seem to care about that. Though give him ten years and he may find he's had a bellyful of freedom. Others have. I calculate it'll take him at least that long, though. He always was the thickest of you boys."

"Oh," said Ethan in a very small voice. He tried to look properly grieved. He tried very hard, twitching the corners of his mouth back down by main force. "Well"—he cleared his throat—"perhaps it's for the best. Some men just aren't cut out for paternity. Better they should realize it before and not after they become responsible for a son."

He turned to Terrence Cee, his grin escaping control at last. "Here, Dad, I want you to meet someone—I brought us an immigrant. Only one, but altogether a remarkable person. He's endured much, to make it to refuge here. He's been a good traveling companion for the last eight months and a good friend."

Ethan introduced Cee; they shook hands, the slight galactic, the tall waterman. "Welcome, Terrence," said Ethan's father. "A good friend of my son's is a son to me. Welcome to Athos."

Emotion broke through Cee's habitual closed coolness: wonder and something like awe. "You really mean that... Thank you. Thank you, sir."

Two of the three moons rose together that night over Athos's Eastern Sea. The little breakers murmured beyond the dunes. The second floor verandah of Ethan's father's house gave a fine view over the moon-spangled waters of the bay. The breeze cooled Ethan's blush, as the darkness concealed its color.

"You see, Terrence," Ethan explained shyly to Cee, "the fastest way to gain your paternal rights and Janine's sons, is to devote all your time to public works until you gain enough social duty credits for designated alternate status. There's plenty to do—everything from road repair to parks maintenance to work for the government—maybe sharing some of your galactic expertise—to all kinds of charity work. Old men's homes, orphanages for the bereft and repossessed, animal care, disaster relief services—although the army handles most of that—the choices are endless."

"But how shall I support myself meanwhile?" objected Cee. "Or is support included?"

"No, you must support yourself. To gain designated alternate points the work must be over and above the regular economy—it's really a kind of labor tax, if you want to think of it that way. But I thought—if you will allow me—I can support you. I make plenty for two as a Rep Center department head—and Desroches and the Chairman have hinted that I may get the Chief of Staff post at the new Rep Center for the Red Mountain district, when it goes into place year after next. By then, with diligence, you'll have your D.A. status. And then it can go really fast, because," Ethan took a breath, "as a designated alternate parent, you can become a Primary Nurturer to my sons. And being a Primary Nurturer is, bar none, the fastest way to accumulate social duty credits toward paternity." Ethan faltered. "I admit, it's not a very adventurous life, compared to the one you've led. Sitting in a garden, rocking a cradle—someone else's cradle, at that. Though it would be good practice for your own and of course I would be happy to stand as designated alternate parent to your sons."

Cee's voice came out of the darkness. "Is hell an adventure, compared to heaven? I've been to the bottom of the pit, thank you. I have no wish to descend again for *adventure's* sake." His tone mocked the very word. "Your garden sounds just fine to me."

He sighed long. There was a pause. Then, "Wait a minute, though. I got the impression the mutual D.A. business, outside the communal brotherhoods, was sort of like married couples—is sex entailed in all this?"

"Well…" said Ethan. "No, not necessarily. D.A. arrangements can be, and are, entered into by brothers, cousins, fathers, grand-fathers—anyone qualified and willing to act as a parent. Parenthood shared between lovers is just the most common variety. But here you are on Athos, after all, for the rest of your life. I thought, per-haps, in time, you might grow accustomed to our ways. Not to rush you or anything, but if you find yourself getting used to the idea, you might, uh, let me know…" Ethan trailed off.

"By God the Father," Cee's voice was amused, assured. And had Ethan really feared he would surprise the telepath? "I just might."

Ethan paused in front of the bathroom mirror before turning out the light and studied his own face. He thought of Elli Quinn and EQ-1. In a woman, one saw not charts and graphs and numbers, but the genes of one's own children personified and made flesh. So, every ovarian culture on Athos cast a woman's shadow, unacknowl-edged, ineradicably there.

And what had she been like, Dr. Cynthia Jane Baruch, two hun-dred years dead now, and how much had she secretly shaped Athos, all unbeknownst to the founding fathers who had hired her to create their ovarian cultures? She who had cared enough to put herself in them? The very bones of Athos were molded to her pattern. His bones.

"Salute, Mother," Ethan whispered and turned away to bed. To-morrow began the new world and the work thereof.

Editor's Note

Many thanks to William Shawcross of Rotten Apple Press who scanned in the text and to another of Lois' many fans who had provided her with another version of that text. This enabled me to skip the first round of proofreading by comparing these two versions electronically. It was my own fault that this did not save any time in the production process. There is no way to properly thank that most puissant of proofreaders, George Flynn, for the final proofing, so I will simply say: thank you. Any flaws remaining in the text are my fault, not his.

This book was set in Adobe Garamond, Albertus Medium, and Wingdings by Suford Lewis in Aldus PageMaker 6.5.

- Suford Lewis

The New England
Science Fiction Association (NESFA)
and NESFA Press

Books from NESFA Press:

Find details and many more books on our web page: www.nesfa.org/press
Books may be ordered by writing to:
   NESFA Press
   PO Box 809
   Framingham, MA 01701

We accept checks, Visa, or MasterCard. Please add $3 postage and handling per order.

The New England Science Fiction Association:

NESFA is an all-volunteer, non-profit organization of science fiction and fantasy fans. Besides publishing, our activities include running Boskone (New England's oldest SF convention) in February each year, producing a semi-monthly newsletter, holding discussion groups relating to the field, and hosting a variety of social events. If you are interested in learning more about us, we'd like to hear from you. Write to our address above!